BAD TIDINGS

Recent Titles by Nick Oldham from Severn House

BACKLASH
SUBSTANTIAL THREAT
DEAD HEAT
BIG CITY JACKS
PSYCHO ALLEY
CRITICAL THREAT
CRUNCH TIME
THE NOTHING JOB
SEIZURE
HIDDEN WITNESS
FACING JUSTICE
INSTINCT
FIGHTING FOR THE DEAD
BAD TIDINGS

BAD TIDINGS

A Detective Superintendent Henry Christie Novel

Nick Oldham

severn House

This first world edition published 2013
in Great Britain and in the USA by
SEVERN HOUSE PUBLISHERS LTD of
19 Cedar Road, Sutton, Surrey, England, SM2 5DA.

British Library Cataloguing in Publication Data

Oldham, Nick, 1956-
    Bad tidings. – (A Henry Christie mystery; 19)
    1. Christie, Henry (Fictitious character)–Fiction.
    2. Serial murder investigation–Fiction. 3. Police–
    England–Blackpool–Fiction. 4. Detective and mystery
    stories.
    I. Title II. Series
    823.9'2-dc23

ISBN-13: 978-0-7278-8266-0 (cased)

For Belinda

All Severn House titles are printed on acid-free paper.

Severn House Publishers support the Forest Stewardship Council [FSC], the
leading international forest certification organisation. All our titles that are printed
on Greenpeace-approved FSC-certified paper carry the FSC logo.

Typeset by Palimpsest Book Production Ltd.,
Falkirk, Stirlingshire, Scotland.
Printed and bound in Great Britain by
MPG Books Ltd., Bodmin, Cornwall.

ONE

For the moment his fear had subsided.

It was still there, humming in the background like a generator, still bubbling away, but the wild boil of terror had turned into a simmer and for the first time David Peters had time to think about his predicament. Not clearly, because his mind was still in turmoil. But at least now he could take a deep breath – even though the hessian bag over his head, with a drawstring pulled tight around his neck, meant he was inhaling strange-smelling dust particles that gagged his nasal passages and the back of his throat – and try to regain some control of his body.

Bring down the heart rate, moderate the breathing. There was nothing he could do about having soiled himself. That had already happened and the piss-shit stink mixed in with the smell of the sacking.

But for a while, though there was no way of knowing how long his respite would be – minutes, hours, days – he had to use the time constructively.

He had to marshal his thoughts and work out why he was here, hooded and bound, a prisoner trapped in a black space so tight he could hardly wriggle, a space even smaller than a coffin.

What had he done? What awful, terrible thing had he done – or omitted to do – to deserve this?

What did he possess, or what was he thought to possess, that was so valuable that he could end up like this?

If he could work out the reason, then maybe he could work out who was punishing him so severely, who held such a deadly grudge against him, or imagined he had wealth of some sort.

If it was possible to answer any of these questions, the next one would be, what could he, David Peters, do to escape with his life? Even then, before he had worked out any of the answers, he knew that if staying alive meant pleading for mercy and humiliating or degrading himself by licking up shit, he would do it.

Anything to live.

He twisted his hands, the cord around his wrists digging deeply into the skin, restricting the blood flow to his fingers, which tingled. He breathed in unsteadily as his heart began to pound again. He wanted to scream and scream. The parcel tape wound tightly across his mouth and around the back of his head and lower jaw meant his sounds were muted, never to be heard by anyone.

The fear began to rise again.

He was nothing special. He'd never cracked any pots – *never will*, his mother used to chide. He'd grown up and attended the primary school in the small Lancashire village where he'd been born. Then, after leaving the village and moving to a bigger town nearby, he'd attended college and after that became a TV repair man.

Unspectacular was his own description of himself. His only epiphany in life, the only good thing he had ever done, was to foresee the demise of tube and valve televisions and the advent of computers, and move into computer repairs. He took the plunge and invested in a little electrical shop, which became three, then back to two when recession struck. He made a half-decent living and that was all: no pots cracked.

He was in a tolerable marriage – unexciting, dull – had two grown-up kids he adored, but who despised him. He occasionally had a tryst with the dreary woman who managed his second shop when they would sneak into a Travelodge for an evening of dour passionless sex, an escape for both of them from their humdrum existences. But it was only occasional and nothing would ever come of the liaison. They didn't even really like each other.

And sometimes he went for a drink with an old mate.

Mr Unspectacular.

A fully grown, middle-aged man, with a family, a small business, a woman he could hardly call a mistress, certainly not a lover – not in any exciting sense of the word . . . although it had been on a night with her that Mr Unspectacular, David Peters, had something extraordinary happen to him.

He had been kidnapped.

'Did you do those invoices?' Peters had grunted. He was on top of his shop manageress, a woman called Stella Richards. They were making love and Peters had been thrusting distract-edly into her when the thought occurred to him. *Invoices.* He stopped suddenly and asked the question.

Stella's eyes popped open in surprise, almost as though it was a shock to see her boss naked on top of her. She rarely opened her eyes when they had sex, not particularly liking what she saw at the best of times – flab and a bored expres-sion (even at climax) on his face. But he was well built in the cock department and could keep going so that, more often than not, Stella managed an orgasm of sorts.

'What?' she said, screwing up her face, feeling those nice waves inside her start to ebb.

'Those invoices,' he said. 'Did they get done?' He had pushed himself up on his hands, taking his weight off her body.

'Yeah,' she gasped. She closed her eyes, grabbed his wide arse, digging her fingernails deep and slamming him back where he came from, deep inside, and she ground back. Their secret meetings were pretty pointless anyway, but would have been utterly so without an orgasm.

He resumed his movements and her ebb flowed again.

They never spent the night together. Their meetings were simply functional, so within minutes of finishing, David Peters was tugging on his socks (something Stella found irritating, a man who got dressed by putting his socks on first). She remained in bed, the duvet up to her neck, staring at the ceiling.

'. . . And that back room needs a tidy,' he was saying as he stepped into his Y-fronts (another irritation – though they mercifully covered his wide bottom). He continued to list the things that needed doing on the retail front. Their evenings usually concluded like this: back to business, because they had nothing else in common. Just a couple of TV and computer shops.

Peters stopped suddenly as he hopped into his pants. 'You not getting dressed?' he queried, puzzled.

She shook her head. 'I'm staying a while . . . going to have a long bath and read a few chapters of that erotic book that's selling loads.'

'Duh – crap . . . whatever.'

He finished dressing and skipped the awkward moment of parting by simply giving her a wave and slipping out of the room. Moments later he was out on the streets, heading for a nearby pub. He needed the smell of ale and maybe cigarette smoke on his clothes to fool his wife, who thought he was out for his monthly pint with his pal. Not that she was particularly interested, Peters believed, except that if he did get found out she'd probably take him for every penny. So, best to go through the motions.

He never made it to the pub.

David Peters stalked through the small lobby of the motel, neither seen nor noticed except by the CCTV camera above the reception desk that recorded all comings and goings. He exited via the main revolving door and found himself out on a busy street, which came as no surprise to him. It was only nine o'clock – the meeting with Stella had commenced at seven forty-five and lasted just over an hour, foreplay included.

And not only was it still quite early, it was also Christmas Eve – and the Lancashire seaside resort of Blackpool was heaving with bodies, mostly inebriated ones it seemed to Peters.

He paused on the footpath, stepping sideways to avoid some of the revellers, deciding where to go.

He couldn't go home too early, nor too late. It had to be finely judged, so he needed to go to a nice pub for a couple of slow jars, maybe a bag of crisps – Chilli Heatwave Doritos, he knew, did a good job of masking the aroma of recent sex – and then drive home for about elevenish. By that time his wife would be tucked up in bed and he could slide in without incident, even tonight.

Standing there, he experienced that sensation again.

That sixth sense, the one that made his hairs creep on the back of his neck. The one he'd had a few times recently.

The sensation that someone was watching him. There was no evidence of it. No furtive shadows, just a feeling.

He spun quickly, only to come face to face with two drunken men who split either side of him and staggered past.

David Peters chuckled at his own foolishness. Who would be watching him?

He turned and headed towards Blackpool town centre, the two drunks ahead of him bouncing off each other as they progressed, crashing into other people, too. A couple to avoid, Peters thought, and set off to town, only a short distance away.

He turned off Talbot Square onto Market Street, thinking he would cut up Birley Street, past the entrance to the multi-storey car park, where he had left his car, then get into one of the pubs on Corporation Street and find a quiet corner with a pint of lager and spend some time contemplating his dreary existence.

Birley Street was maybe seventy metres long. It was a nothing of a street, just a thoroughfare connecting one busy main road to another. A street that took only a matter of seconds to walk along.

The van screeched past Peters and stopped just ahead of him. He thought nothing of it. Just a small box van based on a Vauxhall Astra.

Instead he was thinking, Mm . . . my life . . . shitty . . .

It was about to get even shittier.

He didn't think about the footsteps behind him. Running.

Nor about the double rear doors of the van being flung open from within. And even if he had thought it through, his conclusion would have been that it was probably a van about to disgorge drunken occupants onto the street. More revellers to add to the thousands already in town.

Except no one emerged from the van.

And the footsteps rushed up behind him.

Then there was the blow to the back of the head which turned his knees to squish. His legs folded underneath him, no longer able to support his weight, and he slumped heavily onto his knees.

His eyes were still open, though. Just briefly he saw a dark shape in the back of the unlit van, but could not make out any features of it.

The pain from the blow to the head, still sending spasms throughout his body, rocked him onto his hands, and his shitty life swirled uncontrollably as he looked down at the cracked pavement, tried to raise his head, focus, concentrate, fight or run.

But then a hood was fitted over his head and drawn tightly around his neck. He was dragged and lifted and he knew he was being bundled head first into the van. His head hit something hard, an inner wheel arch perhaps. His hands were pulled behind his back and then he was punched on the side of his head, hard . . . and neither his mind nor his body seemed to work any more. His eyes rolled back in their sockets, then there was nothing.

The sound of approaching footsteps on floorboards – or at least that's what they sounded like to David Peters.

He went rigid, listening, not breathing, trying to work it all out.

His head hurt still, throbbed. It was sore and there were big, tender swellings on it from the blows he had received.

Bang. That first one from behind had really hurt, made him drop like a sack of shit.

He blinked. Listened. Footsteps. They seemed to be . . . above him. Then they stopped. There was a scraping, scuffling sound. Then the footsteps again, retreating, becoming distant . . . the sound of a door clattering shut, like a garden gate. Not a house door. Then the metallic click of a latch dropping into place and a bolt being slid shut.

Peters tried to work out what to do.

So far he had been kidnapped and regained consciousness.

He wasn't sure, but he thought he hadn't made any noise yet, so perhaps the kidnapper believed him to be still unconscious.

Giving him precious time to think.

Why was he here?

Could it be Stella's husband? Had he discovered their sordid little affair – if it could be called an affair – and was he enraged by it and now wreaking revenge?

Peters thought it unlikely. Stella was convinced he neither knew nor suspected anything. And even if he found out he was unlikely to give a toss, she said, assuring him he was only interested in model railways.

Or had his own wife discovered the affair? Peters thought that was unlikely, too. He covered his tracks well, destroyed receipts, paid cash when he could, didn't make a regular habit of fucking his shop manager and always used a different location for each meet-up. No, the wife didn't know.

So who?

He had no money to speak of. A few grand in the bank, a couple of thou secreted in a building society, some cash – literally – stashed in the loft . . . not nearly enough to satisfy a ransom demand.

Which was the truly worrying thing.

His assets were minuscule. Certainly not worth anyone kidnapping him for and putting themselves in jeopardy. He was worth next to nothing and even if the shops – which he owned outright – were sold, they wouldn't really be worth much either. They were both in crappy areas of town.

So no ransom demand.

A squeak of terror formed at the back of his throat.

This was personal.

And making it personal, logically, meant there would not be a pretty outcome to this.

No exchange. No money drop. No freedom.

He had been taken for some other reason.

His mind churned desperately.

Up until the start of the affair with Stella he had led a blameless life. Unspectacular. No cracked pots. Got married. Had kids. Ran a business. Had maybe done a few daft things as a kid, but nothing that bad and such a long time ago.

He was forty-five and innocent.

He inhaled unsteadily. The smell of the hessian sacking. And something else in the molecules he sniffed up his nose. Something familiar, yet difficult to place . . . an aroma from the dim distant past.

At once his whole body felt as if it had been instantly frozen, dipped into liquid nitrogen.

And he knew.

The latch clattered. Footsteps approached again.

David Peters' heart pounded against his sternum.

The footsteps stopped directly above him.

There was a creaking noise as if an old door was being opened, or the lid of a coffin lifted. Peters felt an inrush of air around him. He could sense someone close by, standing over him. There was the sound of breathing.

He swallowed. He had hoped to do it silently, but the swallow became a loud gulp and because of that, it was now obvious he was awake. No more pretending.

The hessian hood was drawn slowly off his head.

He had expected to be blinded by bright lights, but the world his eyes saw was a dark, shadowy place, with a sinister figure standing over him. The figure squatted down onto its haunches as Peters realized where he had been lying. In a cavity of some sort, underneath a trap door, in a space maybe seven feet long, two feet wide and ten inches high, beneath some floorboards.

His heart whammed and crashed. Bitter adrenalin surged into his system and fear creased him.

The figure spoke. 'Welcome to the chicken shack.'

TWO

Henry Christie opened his eyes at the first low ring of the cordless telephone handset on the cabinet beside his bed. He was on his back, only half asleep, drifting in and out of wakefulness pretty much as per the last seven nights, over which, he claimed, he could probably count on both hands the hours he had slept. Not many. His head twisted to the right – a quick time check of the digital clock, the conditioned response honed by too many years of early morning phone calls and turnouts.

He saw and mentally logged the illuminated display, which read 03:48.

He rolled quietly out of bed, grabbing the phone as he moved, thumbing the 'Take Call' button before the third ring. He was up on his bare feet in an instant, phone clasped to his ear, plodding naked into the en suite shower room, closing the door softly behind him and only then speaking.

'Henry Christie . . .' His voice was nervy as he wondered which of the two matters this could be. He didn't really want it to be either, but there was slight relief when the voice at the other end announced, 'Mr Christie, this is Inspector Howard, force control room . . .'

Henry juddered a short breath. No, he didn't want either call . . . what he wanted was a full night and a long morning in bed for once, and for nothing to happen . . . but the Force Incident Manager's voice made this one infinitely more preferable to the call he could have got. The FIM was calling from Lancashire Constabulary's HQ Communications Room at Hutton, four miles south of Preston. It was the FIM who managed the call-out rotas for the force, deciding which specialist, if any, needed to be turned out to deal with an incident.

Not that Henry was even on a rota that week.

That week – the week between Christmas and New Year – he was technically off duty. Nevertheless he had been out and about all week, from Christmas Eve all the way through to New Year's Eve. He had been involved in a series of incidents that meant what should have been a week of rest and relaxation had been completely ruined by both work and personal business. He'd had less sleep than ten fingers, he claimed . . . at least it felt that way. And he had been waiting for a call each night, and now, on New Year's Day morning at 3.48 a.m., it had come.

Henry listened. Very fleetingly he wondered if the FIM was visualizing him. Did she see a man too quickly approaching his mid-fifties, standing in a chilly shower room, goosebumps all over his naked body, jotting down notes on the writing pad he'd purposely left on the toilet cistern? Probably not . . . the FIM was far too busy to allow such trivial thoughts to enter her head, Henry guessed.

Henry asked questions, clarified any possible misunder-standings, asked her to repeat the location twice. Then he gave some specific instructions to the FIM, who very professionally reconfirmed them, and Henry gave her his estimated time of arrival.

Call over, Henry turned on the shower and stepped into it for a two-minute freshen up, then a shave.

His clothes were already hanging on the door of the en suite in anticipation of the call. It wasn't formal wear – jeans, a shirt, a sweater and leather jacket (with a tie rolled up in the pocket, just in case a degree of formality was required at some stage), thick socks and practical footwear, a cross between trainers and walking shoes.

When fully dressed, he emerged from the room.

He had hoped not to disturb Alison Marsh, his lady friend, but she was fully awake and propped up on one elbow, bedside light on a low setting. She had a concerned look on her face. Henry felt bad about waking her. She had only been in bed two hours and he knew she was as exhausted as he was by the previous week.

'Sorry. Thought I was being quiet.'

'And I thought a gorilla had broken in and was smashing the place up.'

'Sorry . . . I need to go, love.'

'Which one is it?' she asked quietly.

'Work.'

She exhaled. 'Take care.'

He walked to her side of the bed and kissed her cheek.

Henry made his way through the pub, grabbing his Karrimor Chatsworth jacket as he went, knowing it would be cold outside. He let himself out through the front door into the icy blast of the morning in the north Lancashire village of Kendleton. Up until a couple of hours before the place had been heaving with festivities and the pub, the Tawny Owl, being the only hostelry in town, had been the centre of it. And very well it had performed.

Now it was eerily silent. The only visible remnants of the celebrations were streamers, party poppers spider-webbed out across the car park and several of the cars and a few balloons tied to wing mirrors. On the village green across the road, the embers of the bonfire still glowed and smoked and Henry could smell it.

Henry inhaled the chilly air, feeling it sear into his lungs. He shivered, locked the pub doors and trudged over to his car, making the first footprints in a light dusting of snow. The vehicle was a new Audi convertible, the replacement for his previous car which had met its doom in a very ugly incident on the road into Kendleton six months before. That one had been a Mercedes which Henry had loved, and he was now slightly regretting the brand change.

That said, he acknowledged that the Audi was also a great car.

He slid into it, started up and within moments the efficient heating system was belting out hot air. A heated driver's seat also helped matters. Then he was on the road.

Geographically speaking, in terms of the county of Lancashire he was about as far away as he could be from his destination that morning.

Kendleton was tucked away inconveniently in the very north of the county and he had to travel well into the east, but it wasn't a straightforward journey. First he had to get onto the M6 at the Lancaster north junction, then it was pretty much motorway all the way. Head south down the M6, cut briefly onto the M61 at Bamber Bridge, then onto the M65 to travel east into the depths of the county, exit at junction 5, then plough even further east onto the bleak moors above Blackburn on which perched his destination. The village of Belthorn.

Henry didn't need to use a SatNav, and not just because Belthorn had been pretty much his focus of attention for the last week. He hardly ever needed to use one when travelling around the county, except for possibly the last few hundred metres of a journey. Over thirty years of policing the area had given him detailed knowledge of it and its denizens, particularly the criminal variety.

He knew exactly where he was going on that dark, cold morning, the first day of the New Year. He settled down to enjoy the drive along deserted roads . . . and wondered, not for the first time, why he hadn't been strong enough to stand up to the chief constable and refuse the job in the first place, the one that had been the launch pad for everything else that followed over the week. He should have been more assertive and the chief would have had to delegate it to someone else. But he was playing on Henry Christie's weakness.

The bait: two unsolved murders. And like a dim-witted carp attracted by a wriggling worm, there were some things Henry Christie could not refuse, even though his gut instinct was to tell the chief constable to find some other sucker.

He bit the worm, because the challenge of catching a killer was impossible for Henry to swim away from . . .

'Half a bloody job,' Henry had said bitterly. 'Half a bloody job.'

'I know, I know,' the chief constable had responded, accompanied with a 'so what?' kind of shrug. His name was Robert Fanshaw-Bayley, known to most people as FB, although no one of lower rank would ever be so familiar to his face. Therefore, by default, as everyone else in the Lancashire Constabulary was of lower rank, he was always referred to as 'sir' or 'boss', and occasionally – by his deputy or the assistant chiefs – by his first name, when he wasn't chewing their backsides off.

It was possible that Henry Christie, though a mere detective superintendent, could have got away with the informality. He and FB had known each other touching thirty years, ever since Henry had been a PC on the crime car in Rossendale and Fanshaw-Bayley the young, thrusting, obnoxious DI in that neck of the woods, the smug ruler of the roost. Henry, therefore, knew he had certain privileges with FB that others did not, given their intertwined history, but never pushed it. He liked to keep FB at arm's length, as the prospect of cosying up to him in any way made him nauseous.

Because of their shared history – weighted mainly in favour of FB – Henry could have made a stand against the rotund chief. He had done so often, though he rarely gained any advantage from it. He could have said 'No' on this occasion, but FB had the trump card: murder.

They were in FB's office on the middle floor of police headquarters at Hutton, overlooking the sports pitches and the huge building – known as the Pavilion – that housed the Major Crime Unit, and beyond that the wooded campus in which the force Training Centre was located.

'Sit, sit,' FB purred, gesturing towards the leather settee on the other side of his office, positioned against the wall underneath a big, formal portrait of the Queen.

Bristling at his own weakness – and checking his watch tetchily (it was 6.17 p.m. on Christmas Eve) – Henry slouched round-shouldered over to the settee and dropped miserably onto it. FB rose from the dark wood, leather-bound office chair behind his expansive leather inlaid desk – two pieces of furniture that would not have looked out of place in the captain's cabin of the *Cutty Sark*. Scooping up two fat folders, he followed Henry but sat down directly opposite him on one of the armchairs on the other side of a glass-topped coffee table with an ancient map of the world beneath the glass.

Peevishly, Henry folded his arms, his mouth twitching. He had been grinding away full tilt for the last six months and had booked annual leave for the week ahead. He was looking forward to helping Alison, unofficially, at the Tawny Owl, spending a happy week with her and her daughter Ginny, and maybe inviting his daughters, Jenny and Leanne, to spend a couple of nights at the Owl, too. A bit of a 'get-to-know-you' thing.

The two files in FB's arms meant that Henry's plans were about to change, but neither man could have imagined just how much. And, although he didn't know it just then, something else totally unrelated to work was about to happen that would also screw up his week.

FB gave him his most understanding smile as he placed the files on the table. 'Can I get you a coffee? Tea?'

Henry blinked at the offer. *FB doing something for me?* But then he realized it was after six and all of FB's support staff had gone, and there were no lackeys to whip into shape. Christmas Eve meant an early dart for all the HQ office staff. The place was like the *Mary Celeste*.

'Coffee would be good.' Though Henry loved his coffee,

he rarely drank it after 3 p.m. unless he needed to keep going. Something in FB's eyes led him to believe that he might have to keep running tonight.

FB stood up and poured two mugs from the filter machine on top of the dark panelled sideboard. He handed one to Henry, then reseated himself opposite.

'We know why it was half a job, don't we?' FB said.

'Uh – because he got himself in deep criminal shit and investigating murder wasn't his top priority, even though he was an SIO?' Henry answered what he knew had been a rhetorical question.

'That's it in a nutshell,' FB agreed.

They were talking about Detective Superintendent Joe Speakman, a former colleague of Henry's on FMIT – the Force Major Investigation Team – who had become embroiled in various criminal schemes that had ended tragically for him and his family. After stumbling on Speakman's death, Henry had uncovered organized activities stretching from Lancashire to Cyprus and up into Russia. It turned into a complex, wide-ranging investigation that, six months down the line, was still ongoing for a small, dedicated team of detectives headed by Henry. People were still on the run, arrests still had to be made.

FB placed his coffee on the table, then laid his hands flat on the files.

Henry eyed them, fully aware of their contents.

A beat of silence passed, then FB said, 'Two murders, unfortunately dubbed the "Twixtmas Killings" by our esteemed local press.'

Henry nodded. He sipped his coffee. It was bitter, tasted like it had been on the hotplate for a week. He guessed it was FB's emergency supply for when he couldn't click his fingers to get one of his minions to make a fresh one. Henry could not disguise his grimace of distaste. 'Yup,' he said.

FB's eyes narrowed. With his hands still on top of the files, he slid them across to the detective superintendent.

Henry squirmed. 'Last time I inherited something from Joe Speakman, I ended up being shot at, kidnapped, beaten up. My lovely car was written off by a freakin' Russian gangster and my partner was seriously assaulted – and she's only just got through that shit.' An image of Alison's pulped face came into Henry's mind.

But FB reverted to type, giving an uncaring pout and shrug. 'Who'd have known? Still, there's nothing to say that either of these murders is connected with those other shenanigans, is there?' He tapped the files.

Henry didn't flinch, didn't lean forward. To have done so, in terms of body language, would have signalled his acceptance of what was being said, and he was fighting it.

He had worked long, hard, punishing hours for the last six months and knew it was probably taking its toll on his fledgling relationship with Alison. He really needed a week off with her or he could see the whole thing going south . . . and he had something special planned for Christmas that would put everything – his relationship, his life – back on track.

But two murders?

Fuck you, FB, he thought. *You slimy toad.* He knew it was a crap deal getting handed two unsolved, very cold murders . . . but hell! Two murders. How could he possibly resist?

Fuck you, FB, he thought again. However, he continued his little game, even though his mind was already rehearsing his speech to Alison. His *I'm only doing what my boss ordered, I didn't have a choice* speech. Even in his brain, it sounded piss weak.

'What about Don Royce?' he stalled. Royce was one of the other two FMIT detective superintendents.

'Too busy – and he's on call for everything else this week.'

'Reg Carney?' He was the other one.

'Caribbean cruise – already jetting across the water.'

'There's plenty of DCIs who could tackle them,' Henry suggested.

FB shook his head. His double chins wobbled.

The word 'Bollocks' sat on Henry's tongue, but remained unsaid. He squirmed again.

'You're the man,' FB said. 'You've already had involvement with Joe Speakman. You obviously know how Joe's mind worked, how he thought.'

'Thin,' Henry said. 'Try harder. I have a week's holiday booked and a hot-arsed landlady waiting for me.'

FB continued unmoved. 'You've pretty much wrapped up the Speakman thing . . . you need something else to keep you occupied, to ease you up to retirement.'

'How about I have the week off, then look at them?' He nodded at the files.

'You know you can't.'

Henry raised his eyes and looked directly at FB. 'I'm having them, whatever, aren't I?'

'Course you are.'

'Shit.'

Henry knew exactly what was in the files. He'd read them several times just in case there had been some connection to the mess that Joe Speakman had got himself embroiled in. Henry concluded that the two murders were not linked in any way to Speakman's personal debacle – but there was every chance that they were themselves connected. Whichever senior investigating officer inherited them would have to put in a lot of time and effort over the next week because of that connec- tion and because the week was significant in terms of the murders. Henry gazed at the files, nostrils dilating, knowing two things. First, he would not be spending much time with Alison over the next seven days. Second, he had a horrible feeling he'd just been handed the hunt for a serial killer . . . but when FB said, 'You bloody love it, don't you?' Henry had to agree.

He did.

The morning was still black, no sign of dawn, as Henry approached junction 5 of the M65. He was now well into the east of the county – dark satanic mill land (though most cotton mills had been demolished years ago, or turned into 'shopping events') – and as he looked up to his right he could see the silhouette of the village of Belthorn perched on a high crest of moorland on the edge of some very wild countryside. Over to his left was the town of Blackburn and lit up in the fore- ground, about a mile distant, was Blackburn Royal Infirmary. He'd had some real fun there this last week.

He came off the motorway and bore right onto the A6177 Grane Road, which linked Blackburn with the Rossendale Valley.

Less than a mile distant he turned right onto Belthorn Road and drove up towards the village, over the slight rise, then down into a dip before the steep hill that was the main road through the village. To the right was the Dog Inn, but before Henry reached that, he slowed, then stopped. On his right was a narrow tarmac side road and parked across it was a marked police car, one officer on board, controlling all vehicular access.

Two hundred metres down the lane was the location – a factory unit – at which Henry had been asked to attend.

The scene of the crime. Five very evocative words, Henry always thought: *the scene of the crime*.

At that moment, after a long, fast early morning drive across the county, Henry did not know for certain what he would discover.

What he did believe was that, based on his knowledge of the two unsolved murders FB had given him to investigate, the link between them would be confirmed. But the good thing was that this one wouldn't be a cold case. Henry was coming in right at the start. New leads and connections would be generated and – based on what he learned over the week – the killer, he was confident, would be caught. Because he was pretty certain who it was.

A shimmer of excitement scuttled through him.

He checked his watch, which read 04:58. Two minutes to five on New Year's Day . . . what could be better, after the week he'd just had, than attending the scene of yet another horrific murder?

Don't answer that, he thought . . .

The two files were substantial and Henry had to cart them out of FB's office one under each arm, shouldering his way carefully through doors, down steps, eventually emerging at the front of the HQ building and walking across the footpath that dissected the playing field.

He hadn't completely got his head around how he was

going to manage the week ahead, personally or professionally, but he knew that some skilful juggling would have to take place.

What he didn't expect was to be blindsided by something unexpected – which came in the form of a phone call.

His mobile started to ring as he was halfway from HQ to his office, situated in a refurbished former student accommodation block at the Training Centre. With both files clamped tightly underneath his armpits, he couldn't shuffle them without dropping either, so he ignored the ringing and carried on across the sports pitch in the gloom of the evening.

The phone continued to ring as he walked, with the accompanying sound of text messages pinging as they landed. Something was going on.

He struggled up to his middle-floor office in a building that seemed to be deserted and dumped the files on his desk, fished out his phone and slid it open: four missed calls, two texts and a voicemail.

He checked who each was from. One from Alison, two from his daughter Leanne, one from his sister, Lisa. The texts were both from Alison and the voice message from Lisa.

With a feeling of dread, Henry started to listen to Lisa's voice message, knowing it could only be about one thing.

It was one of the fastest drives of his life: Preston to Blackpool. Police headquarters to Blackpool Victoria Hospital, BVH. Twenty minutes.

And then twenty more minutes finding somewhere to park.

And then ten minutes walking from his car to the A&E department and another five to find the patient in a curtained cubicle somewhere at the back.

As he drew aside the heavy plastic curtain, his eyes alighted on the frail figure of his mother in the bed, hooked up to various monitors and drips stuck in veins at the back of her bony hands, and on the faces of Lisa and Leanne, his sister and daughter, at the bedside.

Both women turned and gripped him, suddenly in floods of tears.

Henry consoled them, an arm around each, as he looked at

his mother, her eyes closed and, he guessed, very close to death.

Something cold and rock solid sank in his chest.

He could have driven down the lane, using his rank, but instead he parked the Audi on the main road, pulled the Chatsworth jacket tight, got out and decided to walk. He grabbed his Maglite torch from the footwell and stuffed a few pairs of latex gloves and shoe covers into his pocket, just a few items from the kit every half-decent detective would carry with him.

As he approached the stationary police car, the officer inside got out wearily. Henry flashed his warrant card, even though the PC recognized him.

'I'll let you drive down, if you like, sir,' he told Henry. 'There's plenty of parking outside the unit and quite a few cop cars down there.'

'Maybe later, when I see what's what,' Henry said, ducking under the cordon tape that had also been strung across the entrance to the lane. His mind was already starting to take in the location, trying to assess its importance, and he worked quickly back over the existing murder files as he walked to the scene of what might actually be the fourth murder in the series. And he shook his head at the memory of the past week and all that he had endured . . .

THREE

It had been a heart attack that had floored Henry's ninety-one-year-old mother, Veronica Martha Christie, née Redwood. Fortunately for her it struck when Lisa, Henry's somewhat flaky sister, was paying one of her very infrequent visits. (Cruelly, Henry wondered if the fact that Lisa had turned up had been the reason for the attack.)

His mother lived – still fiercely independent at such a great age – in sheltered housing in Bispham, to the north of Blackpool. She had survived a previous heart attack a couple of years before, but it had become obvious to the family that she had started to deteriorate health-wise in the last six months. She was eating less and less, hardly had any energy in her frail body and was approaching, if not death, then at least the time when she would need to be cared for by professionals.

Henry had seen the decline and begun what he knew would be the very delicate process of convincing his mum that a home would be a much better place for her. This did not go down well – she was convinced that 'a much better place' meant better off dead. 'Because I might as well be dead in an old people's home with all those old codgers about,' she remonstrated. Henry found that, although she was in physical decline, her mental faculties were still top notch and she refused point blank to move. She had access to a warden if necessary and her main meal of the day was delivered by a charity, although it often remained uneaten.

The other problem for Henry was the commitment needed from his family to look after her – a family that now consisted only of himself and Lisa. It didn't help that his mother's decline had coincided with Henry having to investigate the Joe Speakman scenario which took up so much of his time, nor was it helpful that Lisa cringed at the thought of spending too much time with their mother.

'I'm not cut out for that sort of thing,' she grimaced when Henry tackled her. 'Y'know, cleaning up pots with food dried onto them and helping an old biddy get to the loo.' She shivered repulsively at the prospect.

'She's your mum, not an old biddy,' Henry said, trying to keep his cool. At the time he was trying to balance the investigation, plus his newish relationship with Alison that had suffered after her assault, and he felt like he was a daddy-long-legs having its limbs pulled off. It was exhausting for him, even though Alison was wonderful and understanding about it all. And yet . . . he thought the cracks were starting to appear.

It was also hard to get his daughters involved. Leanne, the younger, was too busy flitting from man to man and Jenny lived in Bristol with her husband.

Henry was struggling.

'I know she's my mum,' Lisa whined, 'but things aren't going well with Rik . . .'

'You're going to get freakin' married, aren't you?' Henry exploded.

'And that's the problem. We both have cold feet . . . Well,' she said awkwardly, 'I do.'

'Just keep living together, then,' Henry suggested wearily.

Lisa shrugged. 'I might've . . . kinda, er . . . been seeing someone else . . .' The words became almost inaudible.

Instead of anger or sympathy, Henry said pragmatically, 'Well if you split with him, then you'll have more time for Mum, won't you?'

'You're all heart.'

Henry shrugged. Struggling.

'And I'm thinking of moving back to London, maybe.'

'Shit,' Henry said, sinking in an emotional mire. 'How imminent is all this?'

Lisa shrugged this time.

'Are you splitting or not?'

'I think so . . . things're a bit fraught.' There was real pain behind her eyes, and Henry felt sad for her and Rik. He thought they had confounded everyone and found some peace and happiness.

'You can crash at my house whenever you need to,' Henry offered. 'But,' he said, raising a finger, 'no shagging there, OK? And you start visiting Mum more. For some reason I can't fathom, she still quite likes you.'

The months following that conversation had been hard and tiring. Lisa did split with Rik after a few unpleasant weeks and bedded down occasionally at Henry's house in Blackpool, the one he and his late wife, Kate, had shared for much of their married life. Henry spent too much time at work, and had also gone abroad to Cyprus to follow up connections uncovered whilst looking into Joe Speakman. He visited his mother's flat as often as possible and enjoyed as much time with Alison as he could, but with her running and living at the Tawny Owl in Kendleton, their moments together were limited and unsatisfactory.

And no matter how he tried, he could not convince his

mother to move to a proper care home. It was easier getting a confession from a murderer.

Lisa's visits started strongly, then dwindled as her private life became increasingly messy (Henry keeping well out of it) and her relationship with Rik swung on and off. It was fortunate that she and Leanne had been there when Mother collapsed after suffering shortness of breath, followed by a twinge in the chest that suddenly felt like a sabre had been stabbed through her left shoulder joint. She fell at Lisa's feet.

Twenty minutes later she was in A&E. An hour after that Henry was on the scene, consoling Lisa and Leanne and watching as his mum was transferred up to the cardiac unit.

The second big scare. The first time she'd even denied that she'd had a heart attack and had recovered sufficiently to be allowed home. She had been lucky that time. This time, Henry thought, might be different.

Henry was eventually left alone with his mother, who was under sedation and very much out of it. He sat by her bed for a long time, clasping a thin bony hand in his, looking at her, pain etched across his face.

Two murders – and this, he thought creakily, feeling his mind splitting, wondering if he could handle it all, unsure if he had the mental resilience to do so.

He stood up and stretched, then walked out into the corridor, shuffling along, his mind swirling like thick pea soup. He was heading for the coffee machine when he walked past an office where a young nurse was working hard at a desk, filling in paperwork. Henry had zoomed in on a filter coffee machine on a shelf behind her.

He knocked, and the nurse glanced up with an instant beaming smile that made him feel much better instantly.

'Can I help?'

Henry introduced himself and they chatted for a few moments about his mother, then he broached the subject timidly, scratching his head like Stan Laurel: 'Is that coffee machine broken?'

The nurse glanced over her shoulder, then back at Henry, with a knowing look. 'No, just not had time to fire it up today.'

'If I get the water . . .' He gave her one of his well-used, probably overused, lopsided, boyish grins (designed, he believed, to melt any woman's heart). 'Do you have any coffee for it . . .? I'll gladly pay.'

It worked. A deal was struck and Henry walked down the corridor with the jug to fill it up in the restroom.

On his way back he spotted a small room. He put his nose up to the window in the door and peered through, seeing a space about the size of a police cell with a desk and a couple of chairs in it, with stacks and stacks of files backed high against the walls and no sign of occupancy. There was no computer on the desk, nothing to suggest the room had been used recently.

Back in the nurse's office, filling the coffee machine with water from the jug, then heaping coffee into the filter section, Henry broached the next subject. The office down the corridor.

Won over again by his charm, the nurse rooted in a drawer and produced a key, saying, 'I'm sure no one'll mind.'

With his mother fast asleep and snoring like a chainsaw, Henry went back to his car and recovered the two murder files which he had efficiently scooped up as he'd raced out of his office. Ten minutes after that, in the small office he had commandeered, he opened the first file, the title of which read: MURDER: CHRISTINE BLACKSHAW.

Christmas Eve two years earlier, and a woman in her mid-forties had been staggering through the streets of Blackburn, very much the worse for wear from drink. She was twice married, twice divorced – but had reverted to using her maiden name – and had two children both now in their twenties, each by a different father. Now single, she lived alone in a council flat in the Eanam district of town. She had a job at ASDA and worked long hours to keep her head above water and to pay for an annual two-week burnout in Benidorm. She liked drink and men, but could not hold either.

She had spent the evening with some friends, getting drunk, and just before midnight they had gone their separate ways.

Christine had been making her way to a pub on Darwen Street to meet up with her latest man friend, a relationship that like most of her others was volatile and violent. That said, they had planned to get a Chinese takeaway, hop into a cab back to her flat, eat, watch the box, hopefully not argue, then crash out.

She never made it to the pub.

Her body was discovered a week later stuffed into a wheelie bin behind a derelict shop in the town centre, where it had also been set on fire.

Henry winced a little as he skim-read the pathologist's report. It painted a gruesome picture of the suffering that Christine must have endured before finally being put to death with two gunshot wounds to the head. In short, she had been tortured repeatedly, although there was no sign of sexual assault.

Her body had only been partially burned, almost as though her killer was simply making a statement. She had been tipped and folded into the wheelie bin, then the bin had been stuffed with kindling and balled-up pieces of newspaper and an accelerant had been poured over her and a match tossed in. All this had happened, the pathologist said, after death.

It had only been because her body had been stuffed into the bin that enough of it was preserved to allow the pathologist to make his deductions.

The subsequent murder investigation, led by Joe Speakman, was thorough, as far as Henry could see. Everything had been done. Boyfriends, ex-husbands, one-night stands and family were pulled in and sweated. Leads were followed up painstakingly and everything was done scientifically and forensically. *Crimewatch* even did a short item on it which brought forth a glut of nothing leads.

Six months down the line, the investigation began to peter out. The murder squad was reduced, and even though an investigation room was kept going, Speakman was floundering.

Henry blinked and stretched. He'd been reading for an hour and he needed to check on his mother.

Some Christmas Eve, he thought . . .

He locked the room and walked back to the cardiac unit, which was quiet now. He smiled at the nurse and saw there was still at least one more mug of coffee in the filter machine. He filled up and went to see his mum.

She was still asleep but not now snoring. The monitors seemed to indicate that things were OK for the moment.

'Hi.'

Henry spun around and saw what he thought, not for the first time, was the most beautiful woman ever.

Alison Marsh, owner of the Tawny Owl, whom he'd met on a hike through the village of Kendleton where he had stumbled slap-bang into the middle of a blood-soaked standoff between gangsters. At the time Henry had been married to Kate, and only after her tragic death did anything blossom between him and Alison. In her he knew he had found a gem – and the fact that she owned a great little village pub and hotel only added to her wonderfulness.

They embraced tenderly and Henry seemed to draw energy from her.

When they stepped apart, Alison said, 'How is she?'

'Not good,' he whispered. 'Not on life support, but not good. Last time she had a heart attack, she was certain she hadn't had one. This time she knows. And anyway, what are you doing here? Haven't you got a pub to run? Christmas Eve and all that?'

'Ginny's doing it with her boyfriend, and you know the staff are great, so no worries.'

Henry nodded, nudged Alison out of the ward and led her to his new office, where her eyes alighted on the two files.

'I got collared just as I was about to skedaddle,' he explained. 'FB foisted these on me. Two of Joe Speakman's unsolved murders.' Henry watched Alison closely as he mentioned the name Speakman. He saw a look of dread come over her face. Her memories of what had happened because of Speakman were very fresh and fragile. Henry went on, 'They're connected, we think, and, er . . .' His voice became a man-squeak. 'I'm going to struggle to get time off this week . . . shit, I know.'

Alison's expression had returned to normal.

'Even so,' Henry said hurriedly, 'I'll spend as much time with you as I can. I know it's been a rough few months . . .' His voice trailed off weakly as he thought about how Alison, unwittingly and innocently, had been sucked into Speakman's violent mess and badly assaulted for simply being connected to Henry. She'd had to undergo surgery to reconstruct part of her smashed-up face. It was only now that she was starting to look completely right again, although to Henry she had always been gorgeous anyway.

Henry knew he was on shaky ground with his announcement. Things had been tough for them and they'd been looking forward to the 'Twixtmas' week, just to hang around, do things together, chill.

Alison nodded and gave a long drawn-out 'Okaaay.' Then she said, 'Are we in love?'

Henry said, 'Yes, course, indubitably.'

'I mean, truly, madly, deeply?'

'Yes.'

'In that case, we'll work through it. It's not what happens to you, it's how you deal with it that's the key.' She locked eyes with him. 'How are you feeling?'

'Gutted and drained. I could've done without either, but both together . . .' He swished a hand at the two files, then gestured helplessly in the general direction of the cardiac unit.

'What about tonight?' Alison asked. Henry started to say something, but bit his bottom lip. 'Do you want to stay here in Blackpool to be near your mum?'

'Yeah,' he admitted.

'I'll stay with you then . . . I'll go and sort your house out and I'll be there when you land, whatever the time.'

Henry shook his head in amazement, but then squinted at her. 'Are you sure?'

'Why wouldn't I be?'

'Erm . . .' Oh God, he thought inwardly. Not good at this sort of thing. 'Err . . .'

'You mean because of Kate?'

'Kinda.'

'I know it was her house, but it's part of you as well. She's gone and you've moved on. I know what it means to you and it's fine. It's not like I haven't stayed there before, is it? I even have a key,' she said grinning. 'You gave me one.'

'I know. I just thought you were uncomfortable there.'

'Henry,' she began firmly.

'Fine, fine.' He held up his hands, palms outward, surrendering.

'I'll be there when you get back, whenever that is,' she stated.

Henry blew out his cheeks and looked at the murder files with annoyance, thinking, *Best laid plans and all that crap.*

But he was mostly annoyed with himself for having said yes to FB. If he'd said no, at least all he would have had to contend with was his mother. It would have been hard, but he could have handled that – to-ing and fro-ing to Kendleton and back without having to think about work as well. But two murders on top was pushing it.

And it wasn't as though he could shelve the murders until New Year, as he'd cheekily suggested to FB.

And that sneaky bastard FB knew that.

Henry opened the second file.

Murder number two: David Peters.

A fairly dull middle-aged man who had led, by all accounts, a fairly uneventful life. What made him interesting was that he had been having an affair with one of his employees, and had vanished – on Christmas Eve again, after an assignation with this woman at a motel in the middle of Blackpool – exactly one year after Christine Blackshaw had disappeared off the streets of Blackburn.

He had been reported missing by his fairly indifferent wife on Christmas Day, not having returned after a drink with his mate, but the police did not treat the matter with much urgency. He was a grown man, it was *that* time of year, and she didn't seem to care very much. She had reported him missing simply because she felt she had to and the turkey was in the oven. At the time of the initial report there was no mention of Peters having an extra-marital relationship.

Only when he hadn't turned up four days later did anyone become concerned.

The missing from home (MFH) file landed in the lap of a keen young PC who would rather have binned it, but decided to do some digging. This is how he, without too much difficulty, discovered Peters' affair and exactly what the man had been doing on the evening he went missing: fucking. Not boozing with an old friend, as he had led his wife to believe.

Even so, this new information led the police to believe merely that maybe he had decided to vanish for a while and contemplate his life, as men of his age often stupidly did.

When his body turned up on New Year's Day, the cops swung into action. Sort of.

The case should have been allocated to Henry because the body had been found in his area of geographic responsibility, but because he was otherwise engaged it was given to Speakman instead.

At the time it obviously wasn't known that Speakman had become embroiled in a whole bunch of criminality that emanated from his purchase of a villa in Cyprus and his association with a crooked local businessman in the north of the county. This meant he didn't concentrate as much as he should have done on David Peters' death. But Speakman did make the connection with the murder of Christine Blackshaw, something he could hardly miss.

Henry read through the pathologist's report on Peters' post-mortem.

The body had been discovered on farmland on the outskirts of Poulton-le-Fylde, near Blackpool. Two bullets to the brain had been what had killed him.

But his body had also been badly burned, set alight having been doused in petrol. The difference between the discovery of his body and that of Christine Blackshaw was that Peters had been found in an unused chicken coop in a secluded copse on the edge of a farmer's field. It was a wooden building that hadn't been used for years, but had been well constructed. It looked as though Peters had been held in this location – in the space underneath the floor – since his disappearance and had spent a week of terror at the hands of the perpetrator before being killed. The coop was then razed to the ground, Peters' body being found in the ashes.

Initially the death was treated as another standalone, but as the forensics, ballistics and scientific teams got together, the links to Blackshaw became clear.

First there was the tie-up with the bullets. The same gun had been used to murder both victims, a .22 calibre which shot bullets into the brain that rattled around the skull like the Tasmanian Devil, but did not exit. Good news for the cops, bad for the offender.

Next link was the general MO. Both victims kidnapped on the same day, a year apart, Christmas Eve. Both held for a week and their bodies found on New Year's Day.

Blackshaw, the female, had been dumped and set alight in a wheelie bin, but Peters was burned where, it was believed, he had been held captive all week. It had never been discovered where Blackshaw had been held.

Both victims were approximately the same age, mid forties.

Both had been born in the borough of Hyndburn . . . but that may just have been coincidental, because thousands of people were born there – though Henry always liked to see coincidences in murder hunts, as they often led to clues. As far as he was concerned a clue in a murder hunt always meant that the killer had made a mistake.

The icing on the cake, though, discovered on the post-mortem slab by the pathologist as he inspected every crevice and orifice, was that the mouths of both victims had been stuffed with chicken feathers.

Henry closed the murder books. He stared vacantly at the wall in front of him, then shook his head and looked at the time. Almost 11 p.m. . . . . Christmas Eve, and he hadn't even had a drink.

'Shit,' he said, his mind turning all this information over and coming back to the feathers. Because not only had there been feathers in the victims' mouths, an examination of their stomach contents revealed that they had been forced to eat the feathers, too.

Henry felt unwell at the thought as he worked through this pivotal piece of information. He was spitting feathers at that moment, desperate for a drink.

Force fed chicken feathers, he thought. He shuffled out his mobile phone and despite the hour dialled a number, which went through to answerphone. He left a curt message, then called another number, also not answered, and left a message on that one too.

Then he stood up and stretched. He walked back towards the cardiac unit, but was almost hurled out of the way as a white-coated doctor shot past him. Henry's insides did a back-flip.

He found a team of doctors and nurses working with urgent efficiency on his mother, one of them desperately pumping her frail chest, inside of which her heart had stopped.

Another nurse stepped forward brandishing the defibrillator paddles which had been powered up.

Incredibly she survived the pounding, then the defib – which jarred her meagre body terribly – and the infusion of drugs, the doctors and nurses doing wonderful work whilst Henry watched wordlessly, an empty feeling inside him.

After they had all gone, Henry sat by her bed and clasped her hand again, stroking it gently, knowing this time she wouldn't be leaving hospital alive.

At 2 a.m., after doing a nodding dog impersonation for several minutes, he knew he had to get to his own bed.

He texted Lisa and his daughters to bring them up to speed with the latest news and noticed that he had also received two texts. Having responded to both, he collected the murder files from his newly acquired office, returned the key to the nurse with grateful thanks and headed home.

It was strange to see the lights on as he drove down the avenue towards it. But it was also good to know that the woman he loved was waiting there for his arrival.

He was up by eight on Christmas Day, having had five hours of dead-black sleep. Alison was already up and making break-fast for them from the paltry resources available. Since being with Alison he had spent less and less time at the house and as a result, fresh food and drink was almost non-existent. Alison managed to find a frozen loaf of bread and a pack of bacon in the freezer, and some ground coffee in a sealed container which still smelled fresh. The tasty Christmas Day breakfast she fashioned from the ingredients was waiting for Henry when he appeared downstairs after a long, invigorating shower.

'Merry Christmas,' Alison declared. They hugged, a move that still sent a shiver of pleasure through both of them.

'And you,' he said.

They stepped apart and suddenly there was a small box in Alison's hand, wrapped in golden Xmas paper. 'Merry Christmas,' she said again and urged Henry to take the present.

'Shit,' he said guilty.

'Go on – open it.'

He did so under her gaze. It was a Breitling watch, which made Henry gasp with admiration. 'You shouldn't have . . . I mean, really you shouldn't.' He slid it onto his wrist after removing the battered Casio digital one he wore for work and admired it. 'It must have cost—'

'Don't go there,' she warned him.

Their eyes locked. Henry said, 'Thanks,' swallowing.

She gave a petite shrug.

'Look . . . I . . . er . . .' he stuttered.

'It doesn't matter.'

'It does, actually.' He held up a finger and dashed into the living room, returning a moment later, a crooked grin on his face and a present of his own in the palm of his hand, his hand clasped tight around the package.

He spoke hesitantly, feeling awkward. 'I didn't quite envisage Christmas Day being like this – two murders and Mum almost in her grave . . . but what is, is,' he shrugged philosophically. He held out his right hand, palm up . . .

FOUR

Two pairs of eyes glowered at Henry Christie. They belonged to police officers of much lower rank than he – a detective inspector, a detective constable – but this disparity in position did not prevent either man staring malevolently and insubordinately at him. Because at that moment in time, both hated him with a vengeance.

'Whaaat?' Henry said innocently as he entered his office

and slid behind his desk, slapping down the two murder files on his ink blotter.

At 9.30 a.m. on Christmas Day, Henry already knew the answer to his somewhat rhetorical question.

He had left a text message for both men the night before, outlining his requirements – that both of them parade for duty the following morning in his office and brace themselves for a tough week ahead.

Christmas Day. A public holiday.

Henry knew that no one else was on duty in FMIT, or covering the Intelligence Unit at headquarters, the departments to which these men were attached. Obviously some staff were on standby call-out rotas, but there wasn't a soul to be seen in either department.

The DI was Rik Dean, his old friend and colleague, and possibly his future brother-in-law, although the recent conversations he'd had with his sister Lisa made him think that union might not be happening – but to be honest, he'd lost track of where they were up to. Henry had fought to get Rik onto FMIT and been successful in his manoeuvrings.

The other was Jerry Tope, a DC from the Intel Unit. Tope, a curmudgeon of a man, grumpy to the extreme right of the dwarf of the same name, had worked for Henry on several occasions over the past few years.

Henry could forgive them their expressions of hatred. He knew how good both were at their jobs – and he knew, of course, he had seriously interrupted their Christmas celebrations.

Neither man responded to his 'What?' question, because they also knew the answer. Both should have been off work that day and the next, and they were none too chuffed about the summons. Financially it wasn't too bad for Tope, because as a DC he could claim double time for the public holiday. But that didn't hold for Rik. Inspectors and above didn't get paid extra for overtime or public holidays, though he would be entitled to time off in lieu, as would Henry. Reality was, though, that neither man would ever find the time to take it off.

'Henry, I'm not being funny, but this better be good,' Rik

grumbled. 'I checked the pads this morning for the last twenty-four hours and nothing's happened to interest FMIT.'

'Yuh, I checked too,' Tope flared up. 'Bugger all's happened – just run-of-the-mill crap. Certainly nothing for a desk jockey like me.'

Henry laid his hands flat on the two files and pushed them forward in much the same way that FB had done the night before. 'No,' he said. 'You're right. Nothing has come in overnight – not yet, anyway. But that doesn't mean we don't have murders to solve, or prevent.'

The four surly eyes opposite dropped to the thick files, both men now with puzzled expressions on their faces.

'Two, to be precise,' Henry went on. He looked at Rik, whose expression changed to one of understanding. Rik had been one of the team working with Henry on Joe Speakman's mess and obviously knew about the unsolved murders still on file. The expression then became one of horror and Henry said, answering the look, 'Foisted on me just before I could sneak out last night. FB's Christmas present – the wonderfully christened Twixtmas Killings.'

'And how come we're involved?' Tope enquired, pointing to himself, then Rik.

'Because . . . because I say so,' Henry returned petulantly, thinking, *I'm a fucking superintendent, that's why!* He could have got narky at that point but instead he softened, not wanting to lose these two guys. 'Look – you're two cops I trust to do a brilliant job . . . I know it's inconvenient . . . Christ, I'm supposed to be off this week,' he said, looking into their eyes, expecting and getting no sympathy. 'The problem is, we – the cops – picked up on it too late that there's a connection between these two murders and, I know it's shit, but I want to be in a position to run instantly with anything that comes in this week . . .'

'Disappeared Christmas Eve, turned up dead on New Year's Day,' Jerry Tope said. He knew the cases, too.

Henry nodded. 'Both of them. Hence the name.'

'Yeah, I know,' Tope said resignedly.

'You didn't work either murder for Joe, though, did you, Jerry?'

'No. Speakman always used the same crew . . . Jenny
Goodwin was his usual Intel cell leader.'

Henry understood this. SIOs liked to use people they knew
and could trust and work with, breaking in newbies bit by bit.
Henry was the same, that's why for intelligence issues he
always went straight to Jerry Tope.

'It's a bit hit and miss, though, isn't it, Henry?' Rik whined.

Henry's gaze turned slowly to him. 'In what way?'

Rik kind of shrugged. From his face Henry could tell he'd
had a heavy night and wondered, briefly, if Lisa had fitted in
anywhere in the festivities. Henry hadn't a clue where she'd
got to.

'Well, as I understand it, from what little I know of these
two murders . . . as Jerry said, they went missing on Christmas
Eve-ish, then turned up dead a week later . . . so, y'know . . .
what's the plan?'

'To work the cases as they stand,' Henry said. 'Two victims
related by gunshot wounds and MO . . . plus I want us to be
on hand to react immediately to anyone who is reported missing
from last night up to New Year's Eve . . .'

Rik's face sagged. 'Do you know how many . . .?'

Henry stepped in and picked it up for him. '. . . how many
people go missing over the Christmas period in Lancashire
alone? Funnily enough, I do. Last year three hundred and fifty
were reported . . . ball park figure.'

'So what do we do? Check everyone?' Rik said.

'No, not quite.'

'So what is the plan, boss?' Tope asked.

'OK.' Henry sat back – trying to think of a plan. 'You
work from here, Jerry. I want you to look at the two victims
we have and see what you can really uncover about what
links them. There must be something, and I'm not convinced
that Joe did a bang-up job in that respect. He got lazy and
distracted because of what was going on in his life.' Henry
knew that a murder investigation rarely came up trumps if
the SIO wasn't fully committed to it. 'We know some things,
but there must be others like . . . I don't know. That's your
job, Jerry. Also I want you to keep an eye on the mispers
that come in. Let's see where we are now, discard any that

don't fit our victims' profiles and any that are obviously not of interest to us. Rik, you and me will do the follow-up enquiries. In the meantime' – he glanced at Rik again – 'we do victim family revisits.'

'On Christmas Day?' Rik bleated.

'Crime doesn't take a holiday,' Henry said glibly, like an advertising slogan.

Rik shook his head in despair.

Henry looked back at Tope. 'I've already been into the control room and checked the chief's daily log,' Henry said, referring to the record compiled by the FIM that highlighted the most interesting and unusual occurrences in the county over the previous twenty-four hours. It was done primarily for the chief's information but was also put on the intranet for anyone else to read. 'There are some mispers who could possibly fit the bill. Check them out first and see what you think, then get back to me. If they're good possibilities as victims, then Rik or me will have a look. Possibility is, though, that if our killer has taken someone, if there's going to be another crime, that is, it's likely that their disappearance won't be remarked on or reported for a day or two, or even later.

'And while you're on with that, start delving into the victims we already have, like I said before.'

'Today?' Tope said, still unable to believe he was at work.

'Yes – today.'

Tope uttered a very hacked off sigh. 'Till when?'

'We'll call it a day when I say so,' Henry said – and gave him a superintendent's look.

Tope's lips twitched as though he'd been wired up to a car battery, but he said nothing, just sighed heavily again, big chest heave, head shaking.

Henry's eyes returned to Rik, then flicked back to Tope. 'There's a coffee machine in the secretary's office, Jerry . . . can you do the honours? There's coffee and everything, even fresh milk.'

Tope blinked. 'Me? Get the brews?'

'Yes, you.' He raised his eyebrows with significance and Tope got it.

'Duh – OK,' he grumbled and left the office.

Henry clasped his fingers in front of him and waited for the door to click shut. He and Rik were left facing each other.

There was an uncomfortable hush.

Then Rik said, 'Is this the bollocking from big brother?'

'You know me better than that . . . plus, I don't actually know what's going on, but it's obviously eating you up.'

'We've split, OK? It's over. That's all you need to know.'

'Fine,' Henry said. 'I'm not a relationship counsellor.'

'So what's this?' Rik made helpless gestures with his hands indicating the office, the location, his presence. 'Called in on Christmas Day. Is it punishment time? I've split with your sister, so you're pissed off with me?'

It was Henry's turn to heave a sigh. 'You're here because you're a good jack and I think we need to be ready to move on this. OK, nothing might happen. It's a waiting game. The killings might be over and if so, good. In the New Year I'll kick-start both investigations and work from scratch. But if you think for one moment you're here because you and my kid sister have fallen out of love, then you don't know me at all, Rik. I'm just surprised it lasted this long in the first place.'

'Thanks for that vote of confidence,' Rik mumbled.

'Your reputation preceded you,' Henry said. He knew Rik had been a serial womanizer and Lisa was much the same where men were concerned. But Henry had come to think they were a match made in heaven, or thereabouts. They had been scheduled to trot down the aisle next summer, but something had gone seriously wrong. The philandering gene seemed to have resurfaced in Lisa. 'That said, I'm truly sorry. I honestly wanted it to work out for you both.'

Rik's shrug was noncommittal. 'Presume she stayed at yours last night?'

'Presume wrong,' Henry said, and looked thoughtfully at Rik. 'I take it you haven't heard about our mother . . . hospital and all that?'

Rik frowned. 'No.'

Henry brought him quickly up to speed, adding that Lisa had been visiting their mother when she'd had her heart attack. 'But I haven't seen her since, Rik.'

'I thought she'd been staying at your place?'

'Not a permanent thing. Sometimes she's there, sometimes she isn't. I always assumed she was back at your flat.'

'She certainly wasn't there last night,' Rik said. 'Not when I rolled in.'

'Which was at . . .?'

'Three-ish. Probably around at her lover's shag-pad,' Rik said bitterly, doing the speech-mark finger tweak on the word 'lover's'.

'Right, whatever,' Henry said, not wanting to get involved, other than to be a brother to Lisa and offer her somewhere to crash if she needed it. 'I hope you work it out, but you are here because of your skill as a detective, not because I want to punish you, OK? I was up till gone two this morning and, trust me, I don't want to be here either – but I have to show willing.'

'Point taken, and sorry about your mum. I hope she pulls through.'

'Thanks.' *She won't*, Henry thought.

The office door opened and Tope reversed in, clutching three mugs of steaming, freshly filtered coffee. He placed them on Henry's desk, then sat down. Henry and Rik grabbed a mug each and sipped the brew gratefully.

'That's bloody excellent,' Henry said as the caffeine immediately hit the spot.

'I logged onto the secretary's computer while I was waiting for the machine,' Tope said, 'and checked the misper figures for this week last year. Three hundred and fifty-two people were reported missing in the period we are interested in. Three hundred and fifty turned up unharmed or at least accounted for, leaving two. One, our victim, David Peters, and another, a girl found dead from an overdose. Mostly they were youngsters who went AWOL after parties. There were about twenty, male and female, in the demographics we're interested in.'

'I think you can assume much the same number this year,' Henry said. 'Did you look at last night's mispers?'

Tope nodded. 'Only quickly . . . my gut is just to keep a watching brief on things . . . a lot could easily roll in hung over or still pissed, tails between their legs. A lot more will be reported towards the end of the day when they haven't rolled in.'

Henry nodded, sipping his coffee. 'The Christmas rush.' He made a decision and looked at the two murder files. 'Let's just spend the next hour going over these two files, make sure we're all acquainted with the scenarios, then' – he looked at Rik – 'you and me will work out strategies for the victims. I'd like to look at the guy from Blackpool – Peters – if that's OK? Just so I'm on hand if my mum needs me.' Rik said that wasn't a problem, he would cover the woman who'd been killed in Blackburn.

Henry's first port of call was to the cardiac unit where he found that his mother was still alive, but sleeping. Leanne was at the bedside, but there was no sign of Lisa. He walked into the small ward and his daughter looked up tearfully, then rose to embrace him. He sat next to her and regarded his mother as he spoke softly to Leanne.

'Have you seen Lisa?'

'No, not at all.'

Henry raised his eyebrows.

'One of the nurses said she wants to speak to you.'

'OK . . . how long are you staying for?'

'As long as.'

'Great Christmas Day,' he said sadly.

'We still haven't exchanged pressies.'

'No, but we will. Later, eh?'

Leanne nodded. 'Jenny's on her way up from Bristol.'

'Yeah – she texted me. Be great to see her.'

'Yeah, I really miss her. Just hope she doesn't bring that dink of a hubby with her.'

Henry chuckled. His eldest daughter's choice of mate hadn't gone down too well with Leanne, but Henry knew he was a decent enough chap, just had nothing about him except a dreary job in banking that made him a fortune. What could Jenny possibly see in such a guy?

'Mr Christie?'

Henry glanced around to see the nurse he'd spoken to the evening before standing by the ward door, the one who'd given him the keys to the empty office. She was back on duty already. She beckoned him and he followed her to her office. She then broached a subject that Henry had been mentally tangling with. A very uncomfortable one.

He emerged drained and dithery, but put on a brave face for Leanne and said he had to nip out to make a phone call.

He dialled Lisa, but the call went straight to voicemail, so he left a short message and also dropped her a text, the gist of both being to call him as soon as possible.

He wondered where she was. No doubt licking her wounds somewhere, or maybe with her new 'lover' – and Henry imagined Rik's speech marks around the word. Henry needed to speak to her sooner rather than later. There was a decision to make here and he didn't want to shoulder it alone.

He then called Alison and asked if she was still in the vicinity. She was – but getting ready to head back to the Tawny Owl. She wasn't planning on opening the pub at lunchtime, but was going to open up from four until eleven, even though it was Christmas Day. The villagers of Kendleton would need some escape from home. She and Henry planned to have dinner together that evening, but that idea had been put on hold.

'Can I catch you before you set off?'

Henry told her he was back in Blackpool visiting a witness, but if she fancied getting to the drive-through KFC on Preston New Road for a coffee in ten minutes, that would be excellent.

He dropped back in to see Leanne, who said she was going to stay for a few more hours. He kissed them both and left.

The coffee served by KFC was pretty good. Henry and Alison had one each and sat at a corner table next to the window. The place was doing healthy business.

'Have you thought about what I asked earlier?' he said.

Alison smiled. 'It was a hell of a big ask.'

'You should've seen it from my side of the court.'

'Did you really, really mean it?'

'Yes,' he said simply, holding her gaze.

'I . . . I feel like I'm teasing you,' she said.

'It's something you need to think about, I get that. Lots of
things to consider, not least of which is the age difference.'

'That's bollocks and you know it.'

'Whatev—'

'But that's not all you wanted to talk to me about, is it?'

'No.'

'Something concerning your mum?'

He nodded.

'DNR?' she guessed.

He nodded again. Do Not Resuscitate. 'Jeez,' he said pain-
fully and rubbed his tired eyes. 'If it ever becomes an issue,
which it will if her heart packs up again – which it will – does
she get pounded and electrified again? Or do we let her die
with some dignity?'

He looked past Alison at the main road, feeling stupid as
his bottom lip quivered. He inhaled a steadying breath. Alison
reached across and laid her fingers on his arm.

'Has your mum ever talked about it at all?'

'No. She thought she'd live for ever . . . she might. But
what do you think?'

Alison paused thoughtfully. 'It might be her time to go,
love. Sometimes keeping people alive is done just for the sake
of others, not for the good of the person in the hospital bed.'

'Yeah, I mean what the medical staff did was fantastic. I
know they don't want to lose people, but it was so . . .
degrading, almost.' He shook his head at the vivid memory
of the doctors and nurses working on his mother's body.
'Crikey,' he laughed, 'it's a tough one.'

'You need to talk it through properly with a consultant, not
a nurse. It's all about quality of life . . . what are the chances
of her ever going home and living any sort of a normal
existence? If it's a good chance, then OK. If not . . .'

'Yuk,' Henry said.

'But there is one thing I do know, Henry Christie.' Her left
hand slid down his forearm and covered his hand. He glanced
down at it and his eyes widened with shock. He looked sharply
up at her. 'Let's get through this, however it pans out, and
then when the time is right you can whisk me away for a dirty,
sorry – romantic – weekend, and then you can ask me to marry

you again. Obviously you'll know the answer already' – she held up her hand and wriggled the third finger, the triple diamonds twinkling in the ring he had given her – 'but I still want it done properly . . . down on one knee . . . ah-ahh – I know you've got bad knees, so I'll help you back up – without anything else for us to worry about but us.'

'Uh . . . I take it that's a yes, then?' he said thickly.

FIVE

Henry dashed back to the hospital to find no change in his mother's condition. Leanne had settled herself in for the duration, saying she would be fine when he explained he had some work to do, but would stay local, maybe fifteen minutes away tops, if needed.

He drove through the still quiet streets of Blackpool, down to the promenade, and found a place to park near the motel at which David Peters had last been seen. Henry had considered going straight to visit the dead man's wife, but decided to start his own investigation from the point at which Peters was last seen alive. Then he would visit the scene where his body had been discovered, on the edge of a farm in Poulton-le-Fylde.

Henry paid his parking fee – nothing was free in Blackpool, even on a public holiday – and walked the short distance to the motel on Talbot Road. He entered and approached the reception desk, not knowing if this was even worth a revisit, a year down the line. But Henry liked to get the feel of a crime, this was the last place Peters had been seen breathing and he wanted to do a mini recreation of events.

He knew from the file that Peters had been in a room with the 'other woman', the lady who managed one of his shops for him. Henry, Rik and DC Tope had had a quick look at the CCTV footage seized from the motel that had captured Peters arriving and leaving the establishment that fateful night. The disk had been in the murder file.

Peters had arrived alone, paid in cash, given a false name

and gone up to the room. This had all been videoed, as had the arrival of the shop manageress twenty minutes later. The two had then indulged in their carnal desires for each other – although, having read the witness statement taken unwillingly from the woman, her recollection had been a bit muted. Peters had departed, about an hour and a half after he'd arrived, and the CCTV showed him skulking out of the motel. The woman stayed for the night, and the camera caught her leaving the following morning.

So Peters had left and then not been seen until his charred body was discovered a week later in the remains of the chicken coop.

Henry mulled all this through his mind as he stood at the reception desk waiting for someone to notice him. He flashed his warrant card enticingly.

A clerk, a young man of mid-European origin, blinked at him with an air of boredom, unconcerned that a cop was at the desk. He was obviously confident that his immigration papers were in order, Henry thought. Henry tried to explain why he was here, but it was either too complicated for the man, whose grasp of English was tenuous at best, or he wasn't terribly interested. A bit of both, Henry guessed.

He did, however, understand the words 'manager' and 'I want to see'.

This turned out to be a smart young lady who was English, and Henry's explanation to her was received and understood. Henry also recognized her from the CCTV footage as the receptionist who had booked Peters in. And she remembered him, but only because the police had been to see her previously and had taken a statement. Henry had read through it while in his temporary office at the hospital. It was an unremarkable piece of writing, confirming what the CCTV showed and nothing more.

He asked her if she recalled anything further that might be of use, but she said no.

The room Peters had used for his little liaison was unoccupied, so Henry asked for the key and went to visit it, even though he realized it wouldn't be of much use to him, other than to get a sense of a victim's final hours.

There was nothing special about it. Just a basic, reasonably comfortable motel room, clear, functional.

Henry sighed as he looked around.

The room where Peters had fucked his mistress, then left alive, and never been seen breathing again – although someone would have seen him, not just the killer, because Peters had stepped out of the motel into a bustling Christmas Eve town. But no witnesses had been found, despite a flurry of press activity following the discovery of the body.

Henry left the room, handed the key back in and exited the motel onto Talbot Road, standing outside the front doors, trying to work out which direction Peters had taken. He had spun a line to his wife that he was out having a pint with a friend that night – a friend who had been tracked down and who denied having had any contact with Peters for over three months and had made no arrangements to meet him that night.

So, having had a shag, Peters left the hotel and was probably killing time before his return home. It was likely, Henry thought, that he would have headed to a town centre pub to have the said drink and ensure his breath reeked of beer.

Henry shivered as a blast of cold wind swept in from the very grey-looking Irish Sea, and seemed to wrap him in a shroud. He wondered if it was the ghost of the dead man, the one who had probably stood in this spot a year before, imploring Henry to catch his killer.

He also wondered if what he was doing was a complete waste of time.

Still, he went through the motions. He turned right and walked slowly towards the town centre, realizing the futility of his actions. Put simply, Peters could have gone in any direction and found a pub. He could have spent hours in one, or going from one to the next, to the next. There were a lot of hours to play with and no sightings to help pinpoint Peters' movements.

Henry walked disconsolately through the streets, shivered again, then made his way back to his car, realizing a couple of things that should have been followed up at the time. First, it was unlikely that the killer was operating alone. From what Henry had seen of Peters in the footage and from post-mortem photographs, he was a biggish guy and for one person to have lifted him from the street was stretching it. He was already convinced that two or more offenders were involved – which gave Henry a bit of heart. Lone killers were notoriously difficult to catch, but more than one equalled weakness. The other thing that Henry wondered about was the name that Peters had used at the motel. Was there any significance in it, or was it just randomly plucked out of nowhere?

His mind swirled with all these thoughts, but he was enjoying the process. Back in the car, he called Jerry Tope.

'This is one of the best Christmas Days I've ever had,' Tope whinged.

'I'm having a doody, too,' Henry assured him.

'Yeah, yeah . . . sorry to hear about your mum, by the way. Rik told me.'

'Thanks. You got anywhere yet?'

'No . . . so far the overnight mispers aren't likely victims. I'm just piecing together what we know about the actual victims. Nothing's really jumping out yet.'

Henry asked Tope to consider his thoughts about Peters' assumed name and the 'more than one killer' scenario, and also asked him to do a national check for similar crimes – kidnaps, followed by bodies being shot and dumped and set on fire, particularly around Christmas time.

Then Henry called Rik Dean to check on his progress on the opposite side of the county. Getting no reply, he left a voice message,

He decided to visit the scene where Peters' body had been discovered, thinking dismally that this had all the hallmarks of being a long drawn-out investigation, not made any easier by coming to it late.

Whenever possible, Henry liked to be in at the death.

Another person not especially happy to see Henry on Christmas Day was Bernadette Peters. She opened her front door suspiciously to him. He gave her his best lopsided grin (it was getting a little overused on that day), which became a 'sorry to disturb you' expression as he introduced himself.

'I'm actually just having my Christmas dinner . . . but, hey, what the hell, it's only an M&S meal for one. I can zap it back in the microwave. Come in.' She stood back and let him walk past her. She was still dressed in her sleeping attire, a long towelling dressing gown tied tightly over her nightdress and a pair of fluffy, tatty slippers.

Henry thanked her and entered the lounge of the house, which was situated in Blackpool's north shore on the boundary with Bispham. It was a careworn semi in need of a lot of TLC.

She had been watching TV with a tray balanced on her knees, on which was her plated-up microwaveable turkey dinner for one. She moved past Henry and picked up the tray, giving him a sidelong glance. 'I really pushed out the boat this year . . . it's usually a Tesco one.' She went into the kitchen.

Henry felt a slight jolt within him. Nothing connected with the investigation, but something that stabbed at his own failings as a man and husband. He had an inner vision of the countless Christmas Days that Kate had been forced to endure without him because of 'work commitments'. He knew she had often prepared meals of proper turkey, slaved over a hot stove, only for them to go to waste, but at the time it hadn't meant anything much to Henry, not being home at Christmas. Kate had always laughed it off. He swallowed dryly.

And here he was again, working on 25 December. His mouth went tight in self-loathing.

Mrs Peters emerged from the kitchen and Henry smiled again, noting that under the drabness of her unkempt appearance, she was very attractive. 'Obviously I don't know why you're here, but I guess it's about David. Can I offer you a brew?'

'That would be great. Tea? Just milk.'

'Coming up. I'll go back in here' – she pointed to the kitchen – 'and you can have a minute or two doing what detectives do – snoop. I don't mind.'

Henry chuckled and said, 'Only on TV.' But when she disappeared, he snooped, taking in the room, the fixtures and fittings, the framed photographs on the fireplace, one of which was of her and her dead husband. Henry picked it up and studied it, wondering how happy she thought they'd been at the time.

'Don't know why I keep it there.'

Henry spun guiltily as she came back in from the kitchen, bearing two mugs of tea, handing one across to him.

'What do you mean?'

She screwed up her face and sat on the settee, pondering the question. 'Dunno,' she frowned. 'I thought we were OK-ish. Not ab-fab, if you know what I mean, just pretty standard. Dull, unremarkable, rubbed along all right, mostly, tolerated each other. Clearly he thought I was a boring cow. Two kids – who, incidentally, I haven't seen for six months – then, Wham!'

Henry took a seat on an armchair.

'He's having a sordid affair and then he's murdered. Double-wham, actually. I'm still not sure I can believe either. He wasn't exactly a Romeo, but mind you, that bitch isn't exactly Angelina Jolie – but hey! These things happen.' She sounded sad, resigned and, despite using the word 'bitch', not resentful.

'You think the two are connected, the affair and the murder?'

'It'd make sense, but I doubt it. Her husband isn't a killer.'

'What about you?'

'If I'd found out about the affair, maybe I would've been.' She looked slyly at Henry. 'Is that why you're here? Has some evidence come to light that says I'm the killer?'

'Now you're teasing me,' Henry chided. 'No is the answer to that, but I am investigating David's murder.'

'Isn't there a link to another murder – a woman in Blackburn?'

'You know about that?'

'I got told – and asked a lot of questions.'

'Do you think he knew the woman?'

'I don't know. I didn't know her . . . that said, it seemed I didn't know very much about him at all.'

Henry nodded sagely, not wanting to say anything trite, like 'No one ever really knows someone else,' just to sympathize with her. He looked at her, saw a lost soul.

'So no ideas?'

'No – and don't think I haven't thought about it.'

'How would you describe your husband?'

'Dour, intelligent enough, not especially creative . . . just a bloke, bit of a country bumpkin in some ways.'

'What about the year leading up to his death? Was there anything unusual about it, did anything unusual happen? Did he change at all?'

'No, seemed the same old self . . . but it wasn't a great year. A bit distant, more than usual. Now whether that was because he was seeing Stella . . . fuck, Stella,' she sneered. 'What a name! Tart's name.' She became thoughtful, then said, 'Maybe he had changed . . . we were both a bit too insulated from each other . . . drifted apart.'

'How long had you been married?'

'Best part of twenty years . . . we sort of met at college.'

'Do you think he kept secrets from you?'

'What, other than the sordid affair? Probably. Don't all men?'

'Not necessarily.'

'I've just been to have a quick look at the place where David's body was found,' Henry said. 'Does that mean anything to you? Is there any reason you can think of as to why he should've ended up there? Is there any significance to it?'

She shook her head. 'Been asked that before. I gave a detailed statement.'

'I know. I've read it. I'm sorry if I'm covering old ground' – actually, he wasn't – 'but sometimes things come back to people and other things start to have meanings that weren't there before. And, of course, I've taken charge of the investigation, so it's important for me to get a handle on it.'

'On Christmas Day?'

Henry's eyes roved quickly around the room. It was decorated in a desultory way, as if there was no heart or feeling behind the hanging baubles or the weary-looking Christmas tree. Nor was there any sign of presents, or wrapping paper. He guessed she was a lonely woman who lived in a grey world. He smiled at her. 'Good point . . . sorry to disturb you, but at least you know that we're still investigating your husband's death. It won't necessarily bring you good cheer, but I hope it reassures you.'

'Do you think you'll get whoever did it?'

'Yes, I do.'

'You sound confident.'

'That's because I am.' And, he thought smugly to himself, Because I'm friggin' good at it.

There was nothing to report from Jerry Tope, other than more grumblings about his spoiled Christmas, but he let Henry know he was still working on the backgrounds of the two victims to see where their paths might have crossed in the past, if at all. He said he was having problems accessing the national database to cross-check the MOs with any similar murders elsewhere in the country. He moaned that he had been forced to revert to Google, which was throwing up a lot of dross. There was nothing of interest on the missing person front, either. He finished by asking when he could go home.

Henry checked his watch, his mind swilling with ghosts of Christmases ruined.

'Finish what you're doing but leave it at a point where you can pick it up straight away when you come back in, and go home. I apologize for dragging you in, so go and have a nice rest of the day with Marina' – that was Tope's mono-browed, moustachioed wife – 'and be in bright and early on the twenty-seventh.'

Henry thought he could actually feel the wafts of disbelief as Tope's eyelids fluttered rapidly.

'You certain, Henry? You mean I can actually have Boxing Day off?'

'Yeah, go for it,' Henry said, ignoring the cheeky irony. 'Have you got some special home-made wine ready?'

'Oh, yeah.' Tope suddenly became enthusiastic. He was a purveyor of home brewing and wine making. 'A special nettle wine. Been laid down for six months. Lovely.'

Henry blanched, but said, 'Go – enjoy, see you day after tomorrow.'

'Oh, did you discover anything interesting?'

'Nah, bit of a waste, really.'

Henry ended the call and checked the time. Three p.m. and the day was already beginning to draw in, dark winter clouds thickening across the sky, spats of icy rain starting to blob down on the car windscreen. He called up Rik Dean, who answered this time and gave Henry a succinct account of his day, which was also quite fruitless. Henry told him to go home, too, and come back in on the 27th when they would start to pull together a murder squad of some description.

Henry then sat in his car, mulling. More than anything he wanted to see Alison again today, especially since things had progressed in their relationship – and though he knew it was very base of him, he was eager to jump into bed with her and consummate the event. He couldn't quite see how that was going to happen, at least not today.

His mother was awake and she watched him enter the room through watery, almost sightless eyes. Leanne was still by the bed, a grim expression on her face. Henry gave her a reassuring wink, then said to his mother, 'Hi, Mum, how you doing?'

'Is that you, Henry?'

'It is.'

'Where have you been?'

'Working, Mum.'

She looked at Leanne. 'Sweetie, can I have a moment with your dad?'

Leanne rose and left the room, grimacing. She touched Henry's arm on the way out. He settled into her vacated chair and asked, 'How are you feeling?'

'Grim,' she gasped, and lay her head back on the plumped-up pillows.

'What do you know?' he asked her.

'Everything . . . my heart stopped, didn't it?'

'It did, so they zapped you and restarted it. Simple. Like jump-starting a car.'

She took a long breath. 'Don't let them do that again, Henry.'

His throat instantly went dry and dread skittered through him, suddenly making him feel very weak. 'What d'you mean, Mum?'

'Henry.' She reached out blindly for him and he took her hand. 'I've passed the ninety mark, outlived your father by fifteen years – and most of the people I've ever known. I'm lucky. I've never been really ill and I don't want to start being a burden on anyone . . . no, shush. I know what would happen. I'm not stupid. I knew I was OK last time . . . this time I know I won't be. I'm tired. My body's had enough and I'd rather go out on top than as a root vegetable.'

'Mum!'

'That said, if I get better – great, but I won't. So if the ticker packs up again, *do not let them restart it*. Hear me?'

Henry stared mutely at their interlocked hands.

'Promise me.'

'OK,' he muttered, not certain if he would or wouldn't.

The subsequent discussion with Leanne was very tense and tearful as Henry brought her into the picture about DNR. It ended with a long hug that made Henry feel quite good, actually. The last few months had been quite fraught with Leanne, especially after she had ended up back home after a disastrous break-up which had been followed by using the house, in Henry's words, as 'a knocking shop', as a series of boyfriends came and went – and always went if Henry was about, hence the friction.

They had patched things up, more or less, and ironically it seemed that his mother's ill-health had helped things between them.

Henry wondered briefly about the living arrangements at his house in Blackpool.

With Lisa there on and off, Leanne a permanent fixture, and his other daughter Jenny on the way up from Bristol (she would want to spend time there with her aunt and little sister, no doubt), and if Alison came and went, he would be completely surrounded by women again, as he had been all his life. He partly pined for a son and often worried why his issue hadn't 'manned-up'.

But that train had long gone, not even worth thinking about.

And as much as female relatives annoyed the crap out of him, he had a bit of a warm glow to think they were all going to be back in one place.

Plus Alison: an addition who had been met with much hostility from Leanne, but who had recently moved into the toleration phase, if not quite acceptance. He did worry about how Leanne might react to the news of the engagement, though. It would probably set her back.

'Chaos,' he thought and shook his head at the prospect.

Leanne looked up at him with moist eyes and said, 'What are you thinking about?'

'Life, death and the universe,' he said philosophically and smiled. 'Let's just see how it all pans out, eh?'

'Hey.'

'Hey you,' Alison replied.

Henry was walking down a hospital corridor, mobile phone attached to his ear, having called Alison on the landline at the Tawny Owl. The mobile phone signal out there in the wilds was iffy at best.

'How's it going?' he asked lamely.

'Good. We're about to open for the afternoon-stroke-evening. The locals are already queued up outside and the dining room's fully booked until eight, which means we'll get through about eighty covers all told. Forty quid a head, plus drinks . . . it's a living. What's happening with you?'

'Mum's awake.' He told Alison of the DNR conversation he'd just had with Leanne, which brought from her noises of genuine sympathy.

She asked what his next move was. 'I really want to be up there with you,' he moaned, 'but I'm going to stay here for the rest of the afternoon. Jenny's imminent and I'd like to see her. And I still need to speak to Lisa, because it'll be me and her who make the final DNR decision. When mum's bedded down for the night, I'll come up.'

'You don't have to. I'll be exhausted, and so will you.'

'In which case you'll be unable to fend off my advances . . . and I'd like to make some.'

Alison giggled. 'OK, look forward to it. What about your work, though?'

'Sacking it for the day, unless something really compelling turns up.'

They exchanged a few lovey-dovey words and ended the call.

The remainder of the afternoon was spent by his mother's bedside. Jenny, his eldest, did arrive, weary and bedraggled from her long journey up from the south-east, but still looking particularly beautiful to Henry. His first child, still very, very special. There were lots of hugs and kisses and tears, then she went to freshen up at Henry's house, promising to return to the hospital later.

One person who failed to appear was Lisa. Henry called her a few times but got no answer.

Only as he walked along another hospital corridor did he have a lurching thought. Here he was, waiting for someone to be reported missing from home who could be the possible victim of a kidnapper/killer, yet he'd never considered that Lisa, his own kid sister, fitted the profile of the previous two victims. She was about the right age – being quite a bit younger than Henry – and had been born in Hyndburn.

He flicked open his phone and called Rik Dean, her ex-fiancé. 'Have you heard anything from Lisa yet?' Henry asked.

'Should I have?' he said, a hurt tone in the words.

'No, maybe not,' Henry conceded. 'That said, I haven't heard anything either and I've been calling her all day. I'm getting a bit concerned.'

Rik uttered a cynical *harumph*. 'She's ditzy and it's not unlike her to do something like this. I mean, she's hardly likely to be our killer's next victim . . . is she?' Rik's voice changed on the last two words as the penny slotted home.

'Life is full of coincidences,' Henry said, 'and I doubt whether she is the next victim, but from a welfare point of view I'd like to know she's OK. She has been pretty cut up about you two splitting,' he fibbed a little.

'It was her freaking fault. Why's she blubbering?' Rik demanded.

'Uh – dunno . . . Look, do you know who the guy is she's . . . er . . . seeing?' It was a delicate question. Henry had never enquired, didn't really want to know if he was honest.

'I do.' Henry could almost hear Rik's teeth gnashing.

Henry waited, nothing came. 'Well, bloody tell me. He might know where she is.'

'Peregrine Astley-Barnes,' Rik said primly.

Henry registered the name. 'As in Astley-Barnes the jewellers?'

'One and the same.'

'The millionaire jewellers?'

'Henry – you're twisting the knife here.'

'Sorry, mate.'

'I wouldn't mind, but she met the stuck-up bastard through her work and then we bought our engagement ring from him.'

Henry was glad Rik couldn't see his grin. The Astley-Barnes family, Henry knew, were diamond retailers, at the very high end of that particular market. They had four stores in Lancashire, two on the coast, two inland, and others in Manchester, Chester and York. They were the kinds of stores with security guards and doors that locked you in – or out – of the shops with thick, unbreakable, plate-glass windows.

'You bought an engagement ring from them? How much does an inspector earn these days?'

'Crippled me,' Rik admitted. 'I wouldn't mind but she'd already started seeing the twat, so I don't know why she let me go through with the purchase.' Lisa made intricate silver jewellery, very exquisite, and sold it through shops like the Astley-Barneses'.

'You got a number for him?'

'Oh yes,' Rik said ominously. 'And car details and bank details . . .'

'Stop right there. I haven't heard that,' Henry said. 'If you're going to get yourself in data protection shit, I don't want to know. Just give me the guy's number.'

As much security as the Astley-Barnes family had, it did not make them immune to becoming the victims of crime. Armed robberies at their shops were infrequent, but when they did happen they were usually very violent affairs resulting in severe beatings for the staff and oodles of rocks being stolen. Nor were the family completely safe in their own homes. Henry had once dealt with what is known as a Tiger Kidnapping, when a member of the family was held hostage while other family members were forced to open up the shops and hand over diamonds, otherwise there would be serious bloodshed.

The problem for the robber on that occasion was that the police had a tip-off and were ready and waiting. In a carefully planned operation run by Henry, the whole gang had been caught and subsequently convicted.

In his dealings with the family Henry had found them to be pleasant and not in the least stuck-up, as Rik insinuated. They were clearly members of the upper class, whose fortunes could be traced back to nineteenth-century diamond fields in South Africa.

He phoned the number Rik had given him. It rang, then dropped onto voicemail. Henry left a short message. Then he called Lisa again and left one for her, too. Hopefully, if the two of them were together, maybe holed up in a shag-pad somewhere, they'd put two and two together and get in touch. As he slotted his phone back into his jacket pocket, it rang.

'Hooray,' he said and answered it, thinking it might be Lisa.

'Henry? It's me, Jerry.'

'Not gone home?'

'I wish.'

'What's up?'

'I might have something . . .'

'I've been looking at the two victims, as you asked, doing the backgrounds and all that. First thing is, Peters was born in September, Blackshaw in December, both in the same year. So they were both the same age as each other, one slightly older.'

Henry listened hard, wishing he was face to face with Tope. Ingesting vital information over a mobile phone line wasn't easy, and Tope had a knack for dramatic suspense that was often irritating.

'And they were both born in Hyndburn.'

'Yes, I know that.'

'Now, I've also been trawling for similar murders in other parts of the country and I've unearthed one that looks similar – but this is from Google, so I haven't got all the details I need . . . but . . . three years ago, Christmas Eve, a female was abducted and turned up dead – shot and burned near Leeds. She was born in the February of the year after our two. In Hyndburn. A woman by the name of Ella Milner.'

Henry screwed up his face, his urge to say, '*And?*' hard to suppress.

'The Leeds MO is similar to ours, so I won't go into it . . . but if you look at the dates of birth it means that the victims were all in the same school year, though not necessarily at the same school.'

'Right.' Henry still didn't gee him along. He picked some flaky skin out of his right ear with his fingernail.

'OK,' Tope said. 'Regarding the birthplaces: all three were born in Hyndburn – except they weren't.'

Henry frowned.

'I've dug through all the records I can and the thing is, their births were registered in Hyndburn, but all three were actually born in their houses in Belthorn, which is a village on the outskirts of Hyndburn, overlooking Blackburn. But it comes under Hyndburn, such are the vagaries of local authority boundaries, hence how the births were registered. Geographically, it's nearer to Blackburn.'

'I know Belthorn. Out on the moors.'

'Exactly, a small place out in the wilds, but with two primary schools, Belthorn School and the Methodist School.'

Henry's ring piece twitched, a sure sign of excitement.

'So, yeah . . . and you know I just said that just because they were the same age, it didn't mean they went to the same school? Well guess what? They did all go to the same school – ta-dah! Belthorn School, to be precise . . . they were all there in the same year. And, in fact, having trawled through the internet, I've even found a picture of the class they were in on some website dedicated to the history of the village. And all three are in it, sat there like little innocent babies.'

'How old would they be?'

'We're talking about the late 1970s, so eleven . . . just before they moved on to whichever high school they went to. I haven't got that far yet.'

'Two things. First, well done, Jerry. Second, why didn't we know this already?'

Tope did not reply. In the background Henry heard a phone.

'Just let me get that, Henry,' Tope said, giving Henry a moment to take in this information. It was a relief of sorts: at least Lisa hadn't been born in Belthorn, if that was the connection between the victims, even though she was in the right age group, and she hadn't been at school in Belthorn, either. Like Henry, she'd been to school in Accrington. Not far away, but far enough.

Tope returned to the phone. 'Henry, that was the FIM just bringing me up to speed with mispers . . . I think we might have one that fits the bill . . . let me get back to you.'

SIX

Henry realized he could say adios to what little remained of his day, but for the life of him he couldn't bring himself to spoil Rik's and Tope's day any further, after having told them they could go home. He asked Tope to email details of the misper to his Blackberry and set off eastwards from Blackpool after first checking on his mother's condition: no worse. Then he called Alison but she was too busy to get to the phone, so he left a message with the word 'sorry' in it numerous times.

A few minutes later he was gunning the Audi east along the M55 out of Blackpool, his phone connected to the handsfree and a mike clipped to his ear, making him feel ridiculous as always.

When he did retire, one of the things he promised himself was to ditch technology updates for ever. He would keep what he had, but stuff the upgrades. It bored him. Rigid.

The Audi responded superbly on the virtually empty motorway, Henry keeping the speed around the eighty mark and trying to enjoy the drive, the feel of the car under his arse and through his hands and feet, and trying not to think about leaving his mother with his daughters, his sister still not having surfaced . . . and Alison getting further and further away in

Kendleton, hoping she didn't lose the engagement ring in the soup of the day. The ring he had bought from Astley-Barnes jewellers, a fact he didn't have the bottle to admit to Rik.

'Jeez,' he sighed. A train wreck of a day.

He had soon joined the M65, heading east as the day continued to darken, clouds thickening like broth. Within thirty minutes of leaving Blackpool, the Audi was climbing up through the village of Belthorn. At the top of the village, he bore right into Tower View – so called because a few miles across the hills to the south was Darwen Tower – though as Henry glanced in that direction there was no way the structure was visible that day.

The tarmac road petered out to become a gravel track, but he only had to travel a hundred metres further to reach his destination, pulling in to the side. He got out, feeling the bitter cold up-here, high on the moors. He walked to the closed wrought iron gates of the large detached house which lay at the end of a curved driveway.

The house was new, large and garishly decorated, festooned with Christmas lights, illuminated reindeer and several huge inflated figures, including Santa himself, Rudolph and a sleigh.

He had been told to use the intercom set into the gatepost and not to enter because of the dogs, and a red-lettered sign on the gatepost proclaimed he had to beware of them.

He pressed the talk button, which buzzed. Then he waited . . . and although he knew his day had already been ruined in more ways than one, this might just make up for it. He could not help but be excited by standing there in the chill of the approaching evening.

After all, it wasn't often a cop got the chance to visit the lair of one of the county's biggest and most ruthless crime families.

'Run that by me again,' Henry had said to Jerry Tope, amazement in his voice.

'I know – incredible, isn't it?' Tope had chuckled at his news.

'You're telling me that one of the Cromer family has gone

AWOL and they're reporting him missing? To the police?'
The rising inflection in Henry's voice reflected his disbelief.

'That's exactly what I'm telling you: Freddy Cromer has
gone missing and yeah, they're reporting it.'

Henry pouted thoughtfully at the news.

'Accrington section have reported it,' Tope explained, filling
in the silence. 'All they've done is send a response patrol and
the PC took the report and circulated it. Just treated it as an
adult gone missing, as they would, and not really attached
much significance to it yet – as they would,' he said again.
'Obviously they don't know what we're up to, which is why
they've done the normal thing. But the FIM spotted it, as it
fits our missing person criteria.'

'Mmm, normal except it's the Cromer clan and Freddy
Cromer isn't the full shilling, as I remember,' Henry said.

'And it's a bit odd they're telling us,' Tope mused. 'Perhaps
because Freddy isn't all there, maybe they're concerned.'

'Should we be?'

'On the face of it, not really. He's apparently stable enough
to go out on the lash, which he did last night, and he just
hasn't landed home. And he hasn't got his keep calm tabs with
him.'

'Does he fit our victim profile?'

'Totally . . . right age group, the Belthorn link – although
I think he was actually born in Preston – and he's even sitting
in the class photo I told you about, like butter wouldn't melt
in his mouth, although we all know he eats car parts. You'd
never guess how he turned out. Looks like an angel.'

'Shit,' Henry said, thinking. 'Runt of the litter.' He made
his decision at that point. 'I'm going up to speak to them.'

A distorted, tinny voice spoke on the intercom and Henry
responded by introducing himself. There was a pause, then
the voice said, 'What do you want?'

'I'd like to speak to Mrs Cromer please. About Freddy. I
believe he's missing.'

'And you are?'

Henry repeated his name and rank.

'Wait there.' The intercom clicked dead.

Henry took a step back and looked through the wrought-iron gate at the house, which was about a hundred metres away. A new build, with various outbuildings, garages and a small stable block, it looked a very nice house, with a view from the rear across the hills to the south which on a clear day must have been outstanding.

Four cars were drawn up outside: an old Jaguar XJS (a real gangster's motor, Henry thought), a new Kia Sportage and a couple of smaller, older saloons, a Mondeo and a van.

The front door opened, light flooded out, and then two dogs rushed out and pelted towards the gate, a figure following them.

They were German Shepherds, big, good-looking, well cared for, mature dogs. They skidded up to the gate, snuffling their wet snouts through the iron railings, but neither barked at Henry. They stood side by side and looked balefully at him through golden eyes.

Henry took a step back and swallowed. Not a great fan of dogs. He could recall the incident over thirty years ago when as a probationer constable, he and his training class had been shown around the police dog training facilities at Moor Farm, Hutton, where the dog unit was based. Being nineteen and stupid he had foolishly volunteered to be a 'robber on the run' from a police dog and after being well briefed, had set off like a hare, convinced he could outrun a well-trained German Shepherd. He had even been given a hundred-metre start, but the dog caught him in a flash. Fortunately a padded protective sleeve had been fitted over his left arm, which he had been told to present to the dog, for it brought him down with the force of a small truck and sank its fangs into the many-layered protection. Even now, Henry could feel the fangs sinking in, causing him to shiver at the memory.

'They won't bite. They're softies,' a female voice came from the darkness behind the two dogs. Henry looked up and saw that the figure who had accompanied them from the house was a young woman, maybe early twenties, dressed in tight jeans, cowboy-style boots, a figure-hugging roll-neck sweater. She was also astoundingly pretty with a rounded jaw, full lips, nice eyes. Her hair was cut into a well-trimmed bob that framed her face.

Henry thought he had come to the wrong property.

The Cromers were a northern English version of a hillbilly criminal family and Henry expected to be greeted by – yes, two hounds from hell – but also pitchfork-yielding rednecks.

The woman stepped between the two dogs, easing them gently away, and placed her face between two perpendicular bars, so it looked as though she was looking out of a prison cell.

Henry fished out his warrant card. 'Detective Superintendent Christie.'

'Janine Cromer,' she responded.

Henry squinted at her, maybe seeing some family resemblance. She looked second generation.

'I've come about Freddy. I'm informed he's gone missing.'

'We've already reported him. A police constable has been up to take details.'

'I know. I'm just doing some follow-up.'

'A detective superintendent?' she questioned, amused.

'A detective superintendent,' he confirmed. 'You going to let me in, or not?'

She surveyed him thoughtfully up and down, her eyes narrowed, weighing him up.

'Because,' he continued, 'I'm not going to stand out here for much longer.'

She unlocked the gate, took hold of each dog by the collar, then turned and manually guided them back towards the house. Henry followed at a respectful distance, knowing he was much slower than he'd been at nineteen, but with his bottom twitching again at the thought of entering the domain of the Cromers. That said, he wasn't foolish enough to think he would see or find anything of interest inside. He guessed that business and home life were kept separate. It wasn't as though he would be shown into a room where the cocaine was being diluted with talc and bagged up or where the cannabis was being grown. That would be something that happened elsewhere – though he had no idea exactly where. The Cromers were rumoured to have at least a dozen cannabis farms, but the police had yet to find even one of them.

Janine led the dogs and Henry up to the house, the dogs

constantly pulling at her as they looked over their shoulders at Henry, tongues lolling, lots of slavering going on, pointy teeth visible. At the door, she held the dogs to one side and indicated for Henry to go into the house ahead of her. He gave them a wide berth and stepped inside, into a wide hallway. A moment later she was with him, having left the dogs outside.

'Nice dogs,' he commented.

'Through here.' She pointed up the hallway to a door on the left which led into a large kitchen. Henry passed another door on his left, from behind which he heard raised male voices.

He went into the kitchen, which was expansive and expensive-looking. There was a double-sized range cooker and a large island unit in the centre of the room on which were the remnants of a buffet. A few plates with sandwiches, bowls of crisps, breadsticks and dips and a wide array of bottles, wine, beer and spirits. Looked like a family Christmas get-together, Henry thought, and maybe the family was in the other room he'd walked past – at least the male members, because here in the kitchen were four ladies. One looked old and wrinkled, two were perhaps mid forties and the fourth in her twenties. All sat at the table, each with a glass of wine in hand.

Their eyes spun to him, this interloper. He flashed a thought: crims' wives, crims' mums – crimwags – then forced a thin smile and said, 'Merry Christmas, ladies.'

Not one of them looked either happy to see him, or happy in themselves. Their faces were all deadly serious, as Henry had seen in the moment before they had turned to him. Each had anger and concern across their faces, but that didn't stop them from regarding him like prey.

'This is Detective Superintendent Christie,' Janine announced. 'He's come about Freddy' – and the tone of her voice meant that she didn't need to add, 'If you believe that!'

One said, 'Well fuck-a-doodle. Just what we need – a cop. Shall we gobble him up?'

Henry's forced smile remained fixed as he quickly tried to work out who was who. The oldest woman was easiest – Granny Cromer, clan matriarch, all-round vicious cow. He knew her face because he'd seen the mug shots a few times, but not recently. She had a long history of violence and debauchery. Knocking seventy, her hell-raising days were over, but only just. This, Henry thought, was Freddy's mother.

The other women were not so easy to pinpoint. One had a Cromer look about her: angular, dark eyed, pretty in an austere sort of way. Henry thought she could be Lizzie – who had once been convicted of attacking another woman with an axe and was known as Lizzie the Blade – but he was not certain. She looked like Granny, maybe was her daughter, maybe Janine's mum. He would have to look at the family tree on his next visit to the Major Crime Unit. The others didn't have any family resemblance and Henry could not place them. Maybe they were friends of the family.

So he thought Janine could be Lizzie's daughter. Janine certainly had a similarity, but now that Henry saw her in proper light, she had a softer edge to her features.

'So why've you turned up?' Granny Cromer asked, interrupting his recollections. She was smoking and blew out a lungful as she spoke, her voice rasping like sandpaper. 'Snoopin'? 'Cos this isn't a job for a detective superintendent. My son's gone missing and I'm worried about him because he hasn't taken his freakin' psycho tablets with him. That's all.' She scowled like a witch.

'Professional service,' Henry said.

'Have we ever had anything to do with you?' she asked, peering suspiciously at him. 'Personally, like?'

'Yes, you have,' Henry said, and caught the look of realization on Granny's face.

'You're the bastard who put Jimmy away!' she accused him.

'It doesn't matter what my past involvement with you was,' Henry said equably, aware that he had entered a nest of vipers. 'I'm here to help now, that's all.' He opened his hands in a gesture designed to say that he was here to offer peace, not war. All he was short of were the butterflies.

Granny's old head shook and her thin corrugated lips sneered at him. 'Yeah, fucking right.'

'So who can I talk to?' Henry asked. 'I mean, you're clearly concerned about Freddy . . .'

'No we're not!'

Henry rotated slowly at the voice and looked at the man now framed in the kitchen door.

Terry Cromer, undisputed head of the Cromer family.

'We're un-reporting him,' he said firmly. 'Thanks for your concern but we don't need any police involvement. We'll find him ourselves.'

'Can I have a word?' Henry said, knowing who he was speaking to and aware that, not two years ago, Henry had put his son away for life on a murder charge.

Henry Christie had been a member of Lancashire Constabulary for over thirty years and he had known about the Cromer family and their activities for most of those years.

Henry's first posting had been as a PC to Blackburn and, at nineteen, he'd had plenty of run-ins with the wild, out of control Cromer family. They had various homes throughout the east of the county and although the core of the family came from Belthorn, some were based on the Shadsworth council estate in Blackburn, an area they ruled with intimidation and havoc, continually at war with other families and criminal factions. Henry had come face to face with a few of the younger Cromers, usually for minor offences and public order incidents.

As they had matured, their activities became more subtle and old father Cromer – Granny's husband – took a grip of the family and realized the potential of drug dealing, especially as he could call on some of the more dumb, but violent members of the family to act as enforcers. He harnessed one of his two sons and they moved into the nightclubs of Blackburn and other towns, taking control of the doors – and therefore the drugs trade – and eventually some of the clubs themselves.

The business expanded quickly, but even old man Cromer could not stop the onset of cancer, which killed him as ruthlessly as any bullet, leaving the son – Terry – in charge of the business.

Terry was the favoured son because the other, Frederick, was always a liability. Weak-willed, mentally unstable and prone to outrageous violence, even against his own family.

Nor did it help that he was built like a brick shithouse. Freddy was farmed out of the way to live in Rossendale with an aunt, but his isolation from the family only increased his paranoia.

Henry had come across Freddy in the mid eighties when, as a teenager, he tried to strangle his aunt, then attempted to kill Henry. It was during Henry's days in uniform, working on the crime car in the Rossendale Valley before he moved on to CID

Frantic neighbours had called in the job after every window of the council house in Rawtenstall was smashed from the inside, closely followed by items of furniture being jettisoned into the garden – and, as Henry drew up in the police car, Freddy's aunt joining the broken furniture from an upstairs window.

Henry was alone, not unusual for a cop down the valley, and he just missed catching her as she slammed down hard and awkwardly onto her pelvis, which he distinctly heard go crack, and which he later learned had shattered into six brittle pieces. He had been doing the obvious, caring thing and bending down on one knee to check out the moaning lady, when Freddy leaned out of an upstairs window and fired an air rifle at him. The pellet thudded into his chest, hitting the personal radio swinging around his neck, one of those Burndept things made of tough plastic, about the size of half a house brick slit lengthways.

Incensed, the younger, angrier Henry kicked open the front door and barged through, only to meet Freddy leaping down the stairs like a silverback gorilla, uttering a terrible demented scream. He launched himself at Henry from the fourth step, landing on him and driving him backwards out of the door, catching the raised threshold with his heel. Henry tipped over, cracked the back of his head – which split – and Freddy straddled and started to strangle him with big, thick thumbs and fingers, about the circumference of pork sausages.

Henry struggled, punching young Freddy on the side of the face repeatedly and as hard as he could, but even though Freddy was only a teenager, he was impossible to dislodge. Freddy's red, rage-filled face still often came to Henry in nightmares, the wild eyes bulging, the sweat dripping, the jagged but smooth-surfaced lines of a burn mark down the side of his face.

Fortunately, backup was en route, though for Henry it couldn't get there quickly enough. Freddy's windpipe-crushing grip was having a serious effect on his vision as blood and oxygen were effectively cut off from his brain and his punches were losing force and coordination, becoming more like weak slaps as Freddy simply rolled with them.

The real ignominy for Henry was that he was going to die at the hands of a deranged teenager, which would only go to prove the old police adage that it was the routine jobs that were always the most dangerous.

First on the scene to assist was the local detective inspector, who just happened to be in the neighbourhood on an unrelated matter. He ran up and kicked Freddy's head like it was a rugby ball – which did the trick momentarily.

Freddy released the killing grip on Henry's throat as he rolled away. Beautiful, fresh, clean, lovely air rushed back into Henry's lungs and he sat up, clutching his throat, but he didn't have time for much convalescence because Freddy simply rolled over a few times, came back up as though he was on starting blocks and charged Henry and the DI.

The ensuing scuffle was messy and a bit dirty.

The DI – a certain Robert Fanshaw-Bayley – got stuck in and he and Henry managed to subdue Freddy, but only by getting him face down on the front lawn and, Henry having dropped with all his weight on one knee onto his spine between the shoulder blades, forcing Freddy's thick arms around his back. They got him double-cuffed: in those days the police were issued with rather flimsy cuffs connected by metal links, not rigid handcuffs, and sometimes it was prudent to put two sets on a violent prisoner, ratcheting them tight into the skin. They then both sat on Freddy, gasping for breath as he continued to squirm and curse underneath them like a trapped crocodile.

'Can't believe this fucker is only a teenager,' FB said, ruddy faced. Even back then he was a big, unfit bloke.

'Big lad,' Henry agreed, massaging his neck.

Freddy was arrested – thrown into the back of the section

van by four officers. Having caused a lot of problems in the
cells down at Rawtenstall nick, not least because he suffered
severe claustrophobia, he was sectioned under the Mental
Health Act and spent much of the rest of his life after that in
secure and non-secure institutions, depending on his state of
mind.

Henry didn't bother to pursue the assault on himself (and
neither did Freddy's aunt, even though she was badly injured).
The main reason was that when Freddy's room at his aunt's
was searched, Henry found fifty beheaded pigeons, the heads
having been bitten off by Freddy, two dead dogs that had been
gutted, four dead cats – hung from the ceiling by their tails
– and numerous rodents that had met their deaths in various
ways, all stacked neatly away in Freddy's sock drawer.

It was plain that Freddy was not remotely stable 'up top'
and to prosecute him would be a pointless exercise, a waste of
public money. It was going to cost the state enough to provide
him with the care and treatment he needed, so Freddy pretty
much disappeared into the system, never to be heard of again.

Until now.

Terry Cromer looked at Henry through half-lidded eyes,
an expression of contempt on his face, and a little surge of
something skittered through the detective. Apprehension and
excitement.

Henry knew about this family. Despite their outward
appearance as country hicks, they had become a well-oiled
money-making machine, very disciplined and ruthless. To
be honest, Henry hadn't had much contact with them over
the years. He was someone who investigated murders – and
if asked, he would say that he had been put on this earth to
do just that.

In an earlier period of his service, Henry had been a
detective sergeant on the Regional Crime Squad, involved in
long-term operations against outfits like the Cromers. Now he
wasn't, and he only really came into contact with such people
when they had some connection with a murder that had been
committed. But he did know that the Cromers were often the
subject of long-range investigations by major crime units; they

may possibly have been so at that moment as Henry stood there, facing off with one of the north-west's scariest gangsters – a man who shared a little of his younger brother's mental state. Henry wasn't routinely kept up to date with ongoing operations, which were often run very secretively.

He could imagine that if the Cromers were the subject of any sort of ongoing job by NCIS or the MCU, he might easily end up being bollocked by someone further up the line for stepping on toes without permission and putting a well-planned op in jeopardy by simply barging up to their house.

Maybe.

But needs must. Everyone had a job to do. He just hoped that he wouldn't come across an undercover cop he might recognize who had infiltrated the family and was having Christmas dinner with them.

So, Terry Cromer.

He was the older brother. Mid forties, and although he was a stocky, muscled guy, he wasn't built to the same proportions as Freddy. But he was still intimidating – or would like to be. He obviously worked out with weights, his arms being all Popeye muscle and tattoos and the tight vest he wore outlining his pecs and rippling six-pack. His shaved head and accompanying snarl harmonized with his tough persona.

He didn't faze Henry, who loved stuff like this. Eyeball to eyeball. Henry and a crim. 'Can I have a word?' Henry had said.

'You're gate crashing our celebrations . . . and to be completely honest with you, no one here's really that worried about Freddy . . . He's nuts, always has been, always will be, and he'll turn up somewhere drunk and incapable, hopefully face down in a ditch.'

Tension is a strange thing. Invisible, yet possible to slice with a sharp knife. And tension surrounded the two men. Henry watched Cromer as he spoke, could smell a whiff of alcohol on his breath, but could tell he wasn't drunk.

Cromer's forehead furrowed as he realized who Henry was. He jabbed a finger at him. 'You're the fucker responsible for getting Freddy sectioned all those years ago . . . and on top of that, you got my lad convicted for murder, too.'

Cromer had a good memory. In terms of the former

allegation, Henry had actually had very little contact with the Cromer family and the sectioning had been done by social workers and doctors. In fact the only time he'd met any of them back then was when he had visited the aunt's bedside at Burnley General Hospital to check on her progress and the family had turned up en masse to visit. Young Terry had been part of that entourage, Henry recalled; then he had been a slim, wiry youth with a cop-hate, sneery attitude well embedded in his psyche.

Years later, of course, he had got Terry's son – Terry junior – convicted of murder. That had entailed a lot of very fractious encounters with Terry senior, but at that time no mention had ever been made of the incident with Freddy many years before.

The murder committed by the junior member of the family had taken place outside a nightclub in Blackpool, when he had stabbed a doorman to death in a frenzied attack witnessed by too many people and had been jumped on and restrained by other bouncers, still with the knife in his hands. A simple enough murder – bang to rights – but one for which the real reason was never properly explained. Henry knew it was about drugs and turf, but neither that nor the murder itself were ever admitted by Terry junior, even in the face of overwhelming evidence that included disturbing CCTV footage of the killing. Not that it mattered, because he was stuffed – and the family did not like it.

Henry's only role had been to oversee the investigation, just to ensure nothing was overlooked. Everyone else did the work, as it should be.

But as SIO Henry could not avoid coming into contact with the Cromers, and at one point he had a stand-up row with Terry senior that almost came to blows in Blackpool police station foyer. Terry's threatening rants then became a personal attack on Henry, who he blamed for taking away his only flesh and blood.

The lad was eventually jailed for life, with a judge's recommendation that he must serve a minimum of fifteen years. The full story behind the killing was never revealed and it was played out as just another night out in Blackpool that had gone sour. As they often did.

And now Henry was back facing Terry senior, a man with

pure hate etched across his features. Henry said calmly, 'I'm simply responding to a missing person report.'

'Fuck off, Christie,' Cromer spat. 'You're just nosying. Just a friggin' excuse to get into my house. I know. I'm not thick.'

'OK, fine, have it your way.'

'Yeah – my house, my way. You're trespassing, so you'd better get out now or else I'm gonna smash your head in.'

'Dad!'

Cromer looked over Henry's shoulder at the young woman who had let Henry into the house. It jolted Henry to learn she was his daughter, mainly because he didn't know that Terry had one.

'Keep out of this,' Terry warned her.

'Dad . . . Gran's worried about Freddy . . . you should be, too,' she said forcefully, standing her ground. 'He is your brother.' She raised her chin defiantly.

Henry saw Terry's right fist bunch up like a rock as he looked at Janine and seemed to want to utter something. His fist shook.

Henry said, 'Look – seriously, we are concerned about him, Mr Cromer. I'm not here nosying, as you put it,' he fibbed a little. He was being nosy, but he also had a right to be there, because he thought there was the outside chance that Freddy was the target for a serial killer.

Should he tell Terry that? As he looked at the man, Henry thought, No, sod it, you bastard. If he gets dead with feathers stuffed in his mouth, then so be it. He actually said, 'Are you bothered or not?'

'Get out,' Terry stated. 'Janine – show him past the dogs.'

SEVEN

Henry had been ejected from a lot worse places. He hadn't expected a warm welcome and they were right to be distrustful of his motives – all crims were – but it was frustrating to be hoofed out without being given the chance to fully explain why he had turned up on the doorstep. He knew he could have forced the issue and made Terry pin his ears back, but that could have been counterproductive.

Their reaction to the possibility that Freddy fitted the profile of a serial killer victim would have either been laugh-out-loud dismissed, or taken so seriously it could have got out of hand. So, Henry had thought as he threw his big Teddy out of his cot, if they wanted to be twats to him, he'd be a twat to them.

The best course of action would be to back out gracefully, then go home and get laid. No contest. Or would have been if it hadn't been for two things.

The first happened as, led by Janine, he walked down the hallway ahead of Terry Cromer. As he passed the door that had been closed when he'd arrived, the one behind which he'd heard male voices, it opened.

Henry could not help but glance to his right.

And just for the instant that the door was open – and it was opened by a man he instantly recognized – Henry glimpsed three other men in what was a large dining room. It was literally a glimpse. A man at the door, three at a table, and on the table a revolver and a sawn-off shotgun, side by side. The door was immediately slammed shut – because, also in that instant, the man who had opened it knew he had been clocked, and Henry could tell from his instantaneous expression of grief that he had committed a faux pas, or in his language, a fucking cock-up.

Henry walked on, internally jolted, but pretending he'd seen nothing. Janine went out of the front door ahead of him and collared the dogs.

As he stepped out, and Terry slammed the door behind him, the second thing happened.

Janine hissed, just loud enough for him to hear, 'Park up the road and wait for me.' Then louder, she said, 'I've got the dogs, you'll be safe.'

Henry didn't acknowledge either statement, but set off for the gate and out to his car, dropping into it and heaving a big sigh. Then, as instructed in the stage whisper, he drove a couple of hundred metres up the lane, did a three-point turn and parked, lights out, engine idling.

Inside him, his own pistons were pumping. *Guns on the table.*

And the dining room door had been opened by none other than Iron-man William Grasson, or Bill the Grass as he was known with irony. Henry knew that in the organizational chart of the Cromer crime business, Grasson fitted in very nicely, thank you, as a violent enforcer, a vicious man once convicted of cutting off another man's little finger with garden shears when chasing up a hundred-pound drug debt.

Henry had recognized him straight away, because Grasson was a difficult man not to know. Although he was an enforcer, he had himself once come a cropper when he encountered a couple of other rival enforcers chasing his debt. They branded him with the triangular and unmistakable imprint of a steam iron, hence the 'Iron-man' epithet. He was scarily recognizable, even to Henry, who had never met the man before.

From what he'd seen of the other men in the room, he didn't know them, but they seemed equally appealing.

Henry worked through the scenario. Not the nicest bunch of people to invite around for Christmas dinner. He guessed that in the normal course of events, guys like these would only be at the family homestead for two reasons – protection or attack.

Or was he being totally preposterous?

Perhaps the Cromers always invited their best staff around at Christmas, then they could all share their war stories for the last year. The best drugs deal I made. That bloke's finger I snapped off. That lad's head I broke . . . that rival's brains I blew out.

Perhaps the guns were merely Christmas pressies.

But knowing what he did about the lifestyles of the rich and criminal, their presence unsettled him.

And on top of that, Janine, daughter of Terry Cromer.

Henry didn't even know he had a daughter.

A deranged, ultra-violent son, yes, but not a daughter, and one who at first glance didn't seem to fit the profile of the rest of the tribe. But that didn't mean anything. Looks could be deceptive.

Just as he was wondering what she wanted, there was a thud and a scraping noise at the car door. Henry jumped, twisted sideways and looked into a pair of menacing eyes. He almost let out a squeak – one of the Cromer dogs was looking at him, leaving a snotty nose print on the window.

Suddenly the head was dragged away sharply as Janine brought the dog under control, leaned forward in its place and looked into Henry's eyes. 'Is it unlocked?' she asked.

He nodded, and she walked around the car and dropped into the passenger seat, trapping the dog's lead in the door so it could not wander off.

Henry looked at her, confirming her good looks. 'Didn't see you coming.'

'Back way.'

Henry could actually smell her, a mix of nice perfume and cigarette smoke on her breath. It was quite alluring in a strange sort of way. He raised his eyebrows. 'So?'

'I wanted to tell you about Freddy.'

'The missing man – or the missing man, not?'

'He's definitely missing and Gran is worried about him.'

'I'll make sure he's circulated.'

'Dad's right, isn't he?'

'About what?'

'You turning up. You're just being nosy, aren't you? Just an excuse to get into our house, isn't it? I mean, a detective superintendent – pah!' She glared accusingly at him.

'Why are you here? Does your dad know?'

'No.'

'Then why?'

'I wanted to make sure you treated Freddy's disappearance seriously and didn't get the huff just because you got kicked out of the house.'

'Every missing person is treated seriously,' Henry told her, 'but what the police do about them is based on the surrounding circumstances . . . so I'll leave Freddy to the local cops and see how it pans out.'

'Just so you know – Freddy's not well.'

Henry stared cynically at her, but desisted from saying, 'He never was.'

'He kind of comes and goes, but for the last few years his medication's kept him stable. But if he doesn't get it he becomes very paranoid and unstable and he can be quite nasty.'

'But why has he been reported missing?'

'He had a big fallout with Dad last night and stormed off into town. He hadn't taken his pills that morning and it doesn't take him long to revert to type. And he definitely hasn't taken any today, either.'

'So he could be chewing carpets somewhere?'

Janine looked fiercely at him. 'Not funny.'

'I didn't know Terry had a daughter.'

'I'm the black sheep of the family. University and a proper job. Never got involved in any of the . . . you know.'

'Shenanigans?' Henry chewed his bottom lip for a moment. 'What's going on?' he asked.

'What d'you mean?'

'In there.' He thumbed at the house. 'Bill Grasson, some more salty-looking dudes and guns.'

Janine's face constricted. 'Don't know, don't want to know,' she said, sounding offended. 'I just want to get Freddy back in one piece. Yeah, he could end up eating carpets, as you so colourfully put it, but he could also end up doing someone some harm – or himself. He needs finding.'

Henry recalled Freddy's hands squeezing his windpipe. He sighed. 'Where do I start looking?'

'I could show you. I know some places he hangs around.'

Henry nodded. 'Are we taking the dog?' It was tempting to set off with the beast attached to the car.

'Wait here. I'll sneak Damian back in and be back in ten minutes.'

While he waited, he selected a Miles Davis track on the car's iPod. He'd been trying to get into jazz, but was so far failing. He liked jazz and blues singers, but couldn't quite get to grips with instrumentalists, though he did appreciate their talent. He was becoming convinced it wasn't for him.

He was considering what he should do about the firearms
he'd seen, which, he now assumed, would be hard to find.
It wasn't practical to go back mob-handed with a bunch of
his hairy-arsed colleagues, at least not on Christmas Day,
nor Boxing Day. Getting enough police staff together to
do anything on these particular days would be almost
impossible.

The best thing to do, he concluded, was to hold on to the
knowledge, because it might come in useful at some future
date – if he needed a warrant, for example. Deep down he did
feel he should be bursting in, kicking down their door, just
for the hell of it. He hadn't kicked a door down for ages and
he was going through withdrawal symptoms. Maybe it was
unbecoming for a man of his years – bursting into people's
houses was a young cop's game – but it was addictive.
However, it was now his job to step carefully over the resultant
carnage *after* entry had been gained, not to lead the charge.

The passenger door opened. Janine dropped in alongside
Henry, no dog in tow.

'You sure about this?'

'Yeah – it'll be all right.'

'Where are we going?'

'Head for Blackburn.'

'So – home for Christmas?'

'Something like that.'

'Where do you live and work?'

'Manchester,' Janine said. Henry waited, but she made no
attempt to give him any further information.

'What is work?'

She shrugged. 'A law firm, dealing mainly with accident
claims. Boring but necessary for the time being. I'd like to
get into corporate law.'

'You're a solicitor?'

'Yep.'

'Well, good for you. Criminal law?'

'No,' she said strongly.

'Good for you,' he said again, not sure if he believed a word
of it, though she did seem genuine. That could have something

to do with the fact she was a Cromer. As far as Henry was concerned, they were all pretty much liars.

'Go right here,' she instructed him. He scooped around a roundabout onto Shadsworth Road. 'There's a club in Knuzden he likes,' she explained.

Henry knew that Shadsworth Road dropped down into the area called Knuzden, on the eastern outskirts of Blackburn.

'So what happened to Freddy?' he asked.

'What do you mean?'

'In between the time he almost killed his aunt by dropping her out of a window, strangled me, and got sent to mental institutions, and now.'

'Just that.' She kept her face forward. 'All I know is what I've been told, really . . . I wasn't even born when that happened.' She gave Henry a sly, amused look. 'Which must make you really old . . . I mean, were you really the cop he tried to kill?'

'I was.' Henry could have said it proudly, but he didn't. It was a long time ago and it still mortified him that a teenager had pinned him down. Even a big one.

'Mm, I've heard about it, obviously. But he got moved from place to place. Got better, got out, went mad again, got locked up again. Vicious circle. Eventually they stopped taking him back when the secure units became more scarce with cutbacks and the drugs got better. He's just another care in the community stat, I guess.'

'How long has he been home?'

'Couple, three years. Gran wanted to have him back, but he's too much of a handful when he goes off the rails. And Dad doesn't have any time for him. Usually just beats him up – Dad beats Freddy, that is.'

'Out of curiosity, which one of those ladies I just saw was your mother?' He tried not to put too much of an inflection on the word 'ladies'.

'None . . . she went years back,' she said, but did not elaborate.

Henry drove on. To his right was the huge Shadsworth council estate, a grim sixties throwback that Henry remembered well from his early days as a uniformed cop, and subsequently on a few murder enquiries. And sat alongside him was the daughter of one of Lancashire's best crims. He couldn't resist asking again, 'Come on, what's going on? All the guns 'n' stuff?'

Janine remained silent as they reached the traffic lights at the bottom of the hill, at the junction with the main road that connected Blackburn with Accrington. She said, 'Do a right here and the club's on the right . . . just called The Moss.'

Henry knew it. It had been there for as long as he could remember and didn't look as though it had ever seen any decoration. It was a single-storey, detached premises, constructed of Accrington brick with metal grilles on all the windows which were never removed, and a roller-shutter that covered the door when the place was closed. Henry knew it must have been refurbished at least a couple of times over the years because it had been firebombed twice. It was basically a very grotty working men's club.

He pulled into the almost empty car park.

'Freddy likes this place. They don't mind giving him booze, but they know when to stop – mainly because he trashed it single-handed once after too much.'

'OK,' Henry said and reached for the door handle.

Janine laid a hand on his arm. 'Mr Christie, whatever my family is involved in, I can't help. I don't have any part in it, but I'm not going to grass on them either. They're my family and I care about them. I won't betray them.'

'Fair do's.'

Henry got out and, with Janine beside him, he walked to the front door of the club and entered.

He stood inside the threshold and surveyed the geography and clientele. One long bar served the whole place. There was a small raised stage in one corner with a tatty-looking drum kit on it. Bench seats clung to the outside walls and battered-looking brass-topped circular tables and chairs were scattered throughout. Music played from speakers hung up high and there were eight middle-aged men, in four pairs, sitting either at the bar or the tables, or playing the gaming machine. They all looked to be drinking mild, a type of beer Henry hadn't tasted for a long, long time. For good reason.

Smoke hung in the air. It appeared that the non-smoking legislation did not apply to this particular enclave of society, and each man, without exception, was smoking. That included the barman, who watched Henry and Janine approach with a cigarette dangling from the corner of his mouth.

For a brief moment Henry's feet got completely stuck in something on the sticky carpet and he thought he might not make it across the floor. He had to stop and roll his shoes out of whatever it was. Very sticky.

With his face a picture to behold, he carried on up to the bar.

The man behind it could have been aged somewhere between forty and sixty, but many years of serious drinking and smoking had taken its toll on his complexion and his pock-marked face, bulbous red nose, veined face and watery bloodshot eyes told the story, as did his rasping voice.

'Can I do for you guys?' he asked his new customers. He took a deep drag on his fag and blew a thick cloud up amongst the rows of cleanish glasses that hung above the bar.

'I'm looking for Freddy Cromer,' Henry said, wafting a path through the haze of smoke.

The barman regarded him. 'Who might you be?'

Henry revealed his warrant card and county badge. 'A cop.'

The barman remained unimpressed. 'Don't know him.'

Henry said, 'He's a regular, apparently.'

The barman shrugged, replaced the cigarette between his lips, inhaled and exhaled again.

'What's this? Licensee-customer confidentiality?'

'No. Just don't know the guy. Can I get you a drink?'

'Can I get you the local authority?'

'Already had 'em. Didn't make much difference.'

'Excuse me.' Janine eased Henry gently aside and stepped into the breach. 'I'm Janine Cromer. Freddy's my uncle. Terry Cromer is my dad.' She allowed those names to permeate the barman's smoke-addled grey matter, knowing they carried great weight. 'Was Freddy in here last night? Simple question.'

'Yes,' he answered instantly, a changed man.

Janine waited for more information and when it didn't come, she opened her palms in a gesture designed to encourage him.

'Yes, he was here.'

'Times? Was he drunk? When did he leave? Who was he with?'

'Uh . . . landed about seven, left at midnight. He'd had a few and was alone,' the barman blurted. 'Just normal, I'd say.'

'He left here in one piece?'

'No one messes with him,' the barman said. 'He gets left alone, he leaves others alone. That's how it works with him.'

'I assume you actually spoke to him?' Janine said.

'Only to get him drinks. Other than that he just sat in his usual place – over in that corner by the drums.' He pointed to the spot by the stage.

'How did he seem?' Henry asked.

The barman shrugged. 'Like I said, just usual.'

'Did anyone else talk to him?'

'Not that I recall. Y'know, we were pretty busy last night, Christmas Eve and all that.'

'Yeah – the place looks well festive,' Henry said. The barman shot him a look.

'OK,' Janine said, 'let's go. There's other places he could've gone to.' She took Henry's arm. Henry nodded at the barman but refrained from threatening the local authority again. Like the man said, it probably wouldn't be much use.

Outside it was chilly. Snowflakes wafted gently down from the heavens.

'White Christmas,' Henry said, catching a few flakes in his hand, hoping it wouldn't be too heavy a snowfall otherwise the journey to Kendleton would be a nightmare. They walked over to his car and got in.

'Right,' Janine said stiffly, turning to him. 'Can you now tell me why you're interested in Freddy's disappearance? It isn't a job for a detective superintendent, is it?'

'It could be,' Henry said defiantly.

'Only if he's gone missing in suspicious circumstances – or, God forbid, turns up dead in suspicious circumstances. At the moment none of those things apply. So – were you just being nosy, or is there another reason?'

'Well, I'd be a poor cop if I didn't take the chance to look into the house of a big bad gangster, wouldn't I?'

Janine uttered an exasperated gush of breath. 'I bloody thought so.'

'Actually,' Henry began – just as his mobile phone started to ring. He took it out and answered it. 'Jerry . . . you still not gone home?'

'No – too engrossed,' Jerry Tope said. 'Just had the FIM on again . . . are you still in Belthorn?' Henry said yes, as good as. 'In that case you might want to get to the A&E department at Royal Blackburn Hospital. Shit's hit the fan . . . there's an ARV on the way . . . and Freddy Cromer's turned up saying he's just escaped from a kidnapper. He's also waving a kitchen knife about and has taken a nurse hostage.'

EIGHT

Sending up a satisfying shower of dust and grit in his wake, Henry gunned the Audi off the club car park and accelerated towards the hospital, which was less than two miles away. In fact, on the journey down from Belthorn, they had been within sight of the huge complex for a substantial part of the way, as it was situated high on a hill, overlooking Blackburn.

As he drove, he reached across to the glove compartment, flicked it open and fumbled in it for his personal radio.

'What's going on?' Janine demanded, gripping her seat belt tightly.

Thumbing the PR on with his left hand and steering with his right, Henry said, 'Freddy's at A&E, causing a rumpus.'

'Shit,' Janine uttered.

'And he's got a knife.' Henry tabbed through the PR to tune it to Blackburn division's radio channel, announcing that he was on his way to the disturbance, ETA four minutes. Then he asked for an update.

'Unclear at the moment,' the operator told him. 'No patrols have arrived there yet, but a treble-nine came from the hospital staff saying that a patient had gone berserk and was holding a nurse hostage.' At that, Henry glanced at Janine, who screwed up her face in agony. 'And he's got a knife to her throat, but we don't have much more than that at the moment, other than it's supposed to be Freddy Cromer who was reported missing earlier. Apparently he's a nut job.'

Henry groaned inwardly at the last phrase. Not that it was off the mark, but it was perhaps a little non-PC – and Freddy's niece was sitting alongside him, listening in.

'Who is attending?'

'An ARV and two section patrols. I'm trying to get supervision up there too, but I know they're busy in custody.'

'OK. I'll take charge,' Henry said as a flush of adrenalin hit his system. To himself he muttered, *And doesn't this day just keep giving . . .*

He braked at the red lights, sneaked carefully through them, then stood on the gas. The car almost lifted off and it felt good. He looked at Janine again.

She said, 'A nut job?'

'It's a medical term.'

She glowered at him, unimpressed. 'Doesn't give him much of a chance in the eyes of the cops then, does it? Already labelled.'

Henry glared back. 'Sometimes it's best to go in prepared.' He spoke into the PR. 'If any patrol gets there ahead of me, tell them to take extreme care. Cromer is prone to serious violence and is very unpredictable. Understood?' He looked at her again. 'A label plus ingredients.'

The operator relayed this over the air, but said to Henry, 'You could well be first on the scene. Other patrols are some distance away.'

'Roger,' Henry said, imagining them having to be torn away from their Christmas puddings.

They had reached the point where Shadsworth Road levelled out and Blackburn Royal Hospital was visible across to their right, illuminated by lights in the car parks and spotlights, angled up to the buildings, as well as by the lights showing from the windows.

Less than a minute later Henry pulled in close to the ambulance bays outside A&E. He jumped out and dashed to the boot, in which he kept his equipment, including a lightweight Teflon stab vest which he slid on underneath his zip-up jacket.

With Janine at his heels he ran through the A&E entrance and skidded to a halt at the reception desk. The place was busy and he shouldered his way to the front of the queue, saying 'Police' to the harassed-looking woman on duty there.

Before she could say anything, a white-coated Asian doctor appeared at his side, grabbed his sleeve and pulled. 'This way.'

Henry followed the man, having a rushed conversation as they strode hurriedly along.

'What's happening?'

'A patient is holding one of the nurses hostage in the X-ray department. Come, come,' the doctor urged him to speed up.

'Why is he doing it?'

'We don't know . . . he just became very violent.'

'OK. What's the current situation?'

'They're in the X-ray waiting area. We managed to clear everyone else away, staff and patients.'

'Right,' Henry said, knowing there wasn't time for an in-depth discussion here. He needed to get to the scene and assess what was really going on.

They turned into the corridor leading to the X-ray department and Henry was impressed to see that a couple of porters had placed trolleys across the width of the corridor, either side of the entrance, creating – ironically – a sterile area. Henry giggled inwardly at the notion.

Fortunately there were not many people around here.

The doctor slowed to a walk and pointed to the double swing doors leading into the X-ray waiting area. 'In there,' he breathed.

Henry nodded. He turned to Janine and held up his hand for her to stay back. 'Let me see what's going on.'

She nodded uncertainly.

He sidled past one of the trolleys to the door and peeped into the waiting area through the porthole window. He could see several rows of chairs, the reception desk, and at the back, in one corner, Freddy Cromer sitting next to a young nurse. His left arm was draped loosely around her shoulder, whilst his right hand held to her throat what looked like a paring knife.

He was whispering into her right ear, mouth right up to it, lips almost brushing her lobe, and the girl, no more than nineteen, sat there with a stiff, terrified expression as she nodded in response to something Freddy had said.

The point of the blade dug into her throat, by her windpipe.

Freddy's left hand slid back and grabbed her hair, bunched it in his fist and jerked her head back, exposing the whole of her throat.

Henry could see that the left side of Freddy's face was badly grazed, looking like he'd been dragged along a cinder track. The smooth burn marks on the other side of his face were still visible, the ones Henry had noticed all those years before when Freddy was trying to strangle him. He was wearing a torn shirt, jeans, socks, but no shoes. The jeans were also ripped. And although Henry hadn't seen him for many years, he hadn't aged beyond recognition. Henry vividly recalled his wild eyes. They hadn't changed, rolling in their sockets in an almost comical loony-guy look.

Freddy placed the blade of the small knife across the girl's throat and continued to speak to her in hushed tones, mouth to ear.

Henry wondered what he was saying.

He saw the knife make an indent in her neck.

'Shit,' Henry thought. He opened the door and stepped through. 'Freddy,' he said.

Freddy Cromer's rage-contorted face twisted towards Henry. 'I told everyone to fucking get out,' Freddy growled, 'or I'll kill this bitch.' His lips exaggerated the words he spoke.

'Freddy, what's going on?' Henry said reasonably. He took one step forward.

Freddy yanked the nurse's head even further back, causing her to gasp in terror. His face angled forebodingly at Henry, his lips in a snarl.

'I'll fucking kill her.' His eyes were ablaze.

'No, Freddy, no,' Henry gasped, his hands patting down fresh air, a keep calm gesture. 'What's going on? What is this for? Talk to me.'

Freddy blinked as though some sort of normality had come

rocked dangerously, the impact triggering its internal alarm, setting off an ear-piercing shriek that filled the waiting room. The force of the collision made Freddy release the nurse, though he took a handful of her hair with him, torn from the poor girl's head. She screamed and spun away.

Henry continued to power into Freddy, his senses continually aware of the knife, trying to keep it in vision or at least be spatially aware of where it was, whilst trying to pin Freddy down somehow. The men bounced off the vending machine, then slammed against the wall like two wrestlers.

Suddenly, up close, Henry realized what a well-built man Freddy was. He'd been strong and stocky as a lad, but the years had filled him out with muscle and real strength.

Henry saw the knife rise in the periphery of his vision as the duo rolled across and over a row of seats. He went for the arm and caught it between his hands as it arced towards him. Henry then wrenched Freddy's wrist and smacked the knife down onto the floor as they crashed onto the tiles.

But then Freddy's left arm encircled Henry's neck and drew him up tight as Henry writhed and corkscrewed, still holding the knife-bearing hand, feeling Freddy's hot, rancid breath against his face. Then Freddy inserted two fingers into Henry's eye socket.

Henry squirmed for room. It felt like those thick, sausage fingers were going to pop out his left eye and probe up into his brain, giving him a free lobotomy.

With strength Henry didn't know he had, he spun round and found space for his right hand to shoot up between them, the heel of his hand connecting with Freddy's lower jaw like a jackhammer. Henry heard the hollow click as Freddy's teeth snapped shut and his head jerked back. Henry dropped into a sideways roll and came up onto his feet, his breath rasping, and in a parallel world of thought he wondered what had happened to Christmas Day. Pear shaped? Banana shaped? Shit shaped? Tits up!

Freddy didn't give him time for much cogitation, but went for him straight away, diving for his legs. He moved faster than Henry, driven by inner demons.

Henry went over again and Freddy clambered over him,

and for the second time in his life, Henry found himself being strangled by the same individual.

But this time it wasn't the kid version, although that had been pretty bad. Now the bulk of years and experience and weight and sheer madness were thrown into the mix that was Freddy Cromer. A whole lifetime of mental instability and paranoia were focused on the thumb pads that started to press into Henry's Adam's apple, which constricted under the pressure. His vision blurred, seeing Freddy's features start to become hazy, like looking into a fog.

Then the pressure was released as Freddy seemed to leap sideways off him.

Oxygen and blood, cut off in both directions, started to flow and Henry rolled away, clutching his neck, coughing and gasping.

He clambered up to his knees and saw Freddy was lying on his back, holding his head and groaning, and that Janine Cromer was standing over him like some female Colossus, having given Freddy a flying kick in the side of his head to dislodge him, similar to the one delivered by FB years before.

Henry got unsteadily to his feet to see Janine glaring scornfully at him.

'I take it you haven't been on a hostage negotiator's course?'

'I have – actually,' he spluttered. 'You're supposed to build up a rapport. But there wasn't a lot of time for that, was there?' Henry had to raise his voice because the alarm in the vending machine was still sounding.

Freddy sat up, holding his head miserably between his hands and looking up at Janine like a thrashed puppy.

Henry sneered and pulled his rigid handcuffs out from his waistband at the small of his back. He stepped behind Freddy, forced him face down onto the floor and, without any resistance, cuffed his wrists behind him, using the stacking method – the only way rigid cuffs could be used behind a suspect, one hand higher than the other.

Freddy lay there compliantly, his cheek pressed flat on to the floor, making a strange humming noise.

Henry breathed heavily, hands on hips, and regarded Janine,

his chest rising and falling, his heart pounding a little too erratically for comfort and a dithery feeling enveloping him.

Janine's scornful look turned into a grin. 'You getting past it?'

'Definitely.' With a surge of rage, Henry turned and kicked the vending machine, and suddenly the alarm stopped, leaving an echoing, ringing sound in the room. 'Thank God for that,' he said. He made his way to the nurse who was still cowering in a corner, squatting down almost in a foetal shape with her head between her knees and both hands clasped over her head. 'It's OK,' he said gently, lowering himself alongside her and placing a hand between her shoulder blades. Her whole body trembled underneath his touch. 'It's OK, it's over.'

She looked at him through her fingers.

'It's OK,' he said again, not sure whether she believed him. He was about to say more, reassuring, banal words, when he heard something not too far away that he recognized instantly.

Two dull thuds – *thck-thck.*

Gunshots.

The door to the waiting room clattered open, and a worried-looking porter crashed through and gasped, 'Men with guns. In the corridor. Shooting each other.'

Henry cursed.

Another shot was fired.

There was a slight pause, followed by the sound of bullets being discharged by an automatic weapon, a short burst. Then a scream.

A nurse, another porter and the Asian doctor ran into the waiting room, closely followed by another porter clutching his shoulder as blood blossomed under his hand. He fell to his knees, his face white and horrified with disbelief, staring at the blood. He swooned. His eyeballs spun and he fainted, crashing face first into the hard floor and splitting his forehead open.

Henry watched all this unfold in a matter of seconds.

Then he heard another shot being fired. He dashed to the door, peering out through the porthole, flattening the side of his face to the glass in an attempt to see down the corridor outside. It was impossible, because the door was set into the wall. restricting his view.

'Two guys walking towards us,' one of the porters explained over Henry's shoulder. 'Then there's two more guys behind them. One shouts, the first guys spin round, then all hell shits itself. Bullets everywhere.'

Henry nodded and glanced at Janine, then at Freddy – who was still humming tunelessly to himself. He caught Janine's eye, and could tell that she too knew this was no coincidence. But also, from the look on her face, he could see she was bewildered by the turn of events.

'Where are they now?' he asked the porter.

'They all legged it in the direction of A&E . . . which is where Derek needs to be . . . one of the bastards shot him.' He pointed at his wounded colleague.

Henry scooped up his PR from the floor and cautiously eased a gap in the swing door, one centimetre at a time, edging himself out without completely exposing himself to the possibility of taking a bullet. He might have been wearing a stab vest, but it didn't stop slugs.

The corridor was empty. The two trolleys used by the porters to block it off were still there, abandoned.

He called up Blackburn comms and succinctly brought them into the picture, adding, 'Where's that ARV unit?'

'Should be with you . . .'

'Echo Romeo Seven interrupting,' Henry heard the call sign of the Armed Response Vehicle patrol butt into the conversation. 'I'm on the corridor walking towards the X-ray department.'

Henry recognized the gruff tones of PC Bill Robbins, a firearms trainer and a man he knew well.

'Bill,' Henry cut back in, 'Henry Christie here . . . just take care . . . there's been some sort of shooting incident along that corridor, offenders still on the loose.'

'No problems.'

Henry took a chance to peer down the corridor – still empty. So he stepped out, sniffing the whiff of cordite in the air, seeing a line of four bullet holes in an arc on the wall, made by the automatic weapon he'd heard. And splashes of blood on the wall and floor from the porter's shoulder wound.

Bill Robbins trotted around a distant corner. Full firearms

kit on, a Heckler and Koch machine pistol slung diagonally across his chest, ready for use, his Glock holstered at his hip, Taser, a CS canister, rigid cuffs, extendable baton, PR – the business. Henry felt some relief, but also a bit of concern: firearms officers were supposed to work in pairs.

Bill came up to Henry.

'You alone?'

'Partner's got the shits. He stayed on for as long as he could, finally had to go sick. Bad turkey. So what's happening?'

Henry glanced back through the porthole. Freddy was still face down. The wounded porter was being tended by the doctor and the nurse.

Henry explained quickly, and Bill said he hadn't seen anyone on his way up. Henry said, 'Let's get this porter and the nurse who was held hostage to A&E. I also want to get Freddy out of here and transported to Blackburn cells, then we'll go and have a mooch around for these armed chappies.'

A few moments later, the porter had been gently laid out on a trolley and with Henry propelling Freddy – who was now in a completely different world to anyone else, allowing himself to be manhandled without complaint – and Bill Robbins leading the way, they reached A&E with no further incident.

By this time the section van had arrived and Freddy was shoved into it. With specific instructions from Henry, who handed the van driver Freddy's knife, Freddy was removed from the scene. One less thing to worry about.

He returned to A&E reception, where Janine was waiting. The porter was being attended to and the nurse-hostage was being soothed and treated by her colleagues.

'Any comment?' Henry asked Janine. She shook her head. Not convinced, Henry said, 'But you know what's going on, don't you?'

'Not as such.'

Henry screwed his face up at her. '*Not as such*? That's a yes, then?' He was about to launch himself verbally into her when his PR came to life, the comms room at Blackburn calling him urgently. 'Go 'head,' he said.

'Report of shots being fired near ward C10 at the hospital. That's on level three.'

'Roger – attending with Romeo Seven.' Bill Robbins had heard the transmission and was ready to go. Henry looked at Janine, jerked a forefinger at her. 'You don't go anywhere. We need to have words.' Then he set off behind Bill, bringing his PR up to his mouth, shouting instructions to comms: basically, send everyone they could to A&E, which would be the RV point for this incident, and ensure the patrol inspector got a grip of things.

Henry and Bill jog-trotted away from A&E, up two flights of stairs that took them onto level 3, on which gunfire had most recently been reported. The corridors, in the main, were deserted. Official visiting times to the wards were over and virtually all hospital activity was now taking place on the wards themselves.

Henry was curious as to why Bill Robbins was out and about operationally – his job, after all, was in firearms training. But Henry did know there was a requirement for training staff to perform operational duties from time to time to keep their hands in. Up until recently, as Henry also knew, Bill's authorization to carry firearms had been revoked following a shooting incident over two years before, but now it had been reinstated following a long drawn-out inquiry and – sadly – an inquest at which a verdict of death by misadventure had been recorded and Bill had been exonerated.

But there was no time for discussion.

They came out onto level 3, turned right towards the wards.

The radio chatter was unceasing and all very excitable, so Henry cut across it and told the comms operator to stamp his authority on it as he and Bill approached the scene warily.

They stopped at the entrance to a long, wide corridor, partitioned by several sets of fire safety doors, off which were the wards. Looking along its length, Henry saw it was deserted.

They shouldered through the doors, walking side by side. On the left was the entrance to ward C14. They stopped, glanced into it. No sign of untoward activity. Next along, this time on the right, was the Spiritual Care centre. The door to this was locked.

Next on the left was C10.

Henry moved to his left, up to the wall, fighting the urge to push Bill ahead of him and use him as a human shield.

Bill, his round face serious, had the H&K in a firing position and the two men crept the last metres to the ward entrance, hearing nothing.

They exchanged looks.

Then a terrifying scream emanated from the ward.

There was a gunshot. Henry ducked instinctively as a slug slammed into the corridor wall opposite the ward entrance.

There was the thudding of running feet.

Another shot. Then a man tore out of the ward, running hard and fast, too hard and fast to stop, and slammed into the wall ahead of him, where the bullet had entered the plasterwork only seconds before. He crashed into it with his right shoulder, pushed himself off and ran in the opposite direction to Henry, not even having noticed the two officers, who watched him in amazement. The man was clearly running for his life – on the wall, he had left a thick smear of blood from a wound some-where around his right shoulder.

He was pursued by another man who followed almost exactly the same route, moving so quickly he too hit the wall, bounced off and went for his quarry.

Difference was, this guy wasn't injured.

And he was carrying a handgun.

Fifteen metres ahead of him, the first man stopped and turned, and for the first time Henry saw that he also had a gun. This was in his left hand, and the weapon wavered.

The second man weaved to one side, and holding his own handgun – a large pistol of some sort – in the manner of a film gangster, he fired at the first man.

Four shots, quick succession.

The gun jerked at each discharge.

Each bullet hit the first man in the abdomen, sending him staggering backwards, arms windmilling, his gun flying out of his hand, until he tipped sideways and over.

By which time Henry and Bill had moved.

Bill screamed, 'Armed police – drop your weapon. Armed police – drop your weapon – or I will fire!' The words were loud, clear and unambiguous and Bill could not have been mistaken for anything other than an armed cop – full regalia, including the chequered baseball cap.

But the man was at that moment probably charged with a super-shot of adrenalin. He spun – Henry recognized who it was – not reacting to Bill's words, but driven on by the situation and his own heart rate and red-mist rage.

Bill – rightly – took no chances.

The man had just murdered someone in front of him, may have killed others, might try and shoot at them.

So he cut down Iron-man Bill Grasson with a four-bullet strafe across the chest, sent him pirouetting like a demented ballet dancer down the corridor, where he stumbled and tripped over his own victim, their blood mingling and spreading fast on the highly polished tiled floor.

Bill lowered his weapon, his chest rising and falling.

'Fuck,' he said. 'Times like this I wish I'd had the shits, not my mate.'

NINE

As a police manager, the key to success at an ongoing, complex incident was to detach yourself from it, keep an overview, bring calm to chaos and in the process keep a firm eye on securing and preserving evidence. But above all, to ensure that people were safe and the danger had passed.

It was easy to become an imitation of Miracle Mike, the Headless Chicken, particularly when blood was being splattered – but as soon as Bill pulled the trigger on his MP5 and two people lay dead at his feet, Henry went straight into auto-mode, took charge of the scene and imposed his authority.

Once it was confirmed that the two men in the corridor were first, no longer a threat and second, dead, Henry went to check there was no further danger in ward C10. There wasn't, but there was another dead body also containing several chunks of lead. And he needed to confirm that no one else had made good their escape. The process itself was just like dealing with a burglary scene, using the same skill set – but with the addition of more blood, emotion and chaos.

Once all that was established, Henry seized Bill's weapons and sat him in a nurses' office on ward C14, got him a cup of tea, then carried on with the job in hand.

And despite people having lost their lives, and his day being ruined, Henry relished it.

What astonished him as he began to piece it all together was that as well as knowing Bill Grasson, who he'd seen earlier at the Cromers', trying to stop Henry from getting an accidental eyeful of a table full of guns, he also knew the other dead men.

As he looked down at them, one in the corridor, the other in the ward, he couldn't help but say, 'Well, well, well.'

Because they were members of the Costain family from Blackpool. Rather like the Cromers, Henry had known the family for much of his police service, but unlike the Cromers, he had had regular contact with the Costains because of their geographic location and nefarious activities. They were a very extended family of several generations, mainly resident on one of Blackpool's most crime-ridden council estates – Shoreside. From ragged beginnings, they had become an organized gang and largely controlled the supply of drugs in Blackpool and Fylde.

The two members of that family lying dead at the hospital were Stuart and Benji Costain. From the younger end of the family, cousins of the main branch, they were ruthless villains of the highest order, doing a similar job for the Costains to that performed by Bill Grasson for the Cromers.

They were enforcers and tax collectors. Finger breakers and ball busters.

And Henry knew it didn't take the detective of the year – an accolade he had never achieved, incidentally – to know that he had stumbled into a turf war. Either the Costains were expanding onto Cromer territory, or vice versa, or they were in dispute over something else. And if this was the opening salvo, the rest of Henry's festive season was going to be a real hoot.

* * *

It took him two hours to gain complete control, a complication being that the body of Benji Costain was lying in one of the side wards of C10 and there were six extremely old and ill patients in the beds. They had to be relocated into other wards, as well as having their blood-splashed bedding removed, bagged up for forensics, then replaced. Fortunately none of them seemed to have taken a turn for the worse because of the incident, which had happened quite quickly. Henry guessed they probably thought they were hallucinating . . . but even so, each would have to be interviewed soon.

As he worked, he was mentally calculating all the time. Not forgetting that he had a prisoner to deal with at Blackburn police station, a picture started to come into focus of what had happened . . . and one thing he didn't leave out of the scenario was the presence of Freddy Cromer at the hospital in the first place, which Henry suspected might be relevant to what subsequently transpired.

Freddy had been discovered by a paramedic on one of the roads outside A&E, lying in the middle of it in a state of semi-consciousness, injured, but not seriously. He looked like he'd been dumped there.

He was taken into the department, where after a quick triage examination he was sent up to X-ray; not only did he have a facial injury but he was acting strangely, rambling on that he'd been kidnapped, drifting in and out of sense. Because he'd clearly cracked his head, it was thought best to check whether he'd got a more serious injury underneath his scalp.

As he lay on a trolley in X-ray he had suddenly decided that the nurse with him was one of the kidnappers. A knife was produced from somewhere and it all then kicked off.

Henry had arrived soon after and it looked, even though he couldn't be certain, as if the Cromer family had been informed Freddy was at hospital, and Bill Grasson and another – as yet unidentified – had turned up to collect him. They had been confronted by the hoods from the Costain crew and a deadly shoot-out had ensued.

One question was already making the back of Henry's mind tingle: had the Cromers been lured to the hospital? It was just one of the myriad hypotheses tumbling through his grey matter.

Henry snatched a few minutes with Bill Robbins in the nurses' office.

They had known each other a long time, since being PCs in fact, and recently Henry had used Bill on some enquiries. During one of these Bill had come up against two rogue FBI agents turned vigilantes and shot them dead. The killings had been absolutely justified, but it had taken an agonizingly long time for Bill to be exonerated through the justice system. There was then further dithering by the force before he was reinstated as a firearms trainer, and an even longer delay before he got his firearms authorization back. Bill's perception was that, apart from Henry's support, he had been left very much to fend for himself, with the force keeping him at cow-prod length.

And now he'd pulled the trigger again. Killed someone. Again. Not good.

The two men eyed each other acerbically.

'I think I'm a serial killer,' Bill said. He looked ill, and pale.

'No, you just did your job.'

'Again,' Bill said. 'But this time I'll never see a firearm again, will I?'

'No, you won't,' Henry said. That was a truth Bill had to face. 'But you did the right thing.'

Bill nodded vacantly.

Henry left him to his thoughts, backing out of the office as his mobile phone rang. It was the custody officer at Blackburn cells, apologetic, although he didn't need to be.

'Boss, sorry. Know you're busy, but . . .'

'I've got a prisoner to deal with. Yeah, I know.'

''Fraid so. I've got Cromer's solicitors on the blower giving me earache. What do you want me to do with the little fella?'

'Give me twenty minutes and I'll be down there,' he promised, but only because he glanced around to see Rik Dean walking towards him. Someone he trusted to take on the management of the scene. 'Sorry, bud,' he apologized to Rik.

Rik shrugged and said, 'I didn't even get home, actually.' He looked a little uncomfortable. 'Been trying to track Lisa down.'

'Yeah, she's still not got back to me,' Henry said, automatically checking his phone for texts and missed calls, even though he knew there were none. 'Look – I need you to take this over while I go and process a prisoner.' He explained quickly what had happened, knowing that to say it out loud would help him get the story, the chain of events, straight in his mind. He would have to tell it over and over to people including the chief constable (already turned out), the ACC (Ops), turned out too, someone from the Independent Police Complaints Commission – already informed – and a multitude of others he could only guess at. It would soon be a very slick story. 'I'll be as quick as I can down at the cells, got an idea on that score, and then I'll be back. Sorry about your Christmas Day.'

Rik blew out his cheeks. 'Yours looks pretty screwed up, too.'

Suddenly weary, Henry walked back through the hospital. He called Alison – so far away at the Tawny Owl – and was relieved to hear her voice. She sounded tearful and drained, and he heard a little choke in her voice when he told her what had happened and said he thought it unlikely he would get to Kendleton now. It was a tough call to make – she clearly had been looking forward to his arrival at some stage, particularly after a long, tiring day at the pub. The call ended very mutely.

Fuck this job, Henry thought bitterly.

He walked back to A&E hoping that Janine Cromer hadn't got bored and disappeared. He was amazed to see she was still in the waiting room, looking pale, in shock and staring blankly ahead. She shook herself out of her reverie on Henry's approach.

'Right, we need to get down to Blackburn nick and sort out Freddy – and on the way down, you need to tell me what the phrase "not as such" means.'

They were in the Audi, heading down Shadsworth Road towards Whitebirk, the location of Blackburn's new police station. In fact it had been open several years, having replaced the old Victorian one in the town centre.

'You said you didn't know "as such" what all this shit was

about,' Henry said harshly to Janine. 'Not knowing "as such",' he persisted, 'means you know something. So fire away.'

'I . . . I . . .' she stuttered.

'Look, Janine, there's three dead men back there. This isn't just about protecting a family or looking the other way, trying to distance yourself from them. I need to know what you know. This is serious fucking stuff now, and I'll get to the bottom of it, with or without you. If it's without you, don't be surprised if you get dragged into it as well.'

Henry slammed on at a red right.

'Then it'll be without me,' she said. She crossed her arms. Defensive, withdrawing.

Henry angled sideways. 'Your decision.'

She stared dead ahead.

'It's all going to get much worse,' he warned. 'And then worse still. There's no upside to this shit,' he said relentlessly.

'The lights've changed.'

Henry shot through.

Janine said, 'You didn't just turn up at the house because Freddy was missing, did you? You must have known something about all this. Like we said, superintendents don't come knocking just because some nutter goes AWOL.'

'Some nutter?'

'Medical term.'

They glanced at each other and the tension was eased slightly.

'You show me yours and I'll show you mine,' Henry said.

They hit the first roundabout at Whitebirk.

'Honest, I don't really know much. I do keep them at a distance. And they keep me away, too. Just occasional family get-togethers, and Christmas. That's pretty much when I see them.'

'Doesn't mean you don't know things.'

'Only bits. I'm not included in the "family business", whatever that is, OK?'

Now they were at Blackburn nick. Henry drove into the secure parking compound and parked close to the custody office entrance.

'Which bits do you know about? Men with guns bits?'

'There's been a big fallout with a Blackpool crime family
. . . the Costains?'

'Could Freddy have been kidnapped by them?' Henry
speculated.

'Why? I don't know . . . maybe . . . there's a lot of goading
going on, a lot of posturing, some skirmishes. Bit like a
schoolyard scrap, no one really wanting to throw the first
punch. But something did happen at one of the clubs a couple
of nights ago.'

'Clubs?'

'One of my dad's places in Blackburn. It got a bit yucky.
Bouncers, knives and such.'

'Which club?' Henry racked his brain to see if he could
recall any mention of this on the chief's daily briefing or in
the other incident logs. Janine told him and he frowned. 'Was
it reported to the police?'

She uttered a snort of disbelief. 'Yeah, right. What world
do you live in? Cops don't hardly hear of anything that goes
on, they just think they do.'

'OK,' Henry conceded. 'I take it Freddy has no part in this
crap? Y'know, with him being some nutter?'

'Not really. He thinks he's part of it – in some of his lucid
but ludicrous moments. But Dad won't let him near. The
violence that gets used needs to be for a purpose. The violence
Freddy uses isn't for anything. And there are enough nutters
in the business to start with. Adding one who's out of control
all the time would be too iffy.'

So it is a turf war, Henry thought. And he knew it needed
to be stamped on now.

'Now yours,' Janine said.

'Uh?'

'Show me yours,' she insisted.

There passed one of those indefinable moments. The look.
The insinuation. The double meaning. And Henry's guts
lurched. Ten years ago – less – he might have done something very, very stupid, such as fall into bed with the daughter
of a dangerous gangster. Now, in his mid-fifties (an age he
was becoming increasingly vague about), he was above and
beyond such actions. Plus he was so much older than Janine

and he could just imagine her disappointment when she saw his naked body. Even he was disappointed with it. Every day.

He cleared his throat and cleansed his mind of the image. 'I'm investigating the activities of a possible serial killer.'

'You think Freddy is a serial killer?' Her screwed-up face showed her complete amazement at this thought.

'No . . . I thought he could be a victim. He fits the profile of the previous ones – right age, background, all of them killed and their bodies dumped over the Christmas period. And then, hey, Freddy gets reported missing. So yeah, I'm interested in him.'

Still incredulous, but in a different way, she said, 'Are you saying someone's killing off mentally deranged individuals?'

Henry grimaced. 'So he's been promoted to a mentally deranged individual, has he?'

'That's what he is.' She shrugged. 'Call him what you like.'

'But with moments of lucidity?'

She shrugged again.

Henry said, 'No . . . he's just from the right age group and background . . .' Then he suddenly didn't want to say any more. 'That's why I turned up at Southfork, because I was investigating murders linked to missing persons . . . not because I was being nosy . . .'

'Although that played a part, as we've already established.'

'A little.' He squeezed his thumb and forefinger together. 'A teensy bit.'

'I couldn't even begin to imagine a serial killer wanting to nab someone like Freddy. A bit of a handful. If he had the nous it would be more likely to be him,' she said, and stifled a yawn. 'But he hasn't.'

'Let's go and see him. Whatever, it looks as though someone did kidnap him, but for a different reason than to murder him.'

'Which would be?'

'To use him as bait.'

Before doing anything else, Henry ensured that the custody record was straight. Once, way back, he had fallen foul of the system by failing to make the correct entries at the correct

times and had learned a harsh lesson. Once the paperwork
was done, a gaoler brought Freddy up from the cells to an
interview room.

He was silent, sullen and compliant, and sat across from
Henry without making eye contact. One side of his face was
badly scratched, the other bore the burn marks Henry recalled
from all those years ago. Henry asked him what had happened
since leaving the club in Knuzden the previous evening.

Freddy made no response. He was in no frame of mind to
talk, but at least he wasn't violent for the moment. Neither
did he respond to any of Henry's other questions. It was as
though he wasn't hearing a thing, like Henry was simply
mouthing silently at him. It didn't take Henry long to realize
there was no profit in this.

He had Freddy put back in a cell, after which he and the
custody officer chewed over the options available as regards
Freddy's disposal.

Then Henry went to talk to Janine, seated out in a visitors'
room.

'Main problem I have is that he attacked a nurse,' Henry
explained. 'Mental or not, I don't want to brush that under
the carpet.'

'In reality, what would happen to him if he went to court?'
Janine asked.

'Secure facility for a month or two, maybe.'

'So he'd be out again in no time. Truth is, nothing's really
going to happen to him, is it? He might as well be free.'

'I do want to get him assessed. I can't just let him out,
unless you're willing to look after him,' he suggested. That
had been Henry's plan all along: dump him on his relatives.

Janine pondered this. 'I could . . . for a while, anyway.'

Henry knew that putting Freddy through the justice system
would be futile. He would only end up in the social care
system after that, and it had been pointless putting him there
in the first place. In fact there was probably no answer to
someone like Freddy, short of a captive bolt. Henry might as
well kick him out of the door and hope for the best. At the
moment he was just filling up a cell which could be occupied
by someone more deserving.

'I'm going to release him into your custody. How does that sound?'

'Pretty shitty.'

'I'll take that as a nod.'

He led Janine to the custody office, and Freddy was brought back from the cells. When he saw his niece, his eyes widened with pleasure.

'Hi, Freddy.' She gave him a little wave.

His fat bottom lip began to tremble. 'My darlin',' he said.

Henry leaned on the custody counter. 'Freddy – I'm going to release you, but you have to go with Janine, OK?' Freddy blinked at Henry. 'You need to get a good kip and then I'll come and speak to you about what's happened. And you have to behave yourself and take your tablets, OK? Deal?'

'OK,' he whispered. 'I know you, don't I?'

'We've met.' Henry tugged at his collar, feeling the ghosts of Freddy's thumbs on his windpipe, as well as their more recent incarnations. He glanced at Janine. 'I'll arrange for someone to drop you off.'

'Not taking us in the Audi?'

'No – I don't want blood on the seats.' His mobile rang. He stepped away and answered it. It was Rik Dean.

'Couple of things come up I thought you should know about,' Rik said.

'Fire away.'

'Speaking to the nursing staff on C10, it looks like Bill Grasson did all the shooting, no weapon seen in the hands of the guy with him. Grasson took out both of the Costains, it seems. It was chaos, as you know, but that seems to be the picture.'

'OK – that simplifies things to an extent.'

'Yeah. I've also been to the security office and checked some CCTV footage. I've ID'd the guy with Grasson, the guy who did a runner. You'll like this, Henry.'

'I'm champing at the bit.'

'Terry Cromer.'

'Yesss . . . thought as much.'

'We going for him?'

'Oh yeah, strike while the blood's still hot.' He checked

out Janine and Freddy, standing by the exit door. Freddy was hugging Janine, and she was patting his shoulders lovingly, speaking softly to him, whilst looking sideways at Henry. Henry frowned slightly as he watched them, but it was only a fleeting thought, gone in an instant. He jerked his head for her to come to him and she detached herself from Freddy. Henry laid it straight on the line. 'It was your dad with Grasson.'

She swallowed and nodded numbly as though this was not unexpected. 'Guessed so.'

'I need to speak to him – on my turf. Here.'

'Are you going for him now?'

'Yes, I need to.'

'Did he shoot either of those men?'

'I don't know yet,' Henry lied a bit.

'But it's possible.'

'You know it is.'

She sighed tiredly. 'What's your plan?'

'To go and get him now.'

She laughed harshly. 'That won't be easy.'

'Could be with your help. But if you're not willing, I'll go in with a bunch of cops wearing Doc Marten's size elevens in front of me. This is a hot operation and I want to move with the momentum. Easy or hard.' He didn't tell her that the gang of size elevens he was referring to would take about eight hours to pull together. 'What if I get Freddy taken home in a police van and I take you back in the Audi? That way I can exchange Terry for Freddy.'

'Suppose I warn him you're coming?'

'You won't . . . me getting hold of him now will make his life much easier.'

'Are you going up with armed officers?'

'Should I? I'd rather keep it low key.'

'OK – you drive me back. Take Uncle Freddy in a van – and I'll see what I can do. I promise nothing . . . cops coming for him are an occupational hazard.'

'All right . . . tell you what, though, we'll all go in the van. I'll commandeer one.'

*   *   *

Freddy was placed in the back of a section van, reassured by Janine. Henry and Janine sat up in front and Henry started the engine, a little shot of excitement zipping through him. It was a long time since he'd driven a marked police vehicle and there was always something good about it, no matter how crappy the vehicle itself. A million memories flooded back.

He reversed out of the car park and set off towards Belthorn. Alongside him, Janine sat pensively, fingers interlinked on her lap. Henry didn't interrupt her thoughts, which he guessed were conflicted. He did look at her when he heard her chuckle. 'What?'

'Where do you get a phrase like "move with the momentum" from? Sounds like a line from a bad rap song.'

'I'm just good with words. Got an O level in English . . . grade C.'

She laughed, but then her face turned hard. 'I don't think this'll be easy, you know. I may be his daughter, but I have no influence on him whatever. If he kicks off you'll have more than a handful.'

'I've got a chum with me.' Henry jerked his thumb backwards.

They had travelled up Shadsworth Road, the hospital over to their right, and then turned onto Haslingden Road towards Belthorn, at which point a vehicle had taken up a following position behind them.

Janine peered into the side mirror, saw the headlights.

'Just the one,' Henry assured her. 'If it does go all wrong, I'll call for further assistance. Let's hope it stays amicable.'

Janine shook her head, and Henry crossed his fingers. Getting more officers to back him up would be a bit of a conjuring trick, because there weren't any. If Terry got upset, Henry would back off and return later with a mini army.

They drove in silence, up through Guide, across the motorway junction, then right towards Belthorn.

At the top of the hill Henry turned onto Tower View and stopped the van outside the Cromer residence. All the lights were on at the house.

Henry and Janine alighted, and he went to the back of the van, opened the back doors, then the inner cage, and let Freddy out.

Janine took Freddy's arm and steered him to the gate, saying nothing to Henry, who turned and looked at the car that had followed him. It pulled up and Rik Dean got out. The two detectives watched the pair paused at the gates as Janine entered a key code, then pushed through and walked up to the house.

'Beauty and the Beast,' Rik commented.

Henry said nothing; he felt shattered. He was always amazed at his ability to keep going through exhaustion. Years of practice is what he put it down to, but lately he was starting to get more tired more quickly. He needed a real coffee boost. Either that or speed.

At the front door, Janine glanced over her shoulder before she entered, then was gone.

'Have you ever thought how dangerous it would be to shag her?' Rik pondered out loud. 'Dangerous but exciting.'

Henry narrowed his eyes but didn't want to admit his thoughts on that subject. He found it remarkable that, even at times of great stress or life-changing moments, where the most serious things were happening or being discussed, the indomitable spirit of cops meant that there was always time to think about humping – and not to be sexist, he was pretty sure that applied to female officers, too. Henry couldn't actually remember being implanted with this chip when he joined the job, but it was definitely still functioning in him. He wondered if it would deactivate when he retired. He hoped not. It was one of life's great comforts, just to know that when all about you was crumbling and going to rat shit, your thoughts gravitated to your penis. He grinned.

'Think he'll walk out and surrender?' Rik asked.

'Nope,' Henry said absently. 'Not in his nature.'

The two detectives stood side by side at the wrought-iron gates and waited.

The front door opened.

'Here we go,' Henry said.

It wasn't Terry Cromer who emerged, hands held high. It was Janine – alone. She ran towards them and Henry could read from the body language that things weren't great. She ran up to the gates and clung to the vertical ironwork.

'He's not here,' she gasped.

'Where, then?'

Her mouth constricted. 'He's heading to Blackpool.'

Henry understood at once. 'Tooled up? Costains?'

She nodded.

'How many?'

'Don't know.'

'Vehicles?'

'Don't know, either.'

Henry closed his eyes. 'Shit.' All he needed to ice the cake that was the best Christmas Day he'd ever spent was a shoot-out between rival gangs.

'And I haven't told you,' Janine said, spinning away and striding quickly back to the house.

TEN

Even allowing for the time taken to swap the police van for his own Audi, Henry still managed to get to Blackpool within twenty-five minutes – some going, even on roads virtually devoid of traffic. He seemed to be making a habit of breaking all world land speed records across the county.

He exited the M55 at Marton Circle and headed into Blackpool along the A583. His house was on an estate over to his right; more importantly, the council estate that was his destination was on his left.

He turned, slowed right down, his heart still pounding at the memory of the 140 mph he had managed to coax out of his car. Both he and the Audi had loved it – until he lost his nerve and slowed to a more respectable ninety. He entered the estate and slowed to a crawl as a police patrol car came slowly towards him. He flashed it and the cars stopped alongside each other, the drivers opening their windows for a chat. Henry had already asked for an immediate high-visibility presence on the estate to discourage anything that might happen, but Blackpool section was as strapped for staff as everywhere else in the county, especially now – in the early hours of Boxing Day.

One car was as much as could be mustered: one cop, one car, police sign illuminated. Still, better than nothing.

The PC driving the car knew Henry. 'Boss.'

'Pete – happy Christmas . . . anything doing?'

'You too, boss . . . not so far, all quiet on the western front.'

'Anything happening at the Costains'?'

'Party time. Banging music. Youngsters hanging out the door and windows, flashing Vs at me, usual shite. But not the only party on the estate. Whole place is heaving.'

'Let's loop around and have a drive past.'

Shoreside: an estate Henry knew well. It had a terrible reputation for public disorder, criminality and unemployment. Some figures claimed that seventy-five per cent of adults on the estate were out of work and that a benefits culture was endemic. Despite many initiatives, most of which involved throwing truckloads of cash at the place, nothing seemed to change.

The only row of shops on the estate had been systematically destroyed and was now a memory. A community centre was first firebombed, then resurrected only to be completely flattened by kids using a stolen bulldozer, driven two miles onto the estate from a building site.

It was as if the estate was cursed by a death wish.

And lording over it all by means of terror and intimidation was the infamous Costain family. Claiming, spuriously, descent from Romany gypsies, they had landed in Blackpool almost fifty years earlier and settled into a life of crime which grew from almost honourable thieving and burglary through to drug dealing and armed robbery.

Henry had dealt with them for more years than he cared to remember. Perhaps his greatest victory over them was that one of their number – Troy, now sadly deceased – had been Henry's informant for a good number of years prior to his demise. Henry had also dealt with the deaths of other members of the family, including old man Costain who had died in a drive-by shooting completely unconnected with his position as the family godfather. But they survived and prospered. To the best of Henry's knowledge, old man Costain's younger brother – Runcie Costain – had taken over at the helm and piloted them to new levels of criminality. This obviously included expanding their empire across the county.

Henry drove slowly past the Costain home, two semi-detached council houses knocked into a single huge one. It was alive with festive cheer. A group of alcohol-fuelled teenagers in the front garden jeered at Henry and the police car behind. One of them threw a bottle of WKD at them, which landed and shattered between the two cars with a pop. Henry dipped his accelerator automatically and the police car behind swerved to miss the broken glass.

They drove out of sight and pulled up for a chat, leaning against the police car.

'Heard you've had a busy night, boss,' the PC said.

'Understatement,' Henry said.

'Reckon there could be repercussions over here?'

'Every chance. But where, I'm not certain . . . if there are a few higher level Costains here, this could be a target.' He bit his bottom lip. 'I think I need to go and knock on the front door.'

'I'll come with you.'

'No, you just hang on here and watch the cars. I don't want to wind them up unnecessarily . . . but come like the wind if I yell, obviously.'

'Obviously.'

He strolled around the corner, wondering if he should have kept his stab vest on. That would have been like a red rag to a bull and someone would have had to try it out.

He walked confidently to the house, passing the group of teens – or were they kidults these days? – who'd lobbed the bottle. They watched him with snake-suspicious eyes. Henry wished them the season's greetings, and was told to fuck off in reply.

The front door was wide open, but Henry was canny enough to stay outside. He knocked. Youngsters pushed past him rudely in both directions.

A couple on the stairs in front of him were locked in an embrace. The lad's hand was down the girl's panties, hers down the front of his jeans. Some very frantic rubbing was going on, more likely to ignite a real flame than produce unforgettable orgasms.

Henry knocked again, the sound lost in the thump-thump of the music and sounds of revelry emanating from the house. The second time in only a few hours that he had turned up unannounced on the doorstep of a criminal family, both for good, honest reasons. Mostly.

First time because he suspected one of them might be a victim of a serial killer. This time to warn of the possibility of some very nasty reprisals. He then had a thought: the news that two of their family had been taken out in Blackburn might fire an uncontrollable reaction from the Costains, either against him as the messenger or in retaliation against the Cromers.

Suddenly his impulsiveness in knocking at the door sent a shimmer of uncertainty through him. This was not the time to be delivering such news to the family, even if they already knew that Stuart and Benji had gone out tooled up to cause mayhem thirty-odd miles to the east.

The thought that he might just be stepping into a cow-pat of conspiracy to murder now struck him.

It was highly likely that Runcie Costain had sent them on their task. They wouldn't have done it off their own bat.

And – again, Henry thought – had Freddy been used as a lure to draw Terry Cromer out into the open and kill him? Had that been their strategy: kidnap and lure?

Too many questions, not enough answers.

Henry now wanted to reverse out of this situation and reappraise things. He had been acting on impulse, which was often his downfall.

But he also didn't want anyone else to lose their lives.

The words 'rock' and 'hard place' sprang to mind.

The Costains needed to know about the deaths in the family (if they didn't already know), and it was Henry's responsibility to tell them. But at the same time, Runcie might well have been the person who effectively sent them on the mission that led to their deaths.

Question was – should he now execute a flawless, unobserved exit, or finish what he'd started?

In his mind he sifted through this dilemma in milliseconds, signals surging through the dendrites in his head like a mini electrical storm.

His decision was to get out, regroup, then return with backup so that he would be in control of the situation, not be one cop versus a bunch of drunks likely to kick off just for fun.

He needed to establish a very visible police presence on Shoreside to dissuade Terry Cromer from attempting anything. He also had to get a few detectives together and come up very quickly with a well-structured plan. And he needed resources. He needed a lot of things.

So he backed away, stepped over a drunken body that had slumped down behind him and retreated down the driveway.

As he guessed, no one moaned and begged him to stay. One kid told him to fuck off again. Another spat at him, though most of the spittle dribbled down the kid's chin.

He started to walk back to his car, pulling out his PR and calling Blackpool comms.

'Any uniformed officer on any non-urgent call needs to be immediately redeployed to Shoreside,' he instructed. 'Tell them to meet me where the shops used to be on Fairview Road for a quick briefing. I need a hi-viz presence here as of now, not just one lone patrol, everyone in yellow jackets, please.' He waited for the patrol inspector to pipe up and whine, which he did. Henry listened to him, stopping in mid-stride as he explained firmly what he needed.

He stopped on the corner of the road close to where he'd left his car and the uniformed officer. He gave the PC a wave as he talked to the inspector, and as he turned, he looked back towards the Costain house.

'I know it's an imposition,' Henry was saying, trying to schmooze the guy, who was rightfully miffed about someone else deciding how his officers should be deployed. 'But one cop won't be enough.' As he said the last word, a feeling of dread coursed through him. In disbelief, he pulled the PR away from his mouth as he saw a car turn into the road about two hundred metres away, its headlights doused as it did so. 'Shit,' Henry said. He was unable to see the occupants clearly, though there were two of them; they were just black shapes.

The car stopped momentarily.

Transfixed and slack-jawed, Henry watched the car. It was

nothing special. A normal, mid-range saloon. Henry thought it was probably Japanese.

Then he saw something poke out of the front passenger window.

Something like a pipe, or a broomstick handle.

Something like the barrel of a gun.

Henry started to move, a roar on his lips. Reprisal time's here, he thought.

The car suddenly surged forward from a standstill.

Henry ran into the centre of the road, screaming at the people outside the house to get down, waving his arms desperately. No one took any notice of him.

The car's speed increased.

The second salvo in a drugs war, the first one having been fired in Blackburn.

Henry was fifty metres short of the house when the car, hurtling in his direction, drew level with the house.

Over the scream of the engine, Henry heard gunfire. He counted. Six shots, quick succession, as the car shot past the house and then bore down on him.

Part of him was aware of the screams from the partygoers. The images of some of them simply watching the car drive by, mouths open, uncomprehending. Others throwing themselves to the ground, at least one person in his view catching a bullet and spinning backwards like a corkscrew.

And the car coming towards him.

Only metres away. Two seconds at most before impact.

He knew it would strike him about knee level. He half imagined the joints being snapped backwards and the rest of his body smashing onto and splaying across the bonnet, maybe his face hitting the windscreen and then the whole of his body being flipped up and cartwheeled over the car.

He was incredulous at himself for thinking he could have prevented a shooting with a combination of the sheer force of his personality and by waving his hands about. It was never going to work.

He moved – with incredible speed. He vaulted sideways out of the path of the car onto the grass verge, executing a graceless double roll and coming up onto his knees in the starting position.

As the car shot past he whipped his head sideways, hoping to focus his eyes on the driver. Just give me that one second, he prayed, just imprint the profile of that man into my brain.

His eyes locked on. They were still good and sharp. But it didn't matter, even though the driver turned and looked directly at him.

He was wearing a balaclava with eye holes. And he had the audacity to flip his middle finger at Henry.

Henry would be able to describe that to a T to a police artist.

He said 'Shit' again but then his eyes zoomed onto the rear number plate. He memorized the registration instantly, even though the car's lights were out. He continued to watch the back of the car and also the PC, who had been waiting around the corner, drawn out by the sound of shooting and general mayhem. Henry hoped he wouldn't be as foolhardy as Henry himself and jump in front of the car, but, wisely, the officer, in a sort of dynamic pose, watched the car flash by and disappear around the next corner.

Henry shouted into his PR, 'Shots fired Fairview Road outside the Costains'. A drive-by shooting, one vehicle, two male occupants, a Nissan saloon, registered number PK05 . . .' He reeled the number off and gave the direction of travel the car had taken. 'Possible gunshot injuries at the house,' he went on, 'just going to check.'

Henry's hunting instinct was to run back to his car and give chase, but that would only enrage the comms room operators and probably end up being classified as a non-authorized pursuit. It might all go wrong, and if it did, he wouldn't have a leg to stand on. All vehicle pursuits were carefully controlled and monitored by the radio operators, and the FIM and vehicles involved were supposed to be liveried and driven by trained pursuit drivers – and despite his driving qualifications, Henry wasn't one. Such regulations hadn't stopped him in the past . . . but with age came a bit of discretion.

Based on the fact it was now the early hours of Boxing Day and there were almost no cops on duty on the ground, he kissed bye-bye to the Nissan – literally puckering his lips as he ran across the road to the house, telling comms he wanted an ambulance turned out and insisting they rouse the police helicopter.

Next thing on his mind was the possibility of this getting out of hand as a public order incident. A matter like this could easily escalate into a riot and with no cops to quell it, that was not a happy prospect.

A group of drunks gathered around the writhing body on the front lawn. Henry shouldered his way through them, smelling alcohol and weed. He knelt down next to a youth of about nineteen he didn't recognize. The lad was wearing what had been a white T-shirt and had clearly taken a bullet in the right shoulder, his top now soaked red. He writhed and moaned, unable to comprehend what had just happened to him. The people surrounding him were doing nothing to help. They were all drunk or drugged, some of the girls becoming hysterical, and it must have been very weird for them, some sort of psychedelic nightmare.

Henry glanced briefly at their faces.

A girl burst through the circle, the one Henry had seen on the stairs a few moments earlier with a lad's hand down her knickers. Her hands flew to her face and she screamed, 'Donny, Donny, oh my God!' Then she fell backwards in a faint and hit the back of her head on the front doorstep.

'Hey – what the fuck did you do that for?' a young lad demanded of Henry.

'Do what?'

'Push her over, you pig-twat.'

'Fuck off,' Henry said and turned his attention to the wounded boy, who was shaking uncontrollably.

'Fuck you too,' the lad shouted. He kicked out at Henry, who saw the foot coming. Though he was squatting he managed to catch it at the heel and twist, flipping the drunk off balance. He gave a push, let go, and the lad staggered backwards. The can of beer he was holding flew away and he landed diagonally across the girl who'd fainted.

Henry felt a shimmer of apprehension.

The mood he'd picked up a few seconds before had suddenly gone a few shades darker, was now almost black. Confusion, alcohol, a cop, a crowd, a violent incident. Not a good combination.

Once, many years ago, when he'd been a young PC on

mobile patrol, he'd been surrounded by a gang outside a chip shop and they had refused to let him drive away. Two lads were at the front of the car, two at the back, and with about ten others they had started to rock the car, building up enough momentum to roll it over – with him inside. That had been pretty scary; he'd been in lots of similar situations since and had learned that in such cases cops should be in and out as quickly as possible, unless they outnumbered the crowd. Situations were easily inflamed.

He stood up, knowing he wouldn't be allowed to help the injured lad. A can of beer was thrown at him, glancing off his arm. Then about ten people circled him, venom in their eyes.

'You stand back,' he said evenly, firmly, without any fear in his voice. 'This lad needs treatment – and so does she.'

The girl who'd toppled over was sitting up, staring in puzzlement at the palm of her hand, which was covered in blood from the ugly gash at the back of her skull.

Another can hit him, thrown from behind the people around him. Hyenas on a wildebeest.

Out of the corner of his eye, Henry saw the police car that had been parked near his Audi emerging with blue lights flashing. It screamed up and stopped outside, the PC getting out, his extendable baton drawn.

A hail of beer bottles and cans, like weapons from a medieval battle scene, arced at him. Using his baton like a baseball bat, he smashed a couple away with amazing accuracy.

Somewhere in the distance there was the wail of a siren.

Still Henry was surrounded.

'You shot him,' one shouted. 'The cop shot him.'

If he'd had the time, Henry would have exhaled a pissed-off sigh and answered back.

'Yeah, you must've,' another one chorused.

The constable shouldered his way roughly through and stood his ground next to Henry. His face showed fear, but he wasn't going to back down. He held the baton across his chest, ready for use.

'We're here to help,' Henry said forcefully. 'This lad needs sorting, so you guys back off and let me look at his wound.'

'You heard – get back,' the PC echoed.

Two cops had a slightly sobering effect. Overwhelming one was easy. Two made it harder, though not impossible.

The sirens grew louder. Two types – ambulance and police – like a mismatched stereo.

Henry glanced at the boy. He was still now – not dead, but probably going into shock. There was a lot of blood from the wound.

Henry said, 'Is Runcie here?' It was a question thrown to everyone. No one replied. 'I said, is Runcie here?' he demanded again. 'Runcie Costain?'

Suddenly the music from inside, the boom-boom, was turned off. 'I'm here,' a voice bellowed from the door.

As one, the kids turned, and there he was at the threshold of the front door – all five two of him, but built like a pillbox, with eyes to match, oblong slits, and a flat head of closely cropped hair.

Henry had crossed his path only a few times. He was a much more cautious operator than the previous heads of the family and had streamlined the business with layers that made him almost untouchable. Until now.

Henry shouted, 'You know me, Runcie – so get this lot to back off. This lad needs attention and I can't help him if they're in the way.'

'You heard, get back you lot,' Runcie ordered them.

'He fuckin' did it,' one of them growled, just loud enough.

Another beer can was tossed half-heartedly at Henry.

'He's a cop, dick-brain,' Runcie said to whoever. 'Back off.'

Muttering angrily, the little crowd slowly stepped back a few paces, but not with any enthusiasm, staying within striking distance.

'Oh God,' the prostrate youth moaned.

'My head, my friggin' head,' the fainting girl said, now with both hands covered in blood. She swooned again and dropped back, hitting the step with her head in exactly the same place, deepening the wound.

'See to her,' Henry told the PC. 'Towels,' he said to Runcie, who nodded and disappeared into the house.

He did not re-emerge, nor did any towels.

A very long minute later an ambulance and a police van

arrived at the scene. Police numbers increased by one. And the music from inside the house went up to full volume.

The plug dangled in Henry's hand. Silence resonated around the living room. Henry's ears rang, there was still a drum beat in his head.

'I said, where's Runcie?'

The four teenagers sprawled on the settee sneered at him, hate in their eyes. The ones standing around with glasses or smokes in their hands did the same.

Runcie had done a runner, that much was obvious. Henry assumed he'd done the sums, realized that the visit by his boys into Cromer territory hadn't gone well, hence the drive-by, and had either gone 'to the blankets', to coin an old Mafia saying – gone into hiding – or had gone to tool up for more retaliation. Although Runcie hadn't been officially informed that two of his relatives had ended up on mortuary slabs, Henry was under no illusions that he probably now knew that the worst had happened in Blackburn.

Henry had scoured the downstairs of the house, now he was going to have a look upstairs.

Having ripped the plug for the music system out of the wall, he took the lead in his left hand, the plug in his right and tore the wire out of the plug so there was no chance of the noise restarting.

'Party's over,' he announced, trying to hide his glee. It was one of the best feelings a cop could have. This was something he'd done a time or two in his long career and it always gave satisfaction: spoil a good party.

'What! You can't do that.' This was from the lad who had kicked out at him and whom Henry had upended.

He glared at the young man. 'Just watch me.'

He dropped plug and wire onto the floor. 'Where's Runcie?' It was the third time of asking.

'Don't know no Runcie.'

'All right – time to clear out,' he announced.

A few more cops had appeared on the scene and the partygoers were more subdued and compliant now, but still vociferous.

Both the boy who'd been winged and the girl who'd cracked her head open had been taken to hospital, and now Henry was pretty much in control.

The force helicopter was up, the registered number of the Nissan had been circulated and a few road checkpoints established, and he had informed everyone necessary.

He was hoping to have a little quality time to take stock of things, get a proper plan put together . . . but he didn't want to miss the chance of grabbing Runcie, hopefully before both factions met up and more blood was spilled.

Runcie had gone, probably straight out of the back door.

Henry went upstairs.

He found a couple of naked teenagers in a back bedroom, busy with each other underneath a duvet, oblivious to what was going on. They stopped in mid-thrust.

'Out!' Henry said, jerking his thumb. 'Now!'

The small box room was empty and there was a main bedroom at the front, the door closed. For politeness' sake, he knocked and entered a nicely furnished room with a king-size bed and subdued lighting.

Henry turned the light switch and brought proper illumination to the proceedings.

Unless Runcie was hidden underneath the bed, he wasn't there.

But there was a woman in the bed, on the floor around which were several empty bottles of champagne, paper plates with scraps of half-eaten food and overflowing ashtrays. And not only cigarette stubs.

The woman's long black hair was dishevelled, make-up skewiff. She propped herself up and blinked at Henry, unperturbed.

Cherry was Runcie's long-time lady friend and she was a stunner. Henry had met her a few times in passing. Because he made it his business to know about the Costains, he knew she had been a stripper, lap dancer and hooker, not necessarily in that order, and sometimes a combination of all three. She had only recently retired from these 'games' to become a lady of leisure at Runcie's side after having spent a couple of years on his payroll. She'd been promoted to his bed, official eye candy.

She rubbed her panda eyes. 'Ungh – you,' she said. The duvet slid down and Henry averted his eyes like a gent. 'Whazzappenin'?' she mumbled thickly. She scratched her left breast, which was completely exposed.

'Where's Runcie?'

'Fuck shoulda know? He were here.' She exhaled like a horse and reached for a packet of cigarettes on the bedside. 'D'ya wan' 'im for?'

'He's done a runner. I need to speak to him urgently.'

Henry watched her pick up the cigarette packet next to an ashtray overflowing with ciggie ends, spliffs and two used condoms.

'Where is he?'

She placed a cigarette between her lipstick-smeared lips, her eyes bleary. 'No idea.'

'Tell me your best guess, Cherry, or I'll bust you.'

She screwed up her nose and hoisted the duvet back over her boob. 'F' what?'

Henry pointed at the ashtray. 'Mary Jane's still illegal, I believe. And are those traces of coke I see on the dressing table top?'

'You wouldn't.'

'Would.'

'Bastard.'

'Just tell me.'

'Uh . . . prob'ly gone to that club on Withnell Street, I dunno.'

Henry only knew of one club on that road in South Shore. 'John Rider's old place?'

'Yuh, that's the one . . . he's just bought it.'

'Right.' Henry turned to leave.

'Hey!' Cherry called.

He turned back. 'What?'

She flung back the duvet, revealing her completely naked and completely hairless body, which to Henry looked very fine indeed. She rotated and opened her legs wide, allowing Henry to see her very finely shaved pubic area. 'Jig-a-jig? You – me? I'll fuck your brains out for Christmas for free.'

'I'll pass.' Henry raised a hand. Just at the moment Henry's brain was screwed up enough.

ELEVEN

Henry knew the club on Withnell Street too intimately for comfort, but was under the impression it had been virtually abandoned and allowed to fall into disrepair, untouched for years. The previous owner, John Rider, had harboured big ideas for the place, a former casino, with visions of turning it into a lap dancing club. Those visions had come to a very bloody end when one of Rider's rivals had declared his own plans for the club and Rider had been killed in the crossfire. Henry had been deeply involved in the situation – it had almost cost him his life – and returning to the club for the first time in years unearthed a lot of unpleasant memories.

That said, he wasn't surprised someone had taken it over for something. He guessed that the licence for the place would have been kept current by whoever had owned it – Rider's executioners, he assumed. Once a liquor licence lapsed it was hard work to resurrect, as the application process would have to begin from scratch. And any premises with a drinks licence in Blackpool could be a gold mine.

He hurried back to his car, still in one piece after his close encounter with Cherry, and set off towards South Shore. Much of that area of town was quite pleasant, but the two hundred metre wide strip from the Pleasure Beach complex as far north as Central Pier was not the most salubrious of localities. Many of the terraced houses, once proud and clean bed and breakfast establishments, had been turned into rabbit-warren flats, financed by the Department of Social Security, run by seedy landlords and inhabited by the unfortunate and the criminal. Henry disliked to stereotype, but many of the people he came across were lazy third-generation scroungers, living off benefits embedded in their psyche, existing hand to mouth, stealing, taking drugs. Many he didn't come across were decent folk living in harsh times. But the truth of the matter was that

South Shore did have a high rate of crime, drug use was rife, and a lot of kids didn't know their fathers.

The clubs and other drinking establishments didn't help matters.

Most were well run, but a core of them were managed by individuals whose names should never have appeared on a licence, or were fronts for more organized crime, thriving on the weakness of others.

Sitting behind the wheel of the Audi, Henry exhaled a long breath, then inhaled an equally lengthy one in the hope of replenishing the oxygen in his system, which felt very depleted. He knew he was running on fumes.

His fingers gripped the steering wheel as he focused his mind. His intention now was to visit the club and see if Runcie had gone there. Hopefully, he wouldn't be there. That would mean Henry could execute a graceful retreat, brief a few people then dash home – to his house in Blackpool, tantalizingly close, but oh so far away – sleep for four hours, then get back to work, and write off any possibility of seeing Alison.

He considered calling her, decided not to, and started the engine, having arranged to meet the night-duty detective at the club. Henry had decided his approach to finding Runcie would be blunt. He would simply knock on the door and take it from there.

He weaved through streets he knew intimately and emerged on the sea front. He drove north, turning into Withnell Street which ran at ninety degrees to the promenade. He drove past the club, did a three-point turn, then pulled in about fifty metres away, just as the night detective came and parked behind him in an unmarked Astra. The jack's name was Brighouse, a youngish DC Henry knew vaguely and had heard good reports about. He had been busy with a prisoner in the cells when Shoreside was kicking off.

'Some rockin' tonight,' he said to Henry as they walked up to the club.

'One of those nights that make it all worthwhile,' Henry said, with a mouth full of irony.

It was well over ten years since Henry had set foot in the club. Standing in front of the big, solid, ornately carved double doors that were the entrance, he paused and his heart upped a beat for a moment as a palpitation shimmied through him, head to toe. He swallowed.

Brighouse noted his hesitation. 'You OK, boss?'

Henry nodded. 'Yeah – someone's just tangoed over my grave, that's all.'

'Don't you just hate it when that happens?'

Henry shook himself free from the terrible memories and ghosts of the past. He had not thought about John Rider for years, a fact that slightly baffled him. Rider had been a top-rate Manchester gangster who had tried to break free from the shackles of his past, but his ex-buddies wouldn't let go. They had muscled in on Rider's Blackpool dream with fatal consequences for too many people, almost including Henry. Henry was amazed that he had the ability to move on from such life-changing events and still function as a cop. He knew that had to be the nature of the cop mentality, to be able to compartmentalize, to box off sections of the brain, file away the shit and carry on.

Not that he was completely immune to leakage between those inner walls. On occasions, they had disintegrated – big style – and the plumber had to be called in.

But not tonight. Tonight he had accidentally stepped into a violent set of circumstances that needed to be dealt with firmly and swiftly and forcefully, and a tenuous link to the past wasn't going to throw him off the scent.

'I've had dealings here in the past,' Henry said.

'I know,' Brighouse said. 'Bit of a legend.'

Henry shot him a glance, seeing if he was taking the piss. He wasn't, but a concurrent thought struck him: did becoming a legend mean you were over the hill? Was it time to retire? he asked himself again. 'This place hasn't been used in a long time, by the looks.'

'Not that I know of,' Brighouse said. 'So why are we here?'

'Runcie Costain owns it.'

'Shit – does he? I wonder if the licensing lads know about that.'

'He'll have got in under the radar. Probably using a clean front man.'

Brighouse nodded.

Henry put his weight to the substantial door. It didn't move. And there was no way of booting it down. It wasn't some flimsy plywood or MDF door to a bedsit. It was thick oak and properly secured. Henry surveyed it from top to bottom and saw a bell on the wall which had the look of being disconnected. Not that he would have rung it anyway. Runcie wasn't likely to open up and let the boys in, if he was here.

'Round the back,' Henry said.

Brighouse gave him a wary look. 'Boss, I don't want to shit my suit up.'

Henry treated him to his best superintendent's caustic, visual dressing down, all eyes and disapproving mouth, and the young man got the message instantly. Henry refrained from saying patronizingly that he'd ruined more suits than Brighouse had had hot dinners. Probably wasn't a good boast for a living legend to make. Instead he stalked away, turned into the next side road and found the alley that ran parallel to the rear of the club. Another location he knew well.

It was a typical Blackpool South back alley. Empty beer cans, cider bottles, dog shit, discarded fast food packaging and, before he knew it, or could lift his foot up quickly enough, Henry had trodden on a hypodermic needle that crunched like a baked cockroach. His mouth turned into an ugly sneer of anger as he lifted his foot carefully from the broken glass.

Up ahead in the darkness the alley was blocked by a parked car, which Henry assumed might belong to Runcie. He and Brighouse crept towards it, leaving fluorescent street lights behind, entering a dark world. Henry saw there were two cars in the alley, both parked facing the same direction, nose to tail.

With some shock he realized that the nearer one was the Nissan he had seen on Shoreside. His mouth tasted bitter again as his system pumped the last dregs of adrenalin into him. Beyond the Nissan was an old-style Fiat Panda, one with a fold-back roof.

'That Panda's Runcie's,' Brighouse whispered behind Henry. 'I think.'

'And this one's from the drive-by shooting,' Henry said under his breath.

'Oh.' Brighouse sounded uncertain.

Henry continued to creep down the alley, careful where he placed his feet. The driver and front passenger windows were wound down on the Nissan. Even feet away Henry could feel the heat of the engine rising on his face, hear the tick-tick of it cooling. A car with a little engine that had been screwed to the ground.

And – not for the first time that night – he could smell the unmistakable odour of cordite from the discharge of a gun.

'What we gonna do, boss?' Brighouse said hoarsely. His adrenalin was flowing too, but he was probably having his first flush of it that night, so he had plenty remaining.

'Investigate.'

'Does that—?'

Henry wasn't completely sure what the next words were going to be, nor did he ever discover, as the sentence was stunted by the sound of gunfire from within the club. Dulled. Muted. Unmistakable.

The young detective's next words actually turned out to be, 'Fuck-shit!' and he ducked instinctively. Henry was sure they were not the words he'd originally planned to finish his sentence with.

'C'mon.' Henry sidestepped between the cars and went to the door set into the high wall at the back of the club. Highly illegal barbed wire was looped loosely along the top of the wall to deter burglars. Henry flicked the latch on the door and put his shoulder to it. This door, unlike its cousin at the front, was rickety and rotten and loose. It scraped open and he stepped into the rear yard. This was not a particularly large area, but it was a mess of tangled and broken pallets, a few beer kegs and a couple of mega-sized wheelie bins.

When Henry had last been to the club, the back door had been sealed by a huge steel panel, pock-riveted to the brickwork. That had long since been peeled away, revealing the door which led into the kitchen area. Henry headed for this door, seeing it was ajar, his mouth now salty and dehydrated. It was a long time since he'd had a drink of anything.

'Henry – is this wise?'

Ahh, Henry thought. Maybe *that* was what Brighouse was going to say.

Henry ignored him and entered the club. A low wattage bulb lit the kitchen, hanging by a bare wire. Henry crossed to the next door. If he remembered correctly, it opened into a series of corridors at the rear of the premises, off which toilets, offices and storerooms were located. Beyond was the way through to the main part of the club.

As he stepped into the first corridor he was instantly confronted by the charging figure of a hooded man, a machine pistol in his hands; behind him was another, similarly clad figure, this one carrying a revolver in his right hand. The two guys from the Nissan.

The meeting was a surprise to all concerned. If it hadn't been deadly it would have been farcical when Henry and the first man collided headlong into each other. They fell into a tangle of thick limbs and torsos, groans of expelled air rushing out of their lungs.

And behind each man was a second man, of course.

The man with the revolver pointed it at Brighouse and fired. It was an ill-judged, unsupported shot, one handed. The recoil snapped the man's hand high and sent the bullet into the wall above the detective's head.

Not that Brighouse would have been hit anyway. As soon as he had seen the weapon rising, self-preservation kicked in and he dived back into the kitchen like a synchronized swimmer launching into a swimming pool – but quicker and not so gracefully.

Henry scrambled wildly and hit out.

The man he was tangling with whipped the barrel of the machine pistol across Henry's temple, a glancing blow, knocking him sideways. Then the man was up on his feet, and both gunmen hurdled over Henry through to the kitchen and fled out past the terrified Brighouse, who had somehow ended up on his knees in front of the gas cooker, hands held up in surrender.

The man with the revolver pointed it at Brighouse, who clamped his hands together as if praying. 'Don't shoot,' he pleaded. 'I've got a fam . . .'

He did not fire, and they were gone.

Moments later, Henry staggered through the door, holding his face, blood from the gash on the side of his head all over his hands.

Brighouse dropped his praying hands hastily and looked shamefacedly at Henry, who gave him a glare, found his balance and ran out of the kitchen as he heard an engine starting up, a crunch of gears and a squeal of rubber.

Henry sprinted into the alleyway to see the Nissan swerving backwards onto the street, rocking as the brakes were slammed on, first gear was engaged and the car sped away.

By the time Henry made it to the street himself, the car had gone, leaving a trail of burned oil smoke hanging two feet above the road surface. He could hear the sound of the engine diminishing into the night.

'You must think I'm a coward.'

Henry had found some kitchen roll, folded it square twice and was holding it against the cut on his head. The blood had flowed onto his face, neck and collar, but the cut itself did not appear too severe. It just hurt.

'Do I hell. You did exactly the right thing. All you did was get out of the way of someone who took a pot shot at you. Good thinking if you ask me. I'd've done the same if I hadn't run headlong into one of the bastards.'

'You're saying I did right by not tackling them?'

'Yeah, you did right,' Henry said softly. 'Don't dwell on it,' he advised, but he could see that the prospect of being labelled a chicken would haunt Brighouse for some time to come, if not for ever. It was in his eyes. Self-recrimination. 'OK?' Henry said, ending the conversation. 'Let's go see what damage they've done.'

He and Brighouse had not been joined by any backup – mainly because all other available men were now up on Shoreside and there wasn't another cop free within twenty miles. Henry, however, would lay odds that they would be safe now. Whatever had been going on in the club was over with. The job had been done.

He jerked his head at Brighouse to tag along, and they started to make their way through the corridors until they entered the main dance floor and bar area. It had not been touched since

Henry had last been there. He quickly scanned the floor for signs of old bloodstains, then glanced up at the ceiling and saw the large number of bullet holes that had been put there on his last visit by killers trying to murder him and John Rider. They had fired upwards, strafing the ceiling, knowing that the two men were hiding in the rafters. Henry shook his head at the memory. The bullets had obviously missed him. They had killed Rider.

He blew out his cheeks, looked around. Brighouse had strolled over to the bar, which he peered over. 'Oh Jeez . . . here,' he called, and looked at Henry, his face horrified.

Henry walked across, dabbing his face. It was still bleeding and the kitchen towel did not seem to be as efficient at soaking up liquid as the manufacturers claimed. Not blood, anyway.

He went to the open end of the bar and – without surprise – looked down at Runcie Costain's bullet-riddled body. Alongside him was a sawn-off shotgun, a few scattered cartridges and a mangy-looking revolver. His little arsenal, stashed at the club, which he'd hurried down to retrieve and arm himself with after the drive-by, before he was ambushed.

He was on his back, one leg drawn up, between the bar and the shelves. An arc of bullets from the right side of his chest ran up to his left shoulder, probably one burst of the machine pistol that had cracked Henry's head. A curved line from his liver, across his sternum, shredding his lungs and heart, and into his left shoulder, most of which seemed to have been blown away. They must have caught him by surprise, because he had a half-smoked cheroot clamped at the corner of his mouth, still smouldering. He was lying in a steady growing pool of crimson, oxygenated blood.

'Holy . . .' Brighouse uttered as it truly sank in what he was seeing. It had taken his mind a few seconds to completely assimilate it. Then he started to gag. He pitched away from the bar and ran across the dance floor to its far edge, where he dropped to his hands and knees and heaved up copious amounts of half-digested Christmas dinner. It reminded Henry he hadn't yet been lucky enough to have his.

But at least the crime scene remained sterile thanks to

Brighouse's thoughtfulness in spewing up as far away from it as he could manage.

Henry walked over to him and gave him a fatherly pat on the back.

The Force Major Investigation Team maintained a pokey office at Blackpool nick, tucked away in a corridor few people ever seemed to venture down. Nominally it was Henry's office, but he let any of the FMIT team use it as necessary. The department only had a toehold because that was all they needed. When anything major happened in a division which called for FMIT involvement, such as a murder or other serious crime, it was up to the division to provide most of the staffing, resources, space and money. The team, which had such a grand-sounding name, was actually a very tiny department based at headquarters, headed by four detective superintendents (though only three at the moment because of Joe Speakman's sudden departure) with a couple of DCIs and DIs, some support staff – and that was about it.

Divisional commanders – the chief superintendents who ran the geographical divisions – were supposed to find the staff and funding for major investigations from their own budgets, but it wasn't always so clear cut, and they could be awkward about it. The FMIT supers had to be skilled in negotiating and prising cash out of tight-fisted commanders whose budgets were already stretched in a force that had recently been compelled to save over £20 million by a cost-cutting central government.

For a force the size of Lancashire's, such cuts were excruciating. Posts were slashed, people lost jobs, were made redundant. HQ departments were pared to the bone or abolished. Police stations were closed, or opening hours reduced. Communications rooms were going to be closed and central-ized, as were custody suites. Front-line cop numbers were reduced, Police Community Support Officers were sacked, and, as Henry discovered (although he already knew it), the number of officers actually working on public holidays, where pay entitlement doubled, were shaved to a minimum. In other words, there was hardly anyone on duty on Christmas or Boxing Day.

The knock-on effect was that, if there was a big incident – and there had been two – it was a struggle to police them.

Which was why, at 6 a.m. on Boxing Day, Henry was sitting in that dank FMIT office in a disintegrating police station, still dabbing his endlessly bleeding cut and rubbing his half-strangled throat, trying to get the county's act together.

At least he was being assisted by a much-needed mug of good filter coffee.

He had just finished a dispiriting phone call to the divisional commander at Blackburn, scene of the first shootings at the hospital – which included, of course, a fatal police shooting. Prior to that he had also spoken to the Blackpool divisional commander, on whose patch there had been a drive-by shooting and a murder.

The crime scene in Blackburn was easier to contain, being in the hospital; those in Blackpool not so, mainly because of the outdoor nature of the drive-by. That was skewed because the more criminally minded inhabitants of Shoreside were bubbling with mischief fuelled by the rumour that the police were behind it all. There was no logic to it, they simply wanted a confrontation, and the likelihood was that Shoreside would become a battleground later in the day.

The chief superintendent's perspective was that he wanted to keep the streets safe; neither Runcie's death nor the wounding of one of the partygoers (a completely innocent lad, incidentally) really mattered very much. His priority was maintaining short-term public order, and if extra staff had to be brought on duty, that's what they would be doing, not investigating the death of a toerag. He didn't actually say the 'welcome death' of Runcie Costain, but Henry caught the insinuation – which riled him: no one's death was welcome in Henry's book. The commander suggested that as the whole thing had kicked off in Blackburn, then any investigation should be run from there . . . with their money, not his.

Henry thought he had a point. Although the commander at Blackburn saw the logic, he wasn't impressed by starting a murder investigation on Boxing Day, because even a very basic Major Investigation Room would need a lot of staff. 'And I don't have the freakin' money,' he bellyached.

And Henry knew that he needed enough staff to be able to carry out some coordinated raids, because he didn't want Terry Cromer to get comfortable. He wanted to start harrying him now, this minute, with lots of cops with big boots kicking down doors behind which Cromer might be hiding.

The chief super pleaded with him to keep a lid on it for a day, so that it would cost less.

Henry had already deployed a plain police car to park discreetly within view of Cromer's house in Belthorn, just watching and waiting for him to possibly sneak home. Henry doubted he would be daft enough to do that, unless he felt brave enough to bluff things out, but you could never tell. On the whole, most criminals were just slightly more dim than the cops who chased them, and they often did silly things, like go home.

But to the chief super it was a cop sat on his backside in a car doing nothing for double the wages. An expensive resource, though Henry appeased him by offering to pay half from the meagre FMIT budget.

After his conversations with the chief supers, Henry was even more whacked. He breathed, 'Talk about bad tidings,' as he tried to work out what best to do – what was a 'must', a 'should' or a 'could'. How he could keep people happy by not spending their money. Budgets were a complete minefield. In times past – those hallowed days of limitless government spending – there always seemed to be a spare pot of cash lying about. No longer.

'Bad, bad tidings,' he whispered again. He leaned back in the rickety office chair that some thieving bastard had left behind in place of the half-decent chair that used to be there. He chugged back through the day he'd just worked, almost twenty-four hours of it.

His mobile phone rang, interrupting his thoughts. It was Rik Dean calling from Blackburn, updating Henry on the hospital shootings, which Rik seemed to have well under control.

From all that Rik said, it was Bill Robbins that bothered Henry the most. Rik said that he'd sent Bill home despite having spoken to some 'stuck-up bint' from the IPCC who insisted that Bill should be arrested on suspicion of murder.

'I told her to fuck off,' Rik said crossly. 'Poor sod's gone home in a bloody Michelin Man suit because all his other stuff's been bagged up for forensics. He's formally had his firearms authorization revoked, he's been swabbed for gunshot residue and DNA and the bitch wanted him locked up to give her the chance to travel up from London. Stuff that! I've arranged for him to come into FMIT at three this aft with a brief, to be interviewed there.'

'Sounds good. How is he?'

'Broken,' Rik sighed bleakly. 'You know, you shoot and kill once – that's OK-ish, if you did the right thing, which Bill did. But do it again, whatever the circumstances, it's the high jump. The force was bad enough with him last time. This time they'll make Pontius Pilate look like the Good Samaritan.'

'I won't let that happen.' Henry was absently spinning a full three-sixty degrees on his chair and as he looped back to face the office door, he jerked to a halt when he saw that Fanshaw-Bayley was filling the door frame.

'Everything else sorted?' Henry asked Rik.

'Yeah . . . Home Office pathologist has been for a look, but it's unlikely the PMs will get done today . . . public holiday and all that.'

'Tell me about it,' Henry said.

FB entered the office and helped himself to a mug of coffee from Henry's filter machine, then parked himself on an office chair. His weight made the pneumatic workings drop down a level with a fart-like thud. He spilled his coffee on the carpet and shot Henry a dagger-like look as he pumped himself back up, muttering, 'Shit.'

Henry didn't want the phone call to end. 'Anything else I need to know about?'

'No . . . is someone taking this over from me?' Rik wanted to know.

'No.'

'How does that work, then?'

'We stay on duty.'

Rik guffawed uncertainly. 'Good joke.'

'No – seriously.'

There was a beat of absolute silence.

'Gotcha,' Henry said. He was feeling a bit light headed.

'I've arranged for someone to keep track of things so we can get home and grab some sleep – but I want us back this afternoon, probably for another long day.'

'Um, all right,' Rik said. 'What's the point of having a personal life when you can be a cop, eh?'

Henry glanced at FB. 'Talking of which, have you heard from Lisa?'

'No.' It was a blunt reply. Only one syllable, Henry thought, but it was incredible what could be read into it. Anger. Hurt. Frustration. Fear . . . Henry's heart, unusually, went out to Rik, who had a lot of years womanizing behind him but then had found someone to really love – someone who, with years of man eating behind her, had rapidly reverted to type.

'OK,' Henry said, not having time to go there. 'DCI Leach should be with you soon. Brief him, then get to bed and be at FMIT at Hutton about one this afternoon. We'll have to run this thing from there for the time being.'

'Eh?'

'Don't ask. I'll sort out some staffing, but it'll be all our people, not division's at the moment . . . It's all about the money, money, money,' he said with sad cynicism. 'Pushing bodies across boundaries.'

'Yeah, understood.' Rik knew what Henry meant. In days gone by, when dead bodies – usually old alcoholics – seemed to turn up face down in canals much more regularly than they did in the present day, the officer who found the 'floater', if it was close enough to a divisional or force boundary, would often spend hours launching rocks into the water in the hope that the ripples would send the body over the border. Then the police over there could deal with it, though occasionally the reverse happened and somehow, mysteriously, the body would be found in its original location. The good old days, when bobbies really were bobbies, skilled at ducking, diving and avoiding work.

'It'll be cheaper all round if we can run it from FMIT, at least until New Year kicks in. We're a bit of a halfway house here, between Blackburn and Blackpool.'

He ended the call and smiled at FB. After a pause of consideration, FB said, 'What I don't get, Henry, is how I give you a simple cold case to deal with and next thing I know, you're in the middle of a real shit storm.'

Henry could have argued the point. He hadn't done any of the stirring, but he was definitely at the centre of a vortex.

His last phone call, using the hands-free in the car, was to Bill Robbins. Unable to sleep, Bill was out walking his dog in the woods close to where he lived in the countryside at Hurst Green, between Longridge and Clitheroe, near the River Hodder.

Bill sounded thoroughly depressed.

'You know, when that bastard swung around with his gun, I actually thought twice about pulling the trigger. I also thought, should I just try and wing him? That was the worst part. In that fucking microsecond, all the shit went through my noggin, as well as the implications of shooting him. Knowing I was right, that I didn't have a choice, that I had to shoot to stop him, not try and be fancy by just shooting him in the shoulder. I knew there would be months and months of shite to come.'

Henry listened, feeling very sorry for him. It was a tough call being an authorized firearms officer, but when it came to *that* moment, the one when the trigger had to be pulled, lives had to be saved, lives had to be taken, the resultant fallout had to be lived with. Authorized Firearms Officers were under no illusions about that, but no amount of training could prepare anyone for it.

'Like I said, though,' Bill went on, 'it was the hesitation that was a problem. If that dickhead had been any good, we could both be dead, Henry, and it would've been my fault.' He sounded totally distraught.

'Bill, you did exactly the right thing. I'll back you up one hundred per cent, like I did last time. I'll give a statement to IPCC, too. I've just had a long discussion with FB and he promises the full backing of the force.'

'Excuse me if I vomit disbelief,' Bill said.

'It will be OK,' Henry insisted.

'Yeah, right . . . I know you'll be there for me . . . it's the other twats that worry me. I need to go, Henry, get my dog . . . it's got something horrible in its mouth.' He finished the call abruptly, just as Henry drew up on the driveway of his house.

Parked on the road, much to his relief, was Lisa's Mercedes. On one side of the drive was the tiny SmartCar that Leanne had inherited from Kate. Also on the road was Jenny's car. But best of all – and completely unexpected – was the sight of Alison's newish, sporty Hyundai.

He was coming home to a houseful of women.

TWELVE

With a nice, thick, fluffy bath sheet wrapped around his middle, Henry stepped out of the shower, then walked through to the bedroom from the en suite. Alison sat on the edge of the bed, waiting for him. The shower had cleansed him of a full day of grit and sweat and he felt almost human. Tired, sleepy, but better, even if the blow to the side of his head was still open and bleeding.

Alison tapped the bed next to her. 'Let me have a look at that.' On the bed was the small medical kit she always carried in her car.

Henry sat beside her and angled his head. 'Again, thanks for coming . . . a wonderful surprise,' he said as her fingers went to the cut and she peered closely at it. She had worked hard at the Tawny Owl until past midnight but had left the clean-up to Ginny and her boyfriend. She had driven to Henry's knowing without having to be told that he wouldn't make it to Kendleton.

'Mm,' she murmured dubiously. There was an accusing look in her eye which put him on his guard. He swallowed nervously. Over the past few hours he had faced a madman who tried to kill him, witnessed fatal shootings, tried valiantly to prevent a drive-by killing, seen a shaved vagina, cracked skulls with an escaping gunman and found a body riddled with bullets. None of these things induced as much terror in him as the look on this woman's face, even if he did love her truly, madly, deeply, passionately.

'You didn't phone or text me,' she said simply, looking

closely at the wound and then squeezing some antiseptic cream into it.

He winced and rubbed a hand towel through his short-cropped hair, which didn't need much drying. He gave her his best remorseful expression. 'Things kind of spiralled out of control.'

'I gathered.' Thin-lipped, not impressed. She rooted through her first aid kit and pulled out a pack of butterfly strips, peeled one free.

'I mean – all night long,' he said.

'And there was no time whatsoever in all those hours to call or text me?' She squeezed the sides of the wound together and gently thumbed the butterfly strip into place.

Henry pouted. 'Somebody tried to shoot me.'

'As you were texting me?' She positioned another strip into place.

'Uh, no, not exactly.'

She applied a third one and inspected her handiwork by taking Henry's chin between her finger and thumb and holding his head to the light. She seemed reasonably pleased by the surgery.

Then she turned his face so it was head-on to hers, eye to eye. '*Just let me know*. I know it's old ground even for us, but I expect to be kept in the loop. Nay – *demand*.' She paused. Her eyes criss-crossed his face. He tried to keep up with her. 'Not a lot to ask, even on busy nights . . . and by the way, I wasn't making light of someone pointing a gun at you.'

'I know.'

'I just want to know you're safe, OK?'

'Point taken.'

She pulled his face to her and their lips met softly, then meshed. Drawing away, she said, 'When are we going to tell your family?'

'About what?' he said stupidly.

She raised her left hand and waggled the significant finger, on which was the ring Henry had placed there what seemed a million years before. His innards sank at the prospect.

'Haven't they seen it? They're women, after all. They home in on things like that. Primed from birth.'

'I didn't have it on when I arrived. I didn't wear it at work just in case it went in the soup.'

'Do we have to? I need my bed,' he said dramatically.

Her look of contempt at his cowardice gave Henry the answer.
'I'll put my dressing gown on.'

When he'd landed home, his daughters had just arrived from
a night at the hospital, reporting that their grandmother had
had a good few hours' sleep. They were downstairs in the
kitchen chatting to Alison, who'd arrived before them, while
Lisa was upstairs sleeping in Jenny's old room; no one knew
where she'd been, but at least she was safe.

Now, half an hour later, they were all assembled in the
lounge, drinking tea, catching up with gossip as a hesitant
Henry and a beaming Alison entered. His three relatives
stopped talking, turned towards the couple, who were holding
hands like gawky teenagers.

Henry cleared his throat, which seemed to have had concrete
poured into it.

'Alison and I have a little announcement,' he said, noting
the instant downward glances of all three women towards
Alison's left hand, then back up at Henry. There was horror
on Leanne's face, delight on Jenny's and despair, or something
like it, on Lisa's.

Responses he expected. Leanne had mostly been very nega-
tive about Alison from the start, constantly making unfair
comparisons to Kate. Henry believed this had something to
do with her own rocky relationships with men. Jenny, from
afar, and who had only briefly met Alison, was pleased for
them. Lisa, Henry thought, was also happy for them, but her
facial reaction puzzled him somewhat.

'Jesus – you're not up the duff, are you?' Leanne blurted
unkindly. 'I couldn't stand some bleeding half-brother or sister,
or whatever.'

Henry tried not to get mad; his mind was muzzed enough
from his night of action. So he forced a crooked, fatherly grin
and said sweetly, 'No, nothing like that.'

He held Alison's left hand aloft like a boxing referee lifting
up the winner's hand.

'We're engaged to be married.'

'Oh, Jesus Christ – even worse,' Leanne said.

Jenny beamed, clapped delightedly, got up and hugged them

both. Tears of joy streamed down her cheeks. 'I'm really happy, Dad. You're great together.'

Alison's bottom lip quivered and her eyelids fluttered. Henry started to blubber a little, too.

Leanne emitted a dreadful moaning noise, showing total disapproval and rolling her eyes.

'Stop it, Leanne,' Jenny admonished her.

Leanne's mouth twisted like wire. Obviously there was an internal wrestling match going on. Then her face softened, and she stood up and embraced Henry as her tears also began to roll. She stepped back from him and turned to Alison. 'It's not you,' she said and opened her arms. The two women embraced.

Henry watched, his own blubbering becoming hard to control, as the girls suddenly decided to examine the engagement ring. Soon they were cooing and clucking over it.

He glanced at Lisa, sitting there with her hands tucked palm to palm between her thighs, her expression forlorn, little girl lost. Their eyes locked.

Henry disengaged his fingers from Alison. He stepped over to Lisa and held out a hand. 'Come on, sis,' he said gently. She took his hand and followed him like a puppy into the kitchen. Henry caught Alison's eye and got a nod from her.

Lisa leaned against the cooker, head bowed.

Henry stood in front of her and tilted up her chin with the tip of his forefinger, forcing her to look at him. 'What's going on?'

Her chin wobbled and she blinked rapidly as tears began to fall in perfect droplets. He could see the weariness in her eyes, smell the stale alcohol on her breath and just a whiff of body odour. None of these things fitted with his perception of his kid sister. As whacky as she was, she was always turned out immaculately, day or night, and always smelled great. But here in front of him was a different creature, tousled uncombed hair, make-up that had run, smeared lipstick. She looked a mess – and, Henry was forced to admit, she looked her age.

She shook her head. 'I've made a terrible mistake,' she admitted quietly.

Henry did not fill the next pause. That was up to her.

'I . . . I thought I wanted something else – as usual,' she

snorted in contempt of herself. 'Always looking for the next best thing. Greener grass and all that. Been doing it all my life – but never looked back before.'

He could not disagree. Although he didn't have a leg to stand on and was in no position to judge, having lost count of the number of times he'd put a bloody good marriage in jeopardy for stupid, cock-driven reasons. He and Lisa were alike in so many ways, not always good ones. 'Tell me,' he said.

'I met Mister Bloody-What's his name . . .'

'Sherbet Lemon, the jeweller?'

'Perry Astley-Barnes, actually,' she chuckled. 'Met him through the business and he's rich and rakish and good-looking, like a character from a bloody Wilbur Smith novel. He's divorced, drives an Aston, got a lot of successful shops, makes a mint . . .'

'Ticks all the right boxes. What's not to like?'

'Nothing. He's actually a good guy. I'm the arsehole.' She took a deep, shuddering breath. 'But I realized I actually had everything I needed in every way with Rik. And I've treated him appallingly.'

'Been there, done that,' Henry said.

'Got the T-shirt,' they said in unison.

'Been out all night, just driving and ignoring the phone, trying to get my head around it all.'

'We've been worried about you.'

'Sorry . . . I've completely screwed up, Henry.'

He looked at his achingly gorgeous sister, who so far had failed to find any real happiness and stability in her life. She had even fled from London back to the north because she'd had an affair with the son of a London gangster whose psychotic ex had put a contract out on her.

That's when she'd run into the arms of Rik, a commitment-phobe if ever there was one. But somehow it had worked. Like two suns colliding and meshing together.

'Maybe it's just cold feet,' Henry suggested. He cupped her face with the palm of his hand and looked deep into her eyes. 'Jitters happen.'

'Will they happen to you this time?'

'No, no they won't,' he said confidently. 'I've found someone very special and I won't do anything to jeopardize it.'

Lisa inhaled another faltering breath. 'Do you think I've messed up completely?' She sounded vulnerable.

Henry shook his head, remembering how Rik had said 'No' not so long ago. 'I think there's a guy out there who loves you like crazy, but he's been hurt badly. That said, he'd have you back in a heartbeat.'

'You really think so?'

'For sure.'

'Oh God.' She buried her face into his chest and sobbed, really let it out. Henry patted her lovingly and realized that he was an amazing couples counsellor after all. Perhaps it was something he could train for after retirement. Or maybe not . . . the idea of working behind the bar at the Tawny Owl was much more appealing.

'So call him before he hits the sack. He's been out working all night, too. Go and screw his brains out, if that's what it takes, tell him you love him and you're sorry and he'll forgive you. He's shallow like that.'

'He's still up?'

'You might just catch him.'

She detached herself from Henry and twisted out of the kitchen door onto the decking out back, taking out her phone. Henry watched her pace back and forth, hand held to her forehead, talking quickly as a connection was made, then gesticulating as she stalked and talked.

Alison materialized by his side, slid her arm though his. 'Sorted?'

'I think I'm hallucinating. Never before have I witnessed Lisa calling and pleading with a man. It's *always* the other way round.'

Lisa punched the air and turned victoriously to Henry, the smile on her face, the relief, instantly wiping away those extra years Henry had seen.

'Just another night on the Henry Christie lurv train,' he said sassily. 'But if I don't get some sleep, I'll collapse.'

Alison tugged his arm. 'Let me tuck you in.'

'Is that a euphemism for something dirty?' he asked hopefully.

'Yes – me tucking you in.'

He didn't even make it to the foot of the stairs.

In a moment of madness on one of his far too frequent visits to a well-known coffee chain, Henry had foolishly invested in a travel flask with their world famous logo on it. Coffee on the go. Of course he had never used it since and it had found its way to the back of a kitchen cupboard. Now, for the first time in its pristine life, it came in handy as he bade farewell to his house full of ladies . . .

He and Alison had been about to say goodnight to everyone, Henry looking forward to being tucked in. He had been about to put his foot on the first step when the house phone rang. He had left his mobile phone upstairs after his shower and these days it was pretty rare for calls to be received on the house phone – usually it was telesales companies cold calling – so he instinctively knew it was work. The landline was always the second means of contact.

He had scooped up the cordless handset and introduced himself, but not in his wildest dreams could he have guessed the content of the call. He'd thought maybe the Nissan had been found, or Terry Cromer had walked into a nick with his hands held high . . . something along those lines.

It was the on-duty FIM, a guy he knew well, hence the informality of his 'Sorry to bother you, Henry . . .'

He was dressed and ready to go within five minutes, during which time Alison made him coffee, found the unused flask and filled it. They managed a peck on the cheek as Henry rushed to his car, grim faced.

Her 'Take care, love' was all but lost on him as he jumped into the Audi, reversed off the drive with a tyre squeal. The words 'Shit, shit, shit' spouted repeatedly from his lips. He didn't even glance back at Alison as he slammed the car into gear and sped away.

There was no short cut to this destination.

Within a minute he was tearing eastwards – towards the reluctantly approaching dawn – along the M55, touching one hundred, sipping his coffee and keeping an ear to his PR, tuned into the appropriate channel. He didn't expect to hear too much over the air about this particular incident, but they knew he was on his way and he'd given instructions that he be kept up to date with any developments.

At the end of the M55 he bore south onto the M6, then exited at junction 31, which spanned the River Ribble, the well-known landmark of the Tickled Trout hotel across to his right on the southern bank. Here, many years before, he'd risked his own life whilst trying to rescue school kids from a submerged bus that had been blown off the bridge into the river. It was an incident that still haunted him occasionally, especially during the dark times. Mostly it was boxed away, compartmentalized.

He took the A59 towards Blackburn, then bore left, still on that road, towards Clitheroe, speeding down the long, straight stretch of road past BAE Systems at Salmesbury. He was aware of the flash of the English Electric Lightning fighter jet positioned on display at the factory gates. The best fighter plane ever, it was often claimed, never to have seen active service. It still looked the business.

The speedo touched a hundred again on that stretch, before he braked for the next roundabout, then accelerated away again, without being daft enough to chance the Gatso speed camera in the forty zone.

At the junction with Ribchester Road, he jumped the red light and turned left towards the old Roman fort. He continued to push his excellent car down the now winding country roads, which he knew well from years gone by. The area held happy teenage memories for him and as he passed the large detached country house that, way back, had been the Lodestar Club and Disco, he gave a quick salute to its memory. He had been in the tiny audience for the first ever English gig of Bob Geldof's Boomtown Rats and had also seen the Sex Pistols there. He had had the privilege of being gozzed on by Johnny Rotten. A night to treasure. He hadn't washed for three days after.

The road descended sharply and he slowed right down to negotiate the narrow bridge spanning the River Ribble. Further on he made a tight right into Gallows Lane – highly appropriate, he thought – and as the road rose and dawn came more quickly, he could see the verdigris-coated copper turrets of

Stoneyhurst College. He sped through the village of Hurst Green, along more tightly winding roads, until he reached his destination of Lower Hodder Bridge and the three police cars pulled into the side of the road in a lay-by just prior to the bridge. Henry drew in behind the last car and got out after one more mouthful of his still hot coffee. The travel mug had been a good buy after all, he thought.

A uniformed constable scurried up to him. 'Mr Christie?'

'That's me. What's happening?'

'There.' The PC pointed. 'He wants to talk to you.'

Parallel to and about fifty metres south of the road bridge was another bridge spanning the River Hodder. This triple-arched structure dated back to Roman times and had once been part of the road connecting Ribchester to Clitheroe and beyond, into the wild and dangerous tribal lands. Now it had crumbled; although still a wonderful piece of engineering and construction, it was nothing more than a passing tourist attraction. It was wide enough to walk over, but there was no access for the general public, with high metal gates at each end, though anyone determined enough could easily get onto it.

The person with enough determination in this case was Bill Robbins, who not many hours before had shot someone to death in the line of duty. Bill had scaled or managed to shuffle around the gate with his dog and was now sitting at the middle of the central arch, his feet dangling in mid-air, some twenty feet above the rushing water below.

With a double-barrelled shotgun laid across his lap, his dog by his side.

There was enough light in the day now for Henry to see Bill clearly. He jumped over a low wall and trudged up to the gate, which had been unlocked by the landowner and was guarded by the patrol sergeant.

'Boss.'

'Mornin', Sarge.' Henry gave a desolate shrug.

'He wants to talk to you, but I've also turned out the on-call negotiator, if you don't mind.'

'No probs.'

They were far enough away from Bill to have a conversation he could not overhear because of the running water below.

'Has he threatened anyone?'

'No – just insisted on talking to you, face to face. But he did tell us to keep back or he'd do it.'

'Do what?'

The sergeant pressed the fingertips of his first two fingers of his right hand up into the soft flesh underneath his chin.

'Oh shit.' Henry knew then that, whatever the outcome, Bill really had had his last day on firearms. There was no pulling back from a suicide threat. 'Whose gun is it?'

'His own. He's a licensed shotgun holder. Does a lot of rough shooting around here, I believe.'

Henry glanced across to the road, where an ambulance arrived and stopped behind his Audi. 'Block the road, divert all traffic. I don't want any gawkers or distractions, Sarge.'

'Will do.' The sergeant hesitated.

'Now,' Henry urged him, and he set to his task. Henry peered through the gate at Bill. Since he'd arrived, Bill had not looked over once, so Henry didn't even know if he realized he had arrived. He simply sat there, head bowed, peering down at the river through his legs.

Henry settled himself about four feet away from Bill on the edge of the bridge, the stone cold and damp, legs dangling. It may not have been the highest bridge in the world, but sitting on it, looking at the water, it seemed a long way down.

Bill had not moved or acknowledged him. The dog, a black Labrador, watched him suspiciously, however.

'Bill,' Henry said.

'You came.' Bill still didn't move, his gaze fixed at a point on the water below.

'Course I did.'

'I'm not sure if I can take this again.'

Henry watched him. The profile of a man he had known for a long time, who he'd always thought of as rock steady. Clearly Henry had no idea of the secret turmoil Bill had been through after the last occasion he'd pulled a trigger and taken someone's life. Henry believed he had done everything in his power for his old friend, but the closed door of Bill's mind, now ajar, revealed that Henry hadn't seen a fraction of what

had been going on in there. He was under the impression
Bill had coasted through it, that all he had been bothered about
was not shooting well enough.

'You have no idea how shitty it was,' Bill said. He looked
sideways at Henry. 'Completely out on a limb, everyone always
suspecting you were lying, everything you said being challenged
and that you were covering up the truth.'

'You were exonerated, Bill. I know it was a tough time.'
Henry had also been through the ringer. 'But you hung in
there like you had to, and the truth did come out. You used
your weapon lawfully, as you did this time. No one said it
would be a walk in the park if you ever had to use your gun,
nobody promised you that.' Henry knew he was being blunt.
He hoped it was the best way. 'And you were reinstated, Bill,
which showed how much faith the force had in you.'

'Doesn't stop it being the shittiest part of my life, Henry.
It turned me into an arsehole at home, nearly split me and the
missus up. I ended up on bloody Prozac, for fuck's sake. Two
weeks of that and you could watch a bulldozer flatten your
house and you'd just shrug your shoulders and say so what.'

Henry did not know about the antidepressants. Nor, he
thought, did anyone else.

'I can't go through it again, H. Not least because I've killed
another man. He was a shit, but he was still a bloke . . . what
was it Clint Eastwood said? Uh, when you kill a man you
take away everything that he ever had and everything he's
gonna be . . . something like that. He could've turned out to
be a community worker.'

'You can't go down that road, Bill. He would have shot you
and me and that was the equation at the time. He'd already
killed one man, then another in front of us. His blood was
running hot and he got what he deserved, and you acted lawfully.'

'Honest, I never thought I'd ever have to face a gunman
again,' Bill went on wistfully, as if he hadn't heard Henry.
'Not really. I mean, what are the odds? Loads of firearms jobs
come in, but they're mostly crap . . .' His voice trailed off.

Henry squinted at him.

Bill said, 'You know what it's like, don't you? The weight
you have to carry around with you . . .'

'Yes, I know. Taking a man's life is the toughest call of all, but your life goes on and you have to deal with it professionally and emotionally.'

Bill's head snapped around. 'Are you saying . . .?'

'I'm saying I know how it feels. I know the temptation is to let it all go to rat shit because the effort to keep on an even keel is so very hard. But, Bill, it's happened. You did the right thing. I saw you do the right thing. I heard you do the right thing. There was no alternative. He gave you no choice. Now it's down to you to deal with it. OK, yeah, you go through shit up here' – Henry tapped his head – 'and at work and in the justice system, but you keep your focus, your dignity, your belief, your professionalism and your life. You seek help if you need it – me, the welfare department, counselling, whatever . . . and you look ahead.'

'I know the IPCC already want to stitch me up. They said I should be locked up.'

'Yeah, and guess what? The force said bollocks.' Henry paused. 'We will be with you, Bill, I promise. I've already spoken to the chief constable and he's completely supportive—'

'Oh, yeah, right . . . until the politics get too tough.'

'Nah.' Henry shook his head. 'As much of a twat as FB is, he'll stick by you. He will,' Henry affirmed gently. 'And so will I, so will your department.'

'Which I'll get booted off.'

Henry could not argue that one. 'I'll see you right,' he promised. 'And I'm not just saying that to get you off here, though my bum is wet and cold. You know me. I keep my word.'

'You struggled last time. You couldn't get me a full-time job on FMIT.'

'That's because of how the department is set up,' Henry came back, slightly cross despite himself.

Bill nodded. 'OK.'

'And I won't promise to get you on this or that department this time. You know I can't . . . but I'll do my best for you.'

Bill continued to nod.

'So what are you going to do now?'

'I'm screwed with guns, aren't I?'

'Do you want the truth or a fabrication?'

'I can handle the truth.'

'Then yes . . . and that includes your own shotgun certificate.'

A huge sigh rattled through Bill's chest. He raised his face to the dawn sky.

'Give me the gun, Bill.' Henry reached over for the shotgun and took it from Bill's grip.

THIRTEEN

Consummate professional that he was, no one would have guessed that Detective Superintendent Henry Christie had only had two hours' sleep in the last twenty-four.

He was back at work at 12.30 p.m., after having got home just before ten that morning and dropped like a block of lead into bed. He had been sensible enough to set his alarm, and as soon as he had done that and snuggled down into bed, alone, and assumed his number one sleeping position – on his right side, left leg drawn up, hands clasped together under his pillow – he fell asleep instantly. When the alarm clock woke him he felt more drained than ever, could easily have turned over and gone back to sleep.

He dragged himself unwillingly into the shower, trying to keep the water from swilling away the butterfly strips that Alison had applied to his head wound, yet wanting the powerful hot water jets to massage life back into his dead face.

His reflected image in the shaving mirror almost made him want to smash the glass with his fist. Then he realized he probably didn't look much worse than normal – an unedifying insight. He looked old and haggard. His eyes were heavily bagged, bloodshot and red raw in the corners. He raised his chin and rubbed his neck, feeling where Freddy Cromer had attempted to throttle him last night. It hurt more now than it did at the time, or perhaps he just hadn't had time to notice it previously. It had all got just a bit frenetic afterwards, and the attempted strangulation seemed tame in comparison to the events that followed.

He shaved and applied moisturizer, something he'd only recently and reluctantly begun to do as his face started falling apart. Then he dressed casually and went downstairs.

Jenny and Leanne were in the kitchen. Lisa was nowhere to be seen and he already knew that Alison had gone back to Kendleton. It was going to be a busy day at the Tawny Owl. It was a special curry day and every table had been pre-booked throughout the day. Henry hoped to be able to make it later. The chef's Indian food was as authentic as it could be without him actually being from the sub-continent, and Henry always hated the thought of missing out on a good curry.

Jenny was going to spend a few hours with her grandmother, reports from the hospital being positive. Leanne would take over later and Henry planned to be there around teatime for a few hours, too . . . not planned – intended. Lisa would do her bit somewhere along the line, too, Henry had decided.

Today, he also decided, other people were going to do the work. He was going to do what a superintendent was supposed to do: delegate. Apart from anything else, he just didn't have the energy to get strangled or shot at again.

Not that he had many staff to play with or order about.

Which meant that today – still, unbelievably, Boxing Day – would be a day of consolidation and forward planning.

The crime scenes needed to be sorted properly, both at the hospital, on Shoreside and at the club in South Shore. That would be the focus of the day, together with working out which relatives needed to be informed and when the post-mortems would be carried out. Tomorrow, when there were more staff, he would think about tracking down Terry Cromer and his mate and getting the bastards arrested – unless something came to light today which required immediate action. He wasn't really pleased by this because he would have liked to go hunting for Cromer, but without staff it wasn't an option. So, all in all, it would be a day of boxing off some of the fundamentals before the investigations really got going next day.

He briefed his handful of staff at FMIT, then retreated to his office and opened the murder book.

Rik Dean appeared a few seconds later and sat down, uninvited, across from him. The two men regarded each other.

Henry said, 'You OK?'

Rik's face broke into a wide beam. 'More than OK, pal.'

'Good,' Henry said and looked down at the empty pages of the murder book that needed to be filled. He picked up a pen.

'Your sister has one helluva hot—'

'Whoa!' Henry threw the pen down and held up his right hand, palm out. The police stop sign. 'Certain things I do not wish to know.'

'Oh, yeah, yeah,' Rik said awkwardly. 'So, anyway – thanks, H.' Then his eyes glazed over and he said, 'Oh, mama.'

'She just needed a nudge in the right direction.'

The door opened and this time Jerry Tope appeared, a thick manila file tucked under his armpit. Henry waved him in and pointed to the spare seat.

'What are your plans for the day, Henry?' Tope asked.

Henry pouted. 'This' – he pointed to the blank murder book – 'crime scene revisits, liaison with the pathologist, see my mum, then I'm going to get a curry at my favourite pub in Kendleton, with my favourite landlady.'

'In that case, what do you want me to do about the original reason we were all summoned together? Something that's been a bit lost with everything else that's happened.'

'The Twixtmas Killings?' Rik said.

'Oh yeah . . . have we had any other missing persons who fit the victim profiles?'

'Not had the chance of a proper sift yet,' Tope admitted. 'Had a quick chat with the FIM, but there's nothing he can see.'

Henry churned it over. He had intended to do nothing that day, apart from direct others, but something nagged at him faintly. 'I might go and have a chat with Freddy Cromer . . . he's sort of a bridge between both incidents, isn't he? That is, the murders and last night's shootings. I wonder how lucid he is today? He might inadvertently give up Terry's whereabouts with a bit of careful questioning.' If Henry had had a handlebar moustache, he would have been twirling it. 'Talking of which, Jerry, can you pull everything together we have on the Cromers and the Costains?'

Jerry nodded. Henry looked at Rik. 'You sort out the crime scenes, will you? And the post mortems . . . I'll follow up Freddy, see what he has to say.'

Henry realized he didn't have Janine Cromer's phone number, but he had a brainwave. When Freddy was released into her custody she had to give the custody officer her mobile number. A quick internal call got him the number and he dialled it from his office phone. It went straight onto voicemail, so he left a short message. He wasn't too concerned.

What had happened overnight was complicated and far reaching, so he took the opportunity to make himself a filter coffee, settle down behind a closed office door – which would remain closed – get the murder book up to date, as he had already tried to do, and put together an investigative strategy. It was invaluable time, an opportunity to step above everything for an overview. The thing was many stranded, a bit like dealing with an excitable octopus, and even if a quick arrest was made, it wouldn't stop there. Because Henry had decided that once and for all, he was going to dismantle the crime empires of the Cromers and the Costains – and have great fun doing it.

It would be his *pièce de résistance* before retiring. Kind of a swansong. He would do it brick by brick. He would go for everything. The clubs. The supply lines. The protection rackets. The finance. The bank accounts. He was sure it would just be like pulling a thread on a woolly jumper.

Clearly it wasn't something he would achieve on his own. It would take many agencies and departments and would require them to pool their knowledge, information and resources.

And probably, he guessed, the first tug of that metaphorical thread was to arrest Terry Cromer and get into his ribs. The threat of a murder charge hanging over the head of even the world's meanest gangster was a very effective bargaining tool.

Then the Cromers would start to crumble.

At the same time he would lean heavily on the Costains. With their head man and two of their hard men lying in mortuaries, this was an ideal time to move in on them and crush the bastards whilst they were running around with no family head to steer them.

Energized by the thought of this little project, Henry spent two solid hours and four coffees planning, from the strategy downwards. (God, aren't I good at this leadership and management stuff, he thought at one point.) He wrote down what he wanted to achieve and how he would go about it – strategy to tactics. (Oh yes, I'm good.) Plus he had an urgent run to the toilet, because the coffee had a less than desirable effect on his bowels.

He knew he would have to pitch his idea to the chief constable. If he could get FB's backing, it would be a goer.

He sat back smugly, placed his pen down and rubbed his hands together, wondering what he could call the operation.

His phone rang to interrupt his thoughts.

'Mr Christie, it's Janine Cromer. You rang, left a message.'

'Thanks for calling back.' Henry sat upright, focused.

Immediately she said, 'I hope you're not going to ask me any awkward questions about my family, because I won't drop them in it.'

'Assuming you know what happened last night in Blackpool, it would be remiss of me not to ask about your father's whereabouts, for obvious reasons. So where is he?'

'I don't know,' she said shortly, 'and even if I did . . .'

'Point taken . . . that said, I do need to speak to Freddy. That's a given. He alleges he was kidnapped last night and he ended up assaulting a nurse – and me.' Henry rubbed his neck. 'How is he today?'

'He's fine. He slept quite well and at the moment, he's content.'

Henry screwed his nose up at that description. *Content?* 'I want to see him. I could have kept him in custody very easily last night, but I didn't.'

'I know, I know, and I'm grateful you didn't. When and where?'

'Blackburn nick, one hour.' Henry had already decided to see Freddy on home turf. 'I want to interview him, get a statement from him and process him properly. I won't re-arrest him unless I have to. He won't be seeing the inside of a cell unless he has to. Do you get my meaning? He behaves – and that is me being very generous.'

'So we have to play along with you, otherwise you'll become a bully?'

'Yep.'

She sighed.

Henry said, 'You can have a solicitor or social worker, or both, present if you wish. And I'll let you stay in the interview, too.'

'How very generous,' she said caustically.

'Yep. One hour, Blackburn police station. If not, I'll come and lock him up.'

Interview rooms in police stations are sparse. A table bolted to the floor, jutting out at ninety degrees from a wall. A cassette tape recorder, affixed to the table because in the early days of tape recording interviews, a lot of less acquiescent prisoners tried to brain officers with the machines if the interviews weren't going their way. Up behind a mesh grille in one corner of the room was a video camera to record particularly important or sensitive interviews, or to allow other officers to watch and listen to interviews through an A/V feed. Henry didn't plan on starring on the small screen that day. Audio tape would suffice.

The Cromers were on time and Henry started the interview quite quickly in the presence of a duty solicitor he knew well, a guy called Richmond who made a great living defending crims. But he was an upright operator, simply playing his part in the criminal justice system.

And Freddy was lucid, friendly, open and quite charming.

Except he claimed he could not recall what happened the night before. The last thing he remembered was going to the club in Knuzden, having a drink there, and walking out of the place. Then nothing. Until he was thrown into a cell. Everything in between was a blank and Henry could not budge him. Freddy had his head bowed and simply shook it as Henry probed until finally sitting back with a despairing glance at Janine, sitting in the corner of the room. He drew the interview to a close and said he now needed to take Freddy's fingerprints, DNA and descriptives.

'I thought you said he wasn't under arrest,' Janine complained.

'He isn't, but whether he recalls it or not, he committed some serious offences last night and I need to process him.' Henry looked at Richmond for support.

Richmond got the message and looked at Janine. 'It's just procedure.'

'I'm not happy with it.'

'Be that as it may,' Henry said.

Richmond said to Henry, 'Are you going to charge my client?'

'I'm going to report the circumstances, let CPS make the decision.'

'OK, that's fine.'

'Freddy – you need to come with me . . . have you had your DNA taken before?'

He shook his head. 'Will it hurt?'

'No . . . it's just a swab to get some spit from your mouth.' Henry collected his paperwork and stood up, as did Freddy. Henry moved to the door of the interview room and Janine stood in front of him, a concerned look on her face.

'Henry, is this really necessary? The DNA and all that? And reporting him? Can't we just let it go? Look – I'll make sure that nurse gets compensated . . . a grand, eh? And you – how about a donation to the police widows and orphans fund?'

He shook his head. 'He has to go through the works, Janine. That's how it is. But if you offered up some compensation anyway, that would be a good thing.'

'You're pretty heartless.'

'No I'm not . . . and nor do I believe he can't remember anything.'

Freddy submitted to the processing and Henry quite enjoyed it. Taking fingerprints, a DNA sample, descriptives and a photo were usually things that more junior officers did. It had been a long time since Henry had rolled someone's fingertips in fingerprint ink and admired the result. There was certainly a skill to it and he was glad to see he hadn't lost it – but the size of Freddy's dabs, large enough to fill each square on the form from edge to edge, top to bottom, made Henry realize just what big fingers the man had. Great for strangulation.

Whilst he did it, Henry made small talk.

'Do you remember junior school at Belthorn, Freddy?'

'Uh?'

'Did you enjoy it? Do you remember any of the kids you went with?'

'Sorta . . . some,' he said.

'How about David Peters? He was your age, wasn't he?'

'Dunno.'

'How about Christine Blackshaw? She was your age, too. Or Ella Milner?'

'I don't know . . . I don't know . . .'

Henry detected a hint of panic in Freddy's response.

'Plonk yourself there,' Henry said and pointed to a chair. They were in the fingerprint room in the custody suite. Freddy sat. Henry rifled through a drawer and found a DNA kit, basically a cotton wool bud in a sealed tube. He completed the name stickers before putting on a pair of latex gloves, twisting the cap off the tube and holding up the cotton bud. 'Just open your mouth and I'll take a swab from inside your cheeks and that's it.'

Freddy complied. Henry leaned towards him and started to take the sample.

'Do you know that David Peters and Christine Blackshaw and Ella Milner have all been murdered? There, done.' He stood back, slid the swab into the tube, sealed it, then placed it in the clear envelope which he also sealed. 'So – do you know that? About those murders?'

Freddy shook his head. 'Why are you asking me questions? You're not allowed to.'

'Just having a chat, Freddy, that's all.'

'Liar.' Freddy's mouth clamped shut.

He led Freddy out to the foyer at the front counter where Janine was waiting, a severe expression on her face. The solicitor was nowhere to be seen.

'He asked me questions,' Freddy blurted to Janine.

'You're just like all the rest,' Janine snarled. 'I'll be making a complaint.'

'Freddy is a witness to what happened last night, and maybe

a victim, but so far he's conveniently forgotten everything. Now, call me a cynic, but I think that's bollocks, whether he's got some acute psychological condition or not. I think you told him to say nothing. That's what I think.'

'Yes, you are a cynic, Henry. Something as traumatic as last night could easily have put up the barriers in his weak brain, so he blocked out the unpleasant, terrifying memory of it all.'

Henry shrugged. 'Perhaps. I definitely need to get him assessed by a shrink.'

'One employed to do the cops' dirty work? Think again,' she sneered.

'And I didn't ask him anything about last night – actually,' he sneered back. 'I asked him about his school days and what he remembered about them . . . which, if you recall, was the reason I turned up at your house in the first place. I was concerned about him possibly being the victim of a serial killer. And, make no mistake, Janine, I'll be coming back to talk to him about that very soon.'

She shook her head hopelessly.

'So where's your dad, love?' Henry chucked in. 'He was a busy man last night.'

She glanced quickly at Freddy, then turned on Henry. 'Love? Fuck me, you're beyond belief, Henry.'

'Where is he? Don't tell me you don't know. You are his daughter.'

'I don't know, and—'

'Even if you did, you wouldn't tell me? And in response to your assessment of me, you, it turns out, are just like the rest of your family. Nice, pleasant, middle class, hard working, honest.' He made a farting sound with his lips. 'You tell me where Terry is and it'll stop a lot of doors being battered down.'

'Fuck you, Henry . . . come on, Uncle Freddy, let's get out of this shit hole.' Her last glance at Henry was almost as cutting as a laser beam in a James Bond movie.

'And you,' Henry said, but not loud enough for her to hear.

His interaction with Janine troubled him, but he wasn't certain why. Maybe because he'd seen her as an 'in' to the Cromers, but then her drawbridge had been pulled up and she'd retreated to the bosom of the family. Not that he blamed her. When the chips were down, families did tend either to stick together or fall apart, he supposed.

A disappointment, but one he should have foreseen. She had been half pleasant with him for her own ends – basically because she had been worried about Freddy, her dear, unstable uncle, when no one else in the family seemed to give a toss, except for Freddy's mother.

What a tangled web, he thought . . . which, of course, he was obliged to untangle.

On the way back to Blackpool he spoke to Rik Dean about the crime scenes, all of which were under control. The one around the Costain house had been quickly dealt with and closed down because of the growing tension on the estate. Even in the pursuit of truth and justice it was sometimes best to back off. The other scenes, at the hospital and the club, were still being combed for evidence and were expected to be sealed for at least another day as the scientific crews did their work. That was fine with Henry. As the manual said, 'You only get one chance at a crime scene.' Rik said that the post-mortems had also been arranged for later that day. He also confirmed that the young lad who'd been shot outside the Costains' had been released from hospital and that arrangements had been made for a detective to interview him the following day.

Henry also spoke to Bill Robbins, who sounded a lot more chilled than he had been on the bridge. Henry had managed to persuade the IPCC to back off from him for another day. They were desperate to get moving with the investigation, but Henry sensed their keenness was inspired by a sense of wanting to be seen to do something rather than by expediency. The press were on their backs about the shooting and, being media savvy, they had to show they were on the case.

Henry talked them out of coming and arranged for interviews the following day, with the promise that they would have full, unrestricted access to anything they wanted because there was simply nothing to hide.

Half an hour later he was back at the cardiac unit at BVH to find his mother sat up in bed, chatting brightly to Leanne and Jenny. After a lot of hugs and kisses, Henry relieved his daughters, who were planning a girls' night out to catch up with each other properly.

Then he sat down next to his mother and took her bony hand between his. It felt cold and brittle. He could easily have crushed it.

'How you doing, Mum?'

'Putting on a brave face. My chest still feels like I've been run over by a steamroller.'

'It will.'

'The girls tell me you've been busy.'

'Just the usual dross.'

'You know, I'm really proud of you, Henry.' Her voice was a gravelly whisper. 'You've achieved so much . . . who would have thought you could even have been a policeman? So shy and introverted when you were a kid, always in your own little world . . . and there was always a bit of Walter Mitty about you.'

That was something his mother had often levelled at him, Mitty being a fictional character who lived in a dream world.

'I just act the part, do what I have to do and then retreat to being the real me when I'm not at work.'

She rested her head on the plumped-up pillows and inhaled a scratchy breath. 'Do you need to tell me something?'

'About what?'

'Rings on fingers.'

'Ahh, that.'

'Yes, that.'

'Er . . . I'm engaged to Alison.'

'Good. She's a good girl. Don't screw it up.'

'I won't.'

She turned her head and looked sharply at him, although Henry could only surmise what she was actually seeing. Just a blur, he guessed. 'You'd better not, otherwise you'll have me to answer to. She's a treasure. I never thought you'd find one as good as Kate again, but I think you have. Bloody look after her.'

'I will.'

'And bring her in to see me before I die . . . I want to see the ring, and you two together.'

'I will . . . but you're not dying.'

With a snort of disbelief, she rested again and asked him what he was working on. He started to tell her but could not say if she was listening or even hearing at all as she lay there, eyes closed, her hand still in his, her chest rising and falling only slightly. Henry droned on, verbally working through the last few days. Any opportunity to get things in order was good for him, but this time it failed to provide him with any investigatory revelations. No light-bulb moments. Just making sense of the muddle.

Partway through this retelling, his mobile phone vibrated. He went out into the corridor to take the call.

It was Lisa, sounding happy and, he supposed, gratified in more ways than one. She said she was coming to the hospital in about an hour, would spend a couple of hours with Mum and then stay on hand locally – and sober – just in case she was needed. She told Henry he could take the night off without worrying if he could have a drink. She and Rik would see to Mum. That was great news for Henry, but he also needed to talk to Lisa about the DNR issue, and he said he would stay until she arrived.

'I thought you'd gone,' his mother said as he settled back next to her.

'Just on the phone.'

She gave him a weak smile and reached out to touch his cheek. 'I was listening to what you were saying, you know. One thing not suffering is my hearing.'

'Oh,' Henry said. 'I thought you were asleep.'

'You know, we used to live in a village.'

'I know.'

Henry's early years had been spent in a tiny village in east Lancashire, not far from Belthorn and not dissimilar. He remembered it as a glowing, glorious time, with harsh winters and long, wonderful summers and hardly anything in between. Deep snow and searing sunshine, one or the other, it always seemed. Running wild, free and unencumbered by any fear.

'You mentioned Belthorn,' his mother said.

'Yes.'

'I know it . . . well, knew it years ago. It's probably bigger now than it was back then. I didn't know it well, but I do know one thing about it, about all villages.'

'And that is?'

'Secrets. All villages have secrets. Lots of them. And they always surface at some time or another. Nothing ever remains secret for ever, and nor do the lies . . .'

And on that observation, Henry's mother fell asleep.

FOURTEEN

Henry was doing what a superintendent was paid so much money to do: sitting at his desk, savouring his coffee and toast (he'd discovered a toaster in his secretary's office a few weeks earlier and had brought in a small toastie loaf that morning, together with some real salted butter), but above all, thinking. He had his feet up, legs crossed at the ankles, and was tilted back in his office chair, hoping it wouldn't collapse. Just thinking, sipping, munching, savouring.

And the words shooting around his head were the ones his mother had uttered before dropping to sleep. *Villages, secrets and lies.* Was this the key to the two murders (and possibly a third one in West Yorkshire) he had been asked to investigate?

Were they the result of secrets and lies?

Something that had happened years before, but like a sleeping virus . . . chicken pox evolving into shingles. It was payback time.

He folded the last piece of toast into his mouth, wiped the corners of his lips, slid his feet off the desk and rocked upright.

If nothing else, he shrugged mentally, it was as good a theory as anything to follow in an unsolved murder case. Just another line of enquiry, a thread of investigation.

He tapped a key on his computer keyboard. The county crest screensaver disappeared and the computer came to life.

He had logged on to the internet, onto the website that celebrated the village of Belthorn, on which Jerry Tope had

class photograph showing a bunch of innocent
ing shyly at the camera. Not many were smiling.
ᴍᴏꜱᴛ ʟᴏᴏᴋᴇᴅ terrified. Henry held his nose close to the monitor
and looked at the children, whose ages ranged from five to
eleven. It was actually a photo of the whole school – a total
of thirty kids – a phenomenon that would simply not exist
in the educational world of today. Thirty was a low number
for just one class now, not the whole school.

There were no names, but Henry could still identify some
of them.

David Peters. Christine Blackshaw. Freddy Cromer. Ella
Milner, the murder victim from West Yorkshire.

Henry could not pick out Terry Cromer and wondered where
he was that day.

Three victims, one madman.

Henry pouted and looked closely through the faces again.
Another one, a little girl, caught his eye. He frowned . . .
something familiar about her. She was sitting with the younger
children at the desks on the left side of the photo, the ages
increasing left to right.

Glancing up he looked at the whiteboard on the back wall
of the office, which bore the names of the two Lancashire
victims. As he looked, he reached for his desk phone and
tapped in a number that he had written on the board, waited
for a connection.

'Hello?' the dull female voice answered eventually.

'Oh, good morning. Is that Bernadette?'

'Look,' she started aggressively before he could say
anything else, 'if you're trying to get me to claim back
payment protection insurance, just sod off . . .'

Henry chuckled. 'No . . . Bernadette, this is Detective
Superintendent Christie here. You know, the cop who interrupted your Christmas Day.'

'Oh, yeah . . . just as bad. Your number shows as unknown.
I just thought . . .'

'It's because I'm calling from my office . . . look, sorry
to bother you again, but have you got a minute or two spare
so I can ask you a few more questions?'

Henry heard her expel a long sigh. 'Go on, then.'

'When I spoke to you,' he began, still peering closely at the monitor, 'you said you'd known David a long time . . . can you tell me exactly how long?'

'Since we met at college.'

'And was college the first time you ever met him?'

She paused, then said, 'Er . . . well, yes, really.'

'Are you sure you didn't go to the same infant school as him?'

'Oh' – something dawned – 'I see what you mean.'

'What do I mean?'

'I suppose you could say I did, for a while at least. We both went to Belthorn School, but we were only there briefly at the same time. He was older than me and I only went there for a few months – just as I started school – and then my parents moved to Accrington from Belthorn. He was four years older than I was and I can't say I knew him, as such. When we met at college later, I didn't even know him at all. It was only as we talked that we realized we'd been at the same school years before.'

Henry rolled his eyes. He was annoyed at himself, annoyed at the detective who had taken Bernadette's witness statement, and tried not to be annoyed at her, too. He knew from experience that people being interviewed by the police usually only answered the questions asked of them and rarely expanded unless pushed. The statement taken from Bernadette Peters was functional but sparse in detail.

'Remind me – you met at college again?'

'Yes. I was in my first year but he was in his last, doing some technical course or other, electronics and such like.'

'Did *he* know you from school?'

'No, as I said . . .'

'OK . . . so how long were you at Belthorn School?'

'Three months, I think. Not long.'

'OK . . . do you know Christine Blackshaw?'

'She was the one shot in Blackburn, wasn't she? You mentioned her before.'

'Yes.'

'Ella Milner – does that name mean anything?'

'No, who's she?'

'Another murder victim. Would you be surprised to learn they were all at Belthorn School?'

'Surprised? The names don't mean anything to me, Mr Christie. I was an itty-bitty kid. But how did you find out?'

He looked at the photograph on his monitor. 'Just as a result of enquiries,' he said mysteriously. Then, 'Do you remember anything at all that David might've been involved in way back then, any sort of incident? Did he ever mention anything?'

'You're clutching at straws, I take it?'

'Following a line of investigation,' Henry said, haughtily this time. 'And the fact that three murder victims were together at the same school, even though that was years before they were killed, seems a pretty good thing to be banging away at, don't you think?'

'That's my hand slapped.'

'Yep . . . so if you do think of anything that David might have mentioned, please give me a call.'

'You're cross now.'

'Yes I am.' Henry hung up after a few words of thanks, and his fingers were still on the phone when his office door was flung open and two faces appeared. Rik Dean and Jerry Tope. Rik was marginally ahead.

Neither man actually spoke, the look on Henry's face reminding them they had burst into a superintendent's office without knocking.

Then Henry said, 'Someone better speak.'

'We've got something,' Rik said.

'Me too,' Tope said, dancing behind Rik, a sheet of paper in hand.

Henry cocked his thumb and forefinger like a pistol and pointed at Rik. 'You first.'

'Shit,' Tope said, crestfallen.

Rik said, 'You'll need your kit.'

After leaving his mother's bedside the previous evening and entrusting her to Lisa, who had turned up looking positively radiant following her reunion with Rik, Henry had driven straight to the Tawny Owl, where he ate the apparently legendary Boxing Day curry (turkey, of course) with a couple of pints of San Miguel, followed by a couple of Jack Daniels on the rocks. He crashed out about midnight with Alison beside him and the newly betrothed couple screwed the last dregs of life out of each other before falling soundly asleep.

Henry woke seven hours later with a bursting bladder, but also completely refreshed and ready for what lay ahead.

Alison watched him get dressed after he came out of the shower.

'This doesn't mean you get out of the "whisking me away, down on one knee" scenario,' she said.

'Good.' He pulled on his jeans, missed the trouser leg and found himself hopping around in a circle in order to keep his balance. He bounced off the wall twice before the second leg found its rightful place. He sat down heavily on the bed and started to pull on his socks. 'But it'll still be busy this week . . . we'll get away next week, promise. A hot city somewhere.'

'How do you think this week will pan out?'

'Dunno. Bit of a waiting game in some respects. First, Mum. I honestly don't think she'll last much longer, even though she rallied a bit yesterday . . . just a feeling,' he said sadly. 'Then we'll see if the Twixtmas Killer strikes again, and today I'll need to pull a big investigation together to sort out the mess of the last couple of days. I'll get in early, brainstorm a bit. Loads of things need covering . . . locations, victims, offenders, post-mortems . . . a manhunt for Terry Cromer and whoever was his partner in crime . . . all sorts. Just want the first hour or two alone to get my head around it.' As he talked he continued to dress, staring at the wall for inspiration, assuming that Alison was enthralled and intrigued by his work. 'Surveillance branch, Intelligence Unit, Fraud, Uniforms . . .' When he glanced at her, she had turned over and seemed to have fallen asleep. 'So, not really interested, eh? Bloody women . . . That said, I did enjoy last night, especially when you flipped over onto your knees and I got behind—'

'Oi!' she interrupted without looking round. 'Save your debriefs for work.'

Henry chuckled, leaned over, kissed her and left.

He was at his office in the FMIT building at HQ three-quarters of an hour later, working out the day ahead.

At 1 p.m. he had a team of detectives in front of him in one of the classrooms at the Training Centre, though not as many as he would have liked; by 2 p.m. they were on the road, fully briefed and tasked. Henry then spent an hour with the IPCC investigators being interviewed on tape, then he was back in his office where he had started pondering about the double murder and had called Bernadette Peters.

'Surveillance Branch picked him up straight away,' Rik Dean explained. 'They'd recently done a job for NCIS on him and Terry Cromer that came to nothing. It seems that this guy and Terry had been doing a lot of to-ing and fro-ing together around the north-west and it's possible he could be Terry's partner in crime for the shootings.'

Followed by an irritated Jerry Tope, Rik Dean and Henry were scuttling across to the garage at the rear of headquarters to pick up one of the pool cars. They were moving quite rapidly and as Rik spoke, Henry scanned the paperwork he had been handed.

Kyle Clovelly was the name of the individual Rik was talking about, and he had been mentioned in Henry's briefing. Late twenties, with a long history of crime behind him, including serious assaults, drug dealing and firearms offences. According to the intel he had recently hooked up with Terry Cromer, mainly it seemed, as a heavy and bodyguard. The information was fairly sparse but a few sharp-eyed cops (and Henry was relieved to learn there were still some out there) had seen him with Cromer entering and leaving clubs in Blackburn. It had been this information that had prompted an NCIS operation, but it had come to nothing, not least because Cromer and Clovelly were surveillance smart.

Since the briefing, a couple of surveillance officers had set off on their own initiative to see if they could track Clovelly down and they'd picked him up in a car driving through Blackburn. They followed him as best they could towards Accrington, the neighbouring town, where he had managed to shake the tail.

Undaunted, the officers had stuck to their task and found the car parked in the West End area of Oswaldtwistle, about a quarter of a mile from the house of a woman Clovelly was supposedly seeing.

'They're not one hundred per cent,' Rik warned, 'but he has been seen to enter and leave the woman's house on a few occasions recently and they guess he'll be there now. They reckon he was just being ultra-cautious about surveillance and they're certain he didn't actually clock them.'

Henry looked carefully at the photograph of Clovelly attached to the paperwork. He hadn't personally come across the man before, but as he racked his brains and put himself back in Cromer's house a couple of nights earlier, he was almost sure that Clovelly was one of the men glimpsed in the dining room when the door had been opened by mistake by Iron-man Grasson.

'Right, good call,' Henry said. 'Let's move as quickly as we can on this. Can you get someone in a plain car to keep nicks on Clovelly's motor and keep the two surveillance bods on the girlfriend's house, if possible. Front and rear ideally.' Rik nodded. 'Let's convene at Accrington nick and put a quick plan together based on who we have available.'

'I love it when a plan comes together,' Tope muttered from behind them. Henry shot him a look. 'Nothing, nothing,' Tope said, holding up his hands in mock defeat.

The semi-detached council house stood in a small cul-de-sac off Thwaites Road in Oswaldtwistle. Clovelly had left his car on a nearby estate and it was still there when Henry, Rik and the small team they had managed to pull together arrived at the end of Thwaites Road. They were still working on the assumption that Clovelly was at the woman's house.

It was almost two hours later. Henry had spent the time poring over intelligence reports, re-checking addresses, confirming the girlfriend's address, and looking at maps and floor plans of similar types of council houses. He wasn't expecting any surprises in the layout, but it was best to be certain.

'I want to try and keep this low key,' he'd explained to the officers he had cobbled together. This not being a public holiday, he had a few more to look at than over the last two days. 'It's not a racing certainty he's there, but that's what we're working on. His car is parked nearby and he's been seen coming and going at the address. We haven't got the staff to go piling in, but if he is there – and he could be armed – I want to be in a position to deal with it.

'I want a discreet perimeter using the support unit, but with every officer in a safe position. The firearms officers' – Henry had two pairs of AFOs to deploy – 'will be ready to move as necessary, once contact has been made and we know what the subject's reaction is going to be.'

'Who's going to knock on the door?' someone piped up.

As much as Henry Christie, detective superintendent, a senior manager in the force, had promised himself that he would delegate everything today, he could not stop himself from blurting, 'That would be me.' And then, internally, he called himself a complete arsehole.

Once they were all in position, Henry drove to the open end of the cul-de-sac, parked the pool car and climbed out. His colleague did the same and Henry watched DC Jerry Tope walk around the car to join him.

At the best of times Henry would have described Tope's facial expression as hang-dog, but now he looked more like a dog that had been hanged.

'Henry, I'm a desk jockey,' he moaned. 'You know, a head-quarters shiny-arsed bastard that operational officers despise . . . from the Dream Factory . . . I interrogate computers, then the rufty-tufty squad go and kick down doors based on what I tell them. I don't do dirty work, knocking on the doors of suspected armed killers.'

Henry grinned at him. 'Yeah, me too.'

Both men wore Kevlar bullet-proof vests under their jackets, which bulked out their chests by a few inches.

'You love it, you pervert,' Tope said.

'You'll learn to love it again,' Henry reassured him.

'I won't. My lair is my desk, my jungle the internet.'

Henry put his arm around Tope's shoulders. 'Stick with me,' he said and ushered the DC ahead of him, along the pavement and up the cul-de-sac.

This was Henry's jungle, had been for over thirty years. Council estates and houses. Some boarded up. One or two with well-kept gardens, but many with rubbish piled up, fridges and other white goods, old bikes and prams. Scruffy kids in the middle of the road, all with very new-looking bikes and mobile phones and designer trainers, scowling at the two intruders walking past them. Most of his business had come from places like this, most of the murderers he had arrested had grown up in such places, and most of the thieves. He knew that criminals were in the minority, but their influence was disproportionate to their numbers and they made others' lives miserable. And sometimes the police didn't help matters.

Henry felt sharp, but also at ease in this environment.

The house was sixth up on the right. A semi, quite substantially constructed, 1960s pedigree.

The two detectives sauntered up to the front door.

'What were you so keen to tell me back at the office?' Henry asked Tope. They had reached the door. Through the earpiece fitted snugly inside Henry's earlobe he heard confirmation that everyone was in position, including two cops who had sneaked into the back garden in case Clovelly tried to do a back-door run. Something not unknown in these circumstances – a villain trying to leg it.

'Oh, nothing.'

Henry rapped on the door using the back of his hand. 'No, tell me,' he insisted.

Tope pouted childishly. 'Just found your serial killer for you, that's all.'

Henry was about to smack the door again but stopped with his hand half an inch from the door. 'Really?'

'Possibly,' Tope said, amending his claim slightly.

Henry beat on the door again. 'Do tell.' He heard some movement from within the house. He put this over the radio and knocked again.

'One of the classmates,' Tope said.

'The kids from the school?'

'Out on licence as we speak . . . been out for two years now.'

'Wow,' Henry said.

'Yeah, what about that?' Tope said proudly.

'Double brownie points,' Henry said. He squatted down, flipped up the brass-plated letterbox and peered into the hallway. He saw nothing, just a bare, uncarpeted hall and stairs. 'Hello – open up, please. Police.' He let the flap drop a couple of times, making a metallic rattle, stood up and thumped the door again, this time with the side of his fist.

The door had a nine-inch square panel of frosted glass in it at about head height. Tope put his face to it, shielding his eyes with his hand, and he saw the outline of a figure tearing down the stairs, skidding along the hall towards the rear of the house.

'Doing a runner,' Tope said excitedly, his voice suddenly high pitched.

'Patrols at the back of the house,' Henry said into his radio, 'he's heading for the back door.'

Tope ran towards the edge of the house but Henry grabbed him and raised his eyebrows.

'Subject emerging from rear door,' one of the officers at the back said.

'What are we doing here?' Tope hissed to Henry, who still had hold of him.

Henry said nothing, just gestured with his hands: *stay put.* Then he pushed Tope to one side of the front door and flattened himself against the wall on the opposite side, still gesticulating for Tope to stay where he was. Tope got the message as the next transmission from the officers out back went, 'Subject exiting, running across the garden towards us.'

'Is it Clovelly?' Henry asked. So far, no one had confirmed that little detail.

There was no time for a reply, because the front door of the house was yanked open and Clovelly himself came out in jeans, T-shirt and trainers. He held a sawn-off shotgun diagonally across his chest, his right hand holding the stock, right forefinger in the trigger guard, left holding the barrels.

Stunned, Henry watched as Tope pivoted, moving hard and fast.

He hit Clovelly on the side of his face, just at the point where the jaw joined the skull in front of his ear.

Henry thought it was one of the hardest punches he had ever seen thrown. Clovelly's face distorted with its power.

Clovelly emitted a roar. His lower jaw jerked sideways, upper and lower sets of teeth grating. The shock of the blow reverberated throughout his body. His head cricked sideways and for a moment, complete blackness engulfed his brain, followed by a dazzling whiteness – and stars. His knees ceased to function and he did a willowy fall.

'I'll have that,' Henry said and deftly snatched the shotgun from Clovelly's non-existent grip as he slumped to his knees, then onto all fours, shaking his head, mumbling and groaning, spitting teeth and blood.

Tope stepped smartly behind him and slammed him down onto his chest, then pulled his arms behind his back, stacking his wrists and fitting a pair of rigid cuffs on him.

'Jeesh, that was pretty exciting,' Tope said in a matter-of-fact way.

Open mouthed, Henry said, 'Told you you'd get to love it again.'

FIFTEEN

'I read a book once,' Jerry Tope explained after Henry's question.

'What – about punching people's lights out?'

Tope snuffled a laugh. 'No, not quite. It was about the Kray twins – you know, Ronnie and Reggie? Nice guys. One of the things they used to do was offer someone a cigarette and as that person was just about to put it into their mouth, at the exact moment when their jaw was slightly relaxed, they'd punch the unsuspecting stoolie on the side of his face at the jaw joint and break the poor sod's jaw. They got it down to a fine art . . . they were both boxers, of course. I was always intrigued by it and I thought I'd give it a shot, especially when he came to the door with a shotgun. Obviously the Krays could hit harder than me, but I did pretty good, didn't I?' he finished proudly. He licked the tip of his forefinger with his tongue and gave himself an imaginary tick in mid-air.

Henry shook his head in amazement. 'Yeah, you did good, Slugger Tope.'

'Went down like a sack o' spuds.' Tope dropped back and started dancing on his tiptoes, throwing punches as though he was shadow boxing with Ali.

Henry watched him, amused. It was as if someone had lit his blue touchpaper and somehow brought him to life. Even though it was six hours later he was still pumped with adrenalin and Henry had never seen this dour man so animated. Now he wanted to fight the world.

'OK, Jerry, time to wind your neck in,' Henry said.

Tope threw one last punch, caught the wall by mistake and howled with pain, doubling over and cradling his fist under his armpit. 'Ooh, that hurt.'

They were standing in the corridor outside Henry's FMIT office at headquarters. Henry ushered Tope in and sat him down.

It was the first time they had stopped since Clovelly's arrest. Henry slid behind his desk, sat down and took a breath.

It had been a hectic six hours and now Clovelly was trapped up in the Blackburn cells, having had a hospital visit during which he had become violent and had to be further restrained. When he arrived at the cells he was pinned to the floor, searched properly, then heaved head first into a cell after managing to assault the custody officer. Not the best of moves for a comfortable stay.

He wasn't going anywhere for the time being.

In the meantime the house had been searched and his car seized. A couple of addresses he was known to frequent were also searched, as well as a lock-up garage in Oswaldtwistle where a very large chunk of evidential gold was discovered: the Nissan that had been used in the drive-by shooting and as a getaway car from the club in Blackpool where Runcie Costain had been shot to death.

Although it seemed unlikely that Clovelly would admit anything when he was interviewed, the forensic side was coming together nicely.

Henry had also arrested the person who had done a runner from the back of the house, hoping to fool officers into thinking it was Clovelly. This turned out to be his girlfriend, dressed in his clothes. Henry held her for harbouring a fugitive – a bit of a weak charge at the best of times – but he bailed her quite quickly when she revealed she was pregnant.

Now he was back at HQ, taking stock, seeing where everyone was up to and preparing for an 8 p.m. debrief.

He looked at Tope, still caressing his wall-scraped knuckles.

'What have you got, Jerry? You told me you found a killer.'

'Possible killer,' Tope corrected him.

'I'm listening.' Henry consulted his watch. 'At least for the next five minutes.'

Tope sat up, cleared his throat and got a grip of himself. 'You remember that school photograph?'

Henry nodded.

'Well – back then school records weren't as good as they should be, it wasn't exactly the age of the computer, but, with due diligence, extremely well-honed computer research skills . . .'

'Hacking, you mean?' Henry knew Tope's skills were unsurpassed.

'That, too,' Tope acknowledged. 'I managed to find out the names of all but two of the people in the photo and did a bit of delving. Some of course were of no interest. Two were dead, not including our victims, that is. Natural causes and a kosher accident. But one was very interesting – and I don't mean Freddy Cromer.'

Henry knew when to say nothing. He waited.

Tope went on. 'Remember a rape and murder quite a few years back? In Darwen? Young girl abducted on the way home from school. Body found a few days later in an industrial dustbin?'

Henry knew it. Even knew the little girl's name – Tina Makinson. Twelve years old. Even though he hadn't been directly involved in the investigation, Henry recalled it being a heartbreaking case. The murderer, found by good, solid detective work, had been one Rafe Liversage, a man whose offences against children had been growing increasingly serious and violent. He had been released from prison only days before he took Tina.

Henry leant forward and tapped his computer mouse. His

monitor came to life, still on the school photograph he had been inspecting before turning out to deal with the arrest of Clovelly. He looked at it closely. His jaw sagged as he focused on one particular boy in the class.

'Shit,' he whispered, raising his eyes to look at a smug Jerry Tope, who licked his finger and ticked the air again.

'He was released on licence seven days before Christine Blackshaw's body was found. They must have known each other,' Tope said. 'Same school, everything.'

Henry thought back, recalling the media coverage of Tina Makinson's murder. The angst of the parents. The massive police searches and an equally big investigation, some seventy detectives grinding on it full-time. Then her tiny, broken body being found behind a factory in Darwen, and soon after, Liversage's arrest. Then his conviction for life – but, such are the vagaries of the criminal justice system, the man was already legitimately back on the streets.

He looked through narrowed eyes at Tope. 'MO?' he said.

'I knew you'd rain on my parade,' Tope said, but not seriously. 'I know it doesn't quite fit what we're looking at, but maybe he has some pent-up, festering grudge against these people. Peters and Blackshaw.'

'Mm,' Henry mumbled. 'What about the Milner woman who was killed in West Yorkshire the year before Blackshaw was killed? Where was Liversage then? In prison, or what?'

Tope had a pained look. 'I don't know for sure. Maybe he'd been out on Christmas leave.'

'See if you can find out.' There could be a grudge thing going on, but he wasn't convinced Liversage was involved, certainly not as an offender. Just a gut thing. 'Whatever, he needs looking at. Have you got a current address for him?'

'From the Probation Service. A room in a bail hostel in Accrington.'

'Right.' Henry pondered this new information. Without doubt Liversage was a cruel and violent man, but he didn't somehow fit what Henry had in mind as the Twixtmas Killer. But he had been known to be wrong on occasion. Liversage needed careful attention. 'OK – tomorrow we pull him, how about that?'

'Can I?' Tope pleaded.

'Got a taste for blood now, have you?'

Henry conducted the debrief in a way, he hoped, that would be clear and logical to all concerned.

The detectives now dealing with the shootings at Blackburn went first, followed by those sorting the drive-by on Shoreside, then Runcie Costain's death in John Rider's old club. There had been lots of people to see, grieving, angry relatives to deal with and keep calm; post-mortems, forensics, crime scenes and a deteriorating public order situation on Shoreside, which was keeping the uniform branch busy.

With Clovelly's arrest, things were going well – although he was still acting 'like a shithead' in custody, it was reported. Terry Cromer was still at large, but Henry was convinced he would be found soon.

In all, he was pretty happy. Next day he had negotiated for more bodies to be drafted in and it would all surge ahead nicely.

He didn't keep the murder squad any longer than necessary, thanking them and telling them to be back for a briefing at nine next morning.

Henry had used one of the classrooms at the Training Centre for the debrief, and as he walked back to his office his mobile phone rang, cutting into his thoughts.

'Mr Christie, it's Bernadette Peters.'

'Oh, hi Mrs Peters, how are you?'

'As well as can be expected, I suppose.'

'What can I do for you?' he asked hopefully.

'You called earlier, remember?'

'Of course I do.'

'You asked about infant school. I might have something for you.'

It was 9 p.m. when Henry drove into Blackpool and around to Bernadette Peters' home. She was waiting for him this time, and although Henry didn't want to be sexist in his thoughts, he had to admit that she scrubbed up well and looked much more with it than when he'd interrupted her on Christmas Day. She was still dressed sloppily, in a baggy T-shirt and tight-fitting

Lycra bottoms, three-quarter length, that showed her shapely legs to good effect. Her hair was pinned back, but touches of subtly applied make-up gave her face a pleasant look – and she was smiling this time. And she smelled nice.

She let Henry in and showed him to the lounge. She sat on an armchair across from him, curling her legs underneath her.

Henry smiled back. He was impatient to get a move on, to see his mother. He had been checking throughout the day and she had been in good spirits. Then he wanted to get back to Kendleton, eat a good meal and chill out in front of the box before bed. He was determined to be asleep before midnight.

'You said you might have something?'

'Oh yeah, yeah . . . I was thinking after your call this morning . . . really going through things in my head. And something came to me.' Henry waited, the smile still affixed. 'It's probably nothing,' she admitted with a derisive laugh.

'Anything could be helpful.'

'I just remember David once reminiscing about Belthorn School and some of the characters he remembered . . . he mentioned mad Freddy Cromer and Terry, his brother.'

Henry blinked, tried not to look too interested. But deep below, his ring piece twitched.

'He said everybody picked on Freddy, including Terry. I don't really remember either of them. Like I said, they were all older than me and I was only there a few months. I think Freddy was a bit backward, or something. He'd probably have gone to a special school these days. But back then, he was just looked on as dim and stupid, I suppose.

'Anyway, one day after school, David and some of the others went to a nearby farm. Don't know which . . . there's a lot of farms up there. They'd heard that some chicks had been hatched, or something. I think it was chicks. In one of the coops on the farm. Chicks? Maybe kittens, I'm not certain.'

'And something happened?' Henry kept his voice level, but he was holding his breath.

'Well, that's where David went a bit vague and I can't exactly recall what he said to me. I think there was a fight or something. Freddy was involved, and Terry and David. I think they all ganged up on Freddy . . .' She looked pained at Henry because her memory was letting her down. 'Sorry . . . vague.'

'That's OK.'

'It was something to do with him being locked in.'

'In where?'

'The chicken coop, or whatever you call them.'

'Who was locked in?'

'Freddy, I think. I think he went totally doolally . . .' She shrugged. 'That's it. Sorry if I've wasted your time.'

'No you haven't,' Henry said, his sphincter relaxing. 'It could be very useful.'

They looked at each other and a beat of silence passed. Then Bernadette said, 'Can I offer you a drink?' It was said shyly, but her eyes were sparkling.

'I must get going,' Henry said, 'but thanks anyway.'

A wave of disappointment washed over her face. Henry could see loneliness in her. 'What you've told me is very interesting,' he assured her. 'It could well have some bearing on David's death.'

She nodded, mouth rigid.

Henry rose and walked to the front door with Bernadette behind him. He reached for the lock, but she stretched past him and placed her hand over his, then manoeuvred herself between him and the door, placing her body between him and the exit.

'I see you're not wearing a wedding ring,' she said quietly, her eyes playing over his face. He swallowed. 'Please stay . . . for a while, at least.'

'I can't,' he said equally quietly, in spite of the surge of blood. He gave her a sad smile.

'I'm lonely,' she said simply.

'And I'm very sorry, but I'm a cop investigating your husband's murder and I'm also a professional. And I'm in a serious, happy relationship.' The words sounded clumsy but were the best he could come up with.

'I'll fuck your brains out,' she promised.

'Excuse me.' He reached for the door and squeezed past her, his face coming within inches of hers. He could see the

glistening of tears in her eyes now. 'That said, I'm very flat-
tered. You're a really nice lady.'

'OK,' she gasped and relented. 'You don't know how hard
that was for me.'

'I think I do.'

He opened the door and sidled out, not even daring to glance
back, trying his best to walk in a straight line. As usual, his
penis seemed to be acting in contravention of his thoughts,
and the subsequent unheralded erection was caught at a very
obtuse angle in his underpants.

Henry was speaking to Jerry Tope via the Bluetooth connection in his car. 'Can you see if you can find the name of the
headmaster or headmistress of the school in Belthorn at that
time? Find out if they're still alive or whatever and if we can
get round to see them as soon as. And it was a church school,
wasn't it? What's the name of the church it was connected to?
And is the vicar still the same one . . . you know the score.'

Tope, who was at home now, swigging his home brew, said,
'Yes – and are we still on for Liversage tomorrow, too? He's
definitely in Accrington.'

'You want to go for him?'

'Yes please.'

Henry grinned at the thought of the change in Tope, who
had suddenly turned into an adrenalin-fuelled super cop. He
ended the call and readjusted his underwear again.

He arrived at BVH at nine thirty and took over from Lisa.
His mother was asleep after an unsettled day with lots of chest
and stomach pains. She had tried to eat but could not keep
anything down. A nurse said she was deteriorating after the
rally and her body was closing down, organ by organ.

He had a long talk with Lisa about the DNR issue without
coming to a conclusion. then, sitting down next to the bed,
and in spite of his determination to get back to Kendleton that
night, he closed his eyes and was asleep within moments.

The vibration of his mobile phone in his pocket roused him
groggily from the deep slumber he had instantly fallen into.
He fumbled for the device, blinking rapidly, standing up and

stumbling towards the corridor to take the call. By the time he got there, it had cut off.

He saw that he had slept through three other missed calls and the arrival of two texts. He cursed, saw it was only 10.45 p.m. – he'd thought it was much later – and scrolled through the phone to find out what he'd missed.

The texts were from Rik Dean. One read: 'THINGS R KICKIN OFF – CROMER V COSTAIN.' Another just 'CALL ME!!!'

'It's like a Fast and Furious film,' Rik said as he and Henry hurtled in Henry's car towards Blackburn.

'Just tell me,' Henry said.

'OK – two cars pull up outside Shady Lady's club in Blackburn, which is operated by the Cromers. Four guys get out, tooled up, shotguns, handguns, bats. They open up at the doormen, who are Cromer employees. Big shoot-out. One guy is hit in the leg. The visitors pile back into their car – stolen, incidentally, from Blackpool, duh – and there's a bloody big baddies' car chase. Guys hanging out of car windows, shooting. One pedestrian clipped, plus loads of parked cars. Next, an unsuspecting cop car gets embroiled and has shots fired at him. Then there's a foot chase through Blackburn centre, like bloody Jason Bourne . . .'

Henry held up a finger. 'Cut the cinematic references please . . . where do we stand now?'

'All seems to have quietened down for the moment.'

'Injuries.'

'Just the doorman, a pedestrian flipped over but OK . . .'

'Arrests?'

'None.'

'Brilliant.' Henry's mouth twisted.

They had reached the outskirts of Blackburn from the M65 side. Henry came off at the exit, but instead of heading towards town, he went to Belthorn.

He was going to pay the Cromers a visit. It was time to crack some heads together.

SIXTEEN

'**Y**ou let me in now,' Henry demanded angrily of the intercom, feeling stupid shouting at a wall. There was no response. He continued, 'Because if you don't, I'll come back mob-handed and tear the fucking house apart in pursuit of a wanted criminal, namely Terrence Cromer.' With that, he lifted his finger off the speak button and stared through the wrought-iron gates at the Cromer house up the driveway. Lights burned. A couple of cars were parked outside. He squinted to see the numbers, but couldn't make them out.

Petulantly he jabbed his thumb three more times on the button. He could be very nasty with his thumb if riled.

A moment later, with a hiss of static, came a tinny, female voice he recognized. 'Wait there. I'll be out in a moment.' Janine Cromer.

He leaned, arms folded, on the front wing of the Audi, next to Rik.

'I'm now getting sorely pissed off with this lot,' Henry said through gritted teeth. 'Not least because I haven't had enough sleep.'

Rik remained silent, brooding. His evening of flesh-based pleasure with Lisa had been rudely interrupted by events and he too was a teensy bit cross.

The front door of the house opened. The two German Shepherd dogs surged out and bounded towards the gate ahead of Janine, who was pulling on a top coat.

The dogs reached the gate and patrolled back and forth, criss-crossing each other's path with a sinuous movement, all the while looking through the railings, teeth bared, growling under their breath at the back of their throats.

'Yes?' Janine demanded. She gripped the gate and the loose sleeves of her coat fell back down her arms, revealing the pale skin of her inner forearms.

Henry pushed himself off the car and strutted across. 'Who's in charge?' he demanded.

'Of what?'

'The family business.'

'We don't have a family business. It's in your imagination.'

'OK, OK,' Henry relented, not wishing to get into an argument on the semantics of the organization of a crime family. 'I need to pass a message to whom it may concern . . . so if it gets to your dad, all the better. Two messages, actually.'

Janine continued to grip the railings, one dog either side of her. Henry glanced briefly down at the dogs, then as he lifted his eyes, saw her white forearms.

'And they are?' she asked.

'First – give yourself up, Terry. We'll get you sooner rather than later.'

Janine yawned mockingly.

'Second, this shit stops. Right fucking now.'

'And that shit would be?'

'Turf wars. Guns. Killings. Blood. Your lot and the Costains. It stops now,' Henry reiterated. 'Before anyone else gets killed. We're going to take a very hard line against you as it is, don't make me step that up any further. Because I will, I promise you, Janine. We will not take any more crap and we will do everything to keep the streets safe from scumbags intent on violence. If there's even a hint of anything further, we will screw you to the floor . . . do I make myself clear?'

'I'm sure I don't know what you mean.'

Henry glared at her, then shrugged. 'And I thought you were different, Janine.'

She did not respond, but held his gaze with her head tilted, and Henry saw a look in her eye and an expression on her face that reminded him strongly of someone.

'Whatever,' he said with exasperation. 'Pass the message, dearie,' he added coldly, 'and don't be surprised when we come knocking.'

She turned and walked away.

Rik sidled up to Henry and said, 'Have you properly checked out little Miss Black Widow?'

'No . . . but I'm going to.'

*   *   *

Henry could have ranted until his face turned a horrible shade
of puce. But it would only have served to wind him up even
more and put more stress than ever on his heart, which he felt
was becoming even feebler by the minute.

Instead, he withdrew from the gates and skidded away in
the Audi, flicking up grit as he went. He was en route to
Blackpool to deliver the same message to the Costains. The
only problem being, who was now their head? Who had
the power now? Who should he target his warning to?

By the time he hit the slip road onto the M65, he had settled
into his driving, taken a few steadying breaths and his mind
was starting to work again.

'Notice anything about her?' he asked Rik.

'In what respect? Fit and dangerous, like I said all along?
Fuckable, but rather like knobbing a black widow spider?
Dangerous as hell?'

'Other than that.'

'No. I'm a simple man,' Rik conceded.

'Her arms?'

'Still no.'

'Her inner forearms, the soft bit from wrist up to elbow . . .
when her sleeve slid back?'

Rik continued to shake his head. 'Best tell me. Not in the
mood for guessing.'

'She self-harms. Lots and lots of razor blade cuts up each
arm, probably hundreds. And probably all over other parts of
her body, too. A lot were old, but some looked recent.'

'Oh . . . and?'

'Why do people self harm?'

'Don't know much about it . . .'

'Usually because of deep-rooted psychological issues and
trauma . . . it's a kind of release, the pain, the blood flow,'
Henry explained.

'Ugh . . . you seem to know a lot about it.' Rik sounded
impressed.

'Not really. Came across it once a while back and read up
on it, that's all.'

'You think it's significant?'

'No idea,' Henry admitted. 'But it's odd and there's always

a back story behind it. I wonder what hers is?' The other thing that was odd, was what he had seen in Janine's face as she'd stared daggers at him.

The car reached eighty-five and he pulled out into the fast lane.

Whether his words had any real effect, Henry could not be certain. He made sure that armed response units were very visible in and around Blackpool and Blackburn in order to get his message across, with orders to cruise by the clubs, and as far as the streets were concerned, everything seemed to quieten down.

What went on behind closed doors, he could not say.

But the lull in overt criminal activity gave him the chance to get a properly structured and staffed investigation under way as, suddenly, the commanders of the relevant divisions became ultra helpful in terms of staffing and resources. Henry didn't know how true it was, but the rumour clinic stated they'd had a very big kick up their backsides from the chief constable's jackboots.

Very quickly Henry had two Major Incident Rooms up and running – one in Blackburn, one in Blackpool – and a coordinating office at FMIT. He was lead SIO and Rik Dean was his deputy, having been promoted temporarily to chief inspector so he could pull rank if necessary.

The day after his visit to the Cromers and the Costains (where he had spoken in no uncertain terms to Cherry, Runcie's girlfriend, who had listened in a very chastened way and did not offer up another view of her shaved lady-region), a very big police operation had begun.

Clovelly, Terry Cromer's running mate, refused to admit to anything, but was placed before magistrates and remanded to police cells for a further seventy-two hours – a three-day lie down – so he could be interviewed further and more evidence found. Whether or not he admitted anything became less important as the scientific side of things put him in the Nissan at the time of the drive-by shooting. And at the scene of Runcie's murder.

To coin a phrase, he was stuffed.

Terry Cromer was still at large, but Henry was relaxed about that. It would only be a matter of time before he was arrested. Several operations were in train to keep under observation addresses he was known to frequent and a surveillance unit was sitting on his house in Belthorn. Or rather lying, waiting and watching from cover in a nearby field, in the manner of an SAS team.

Other detectives and specialists were looking at the hospital shootings, and all in all, Henry thought he had it covered. It felt good. He was loving it. He'd had a couple of half-decent nights' sleep, been well loved up by Alison, who seemed to have a surge of bedroom creativity and energy following the engagement. He also spent a lot of time with his mother, who – true to her nature – was rallying again, though she was still classified as very poorly.

Next morning he was in his office at FMIT, coffee in hand, carefully making up the murder book, having locked himself away successfully for a few hours, phones redirected and a big warning sign on his door.

Eventually he sat back, interlocked his fingers behind his head and for the first time in a while thought about the double murder, which had taken a back seat – again.

He snatched up his phone, jabbed in an internal extension number.

'Thanks for your patience, Jerry old fruit,' Henry said. 'Fancy that look at Rafe Liversage?'

Although Liversage was in the school photograph, Henry didn't really think he was responsible for murdering David Peters and Christine Blackshaw. He was one of the younger pupils, maybe six at the time of the photo, but he had to be dragged in and spoken to.

Jerry Tope landed in Henry's office five minutes later.

An hour after the phone call, Henry and Tope were at the hostel in Accrington, where they learned from the shifty manager that Liversage hadn't been seen for over a week. When asked why this hadn't been reported to the Probation Service, the manager shrugged and said he would do it in the New Year. Residents often went walkabout, but usually returned, no harm done. It made work to report it, then un-report it.

Unimpressed by the lack of professionalism – and his odour
– the two detectives left the hostel, a large, old detached house
on the outskirts of town, and went to stand by Henry's car.

They looked at one another, each knowing the other's
thoughts.

Henry voiced them. 'He's a lying bastard.'

Tope nodded. Their heads swivelled back to the premises,
seeing a curtain twitch at a ground floor window, catching a
glimpse of the manager.

'I'd say so.'

'Let's go back in,' Henry decided.

The manager and Rafe Liversage were arrested in the hostel.
Henry and Tope basically forced their way back in and insisted
that the manager show them all of the rooms, including his
own accommodation.

The man's bolt for the door whilst trying to get his mobile
phone to his ear was a bit of a giveaway. Henry spun him
round and dragged him to the floor, pinned him face down
and spoke into his dirty, hairy, waxy ear.

'Where is he?'

'I don't know what you mean.'

Henry cuffed his hands behind his back, then stepped him
back up to his feet and propelled him to a door marked 'Private
– Staff Only'. This led through to an office and then, via
another door, down some steps to the basement flat where the
manager lived.

The lack of any resistance, the man's total submission, told
Henry what he needed to know. This was confirmed as the
three of them clattered through into the lounge of the flat –
empty – through the kitchen and into the bedroom to find
Liversage dressed only in a grubby grey string vest, sitting on
the edge of an equally disgusting grey bed, one hand mastur-
bating his own flaccid cock, his other hand doing the same to
a young boy who was tied, spreadeagled to the bed with leather
straps, a look of abject terror on his face.

As good an arrest as it was – one of those lucky chances that
often come along as a by-product of a large investigation

– Liversage was soon discounted as a suspect in the double murder. But he was charged with kidnapping and a multitude of sexual offences, all of which would ensure that his prison licence would be revoked and he would be sent back where he belonged. Both Liversage and his accomplice, the hostel manager, were handed over to detectives at Accrington when it became clear they might be responsible for a series of undetected sexual assaults in the area over the last two months.

'Ah well, it was a good try,' Tope sighed.

'Are you getting to like operational duties again?' Henry teased him as they set off back to HQ.

'No chance . . . when *my* arse twitches it's because I've found a way into a website I shouldn't even be on in the first place. I'm not really cut out to be knocking on doors any more.'

Henry laughed. He knew that Tope definitely did his best work for the Constabulary by looking at a computer, although he also knew that the clock was ticking for such people. It was cheaper to employ civilians to do the work and some were already trained, which Henry found sad. Cops brought an indefinable instinct to jobs like Tope's and Henry was firmly of the school of belief, no matter how outdated his stance, that civilians would never have that same intuition. But the world was constantly changing, and not always for the better. For the 'dollar', maybe. And in that respect, Henry also believed that TJF: The Job's Fucked.

Tope showed his value again as they headed towards the motorway.

'Ooh, got something.' He pulled a few neatly folded pieces of paper from his inner jacket pocket and opened them out. 'A vicar and a teacher . . . you asked me to see if I could find them . . . re the school?'

'Oh yes.'

'The vicar who was attached to Belthorn School is called Bateson – but he's retired now . . . But his son is also a vicar and the school is still linked with the same church – and Bateson junior is the vicar. The church is in Oswaldtwistle. Looks like a family business.'

'The son's taken over from the father, dog collar and every-thing?'

'Yep.'

'What about the teacher?'

'No luck so far . . . but we're not far off Oswaldtwistle now. If you fancied, we could call in on spec and maybe the son could direct us to the dad – if he's still alive, that is.'

'I fancy,' Henry said, and at the next set of lights he turned towards Oswaldtwistle instead of heading for the motorway.

They drove through the main street of the little town and soon found the vicarage and church – St Catherine's. Henry knew where it was, having lived in the area many years before. It was early evening when they pulled up on the long gravelled driveway outside a magnificent, but crumbling vicarage, and knocked on the door. It was already dark and cold, and snow was a probability.

'I wonder if the Addams Family is at home?' Tope whispered as a bat flitted above their heads.

From inside they heard the approach of ominous sounding footsteps. The heavy metal-panelled door creaked open, but it wasn't Lurch who answered, but a boyish-looking man in his late forties, with an open dog collar hanging around his neck.

'Mr Bateson?' Henry asked.

'Reverend Bateson,' the man corrected him with a smile.

Henry showed him his warrant card and introduced himself and Tope.

'May we come in?'

Puzzled but welcoming, the vicar stepped politely aside and gestured for them to enter. The entrance hall was huge and ancient, with a tiled floor and a dark wood-panelled wall. 'What can I do for you two gentlemen of the law?'

'Are you still the vicar responsible for Belthorn School?'

'Responsible is too big a word. We're paternalistic, maybe,' he said. 'These days, the phrase "church school" doesn't really mean very much.' He clearly wanted to launch into something more about modern times, and the way that religion was viewed in society and the church's lack of influence in education. Instead he said, 'I try my best.'

'I believe your father held the same position?'

'I took over the parish when he retired, which includes Belthorn School, of course . . . and others.'

As delicately as he could, Henry said, 'Is he still with us?'

Bateson laughed. 'Very much so. Eighty-five and still as strong as an ox, though his mind is . . . you know.' He made an 'eek-eek' sound.

'Oh, great . . . we're investigating the deaths – murders, actually – of some of the pupils who attended the school in the late seventies and I'm speaking to people who might have known them back then, just to see if they remember anything that might give us a hint as to why they were murdered.'

'You mean murdered recently?'

'Yes, over the last three years. It's just too much of a coincidence they all went to the same school, so I need background on them, even though it's so long ago. Someone like your father might know something.'

Bateson looked doubtful. 'You may certainly speak to him. Whether he'll know anything, or be able to recall anything, is a different matter.'

'Alzheimer's?' Tope asked.

'Old age, bad temper and awkwardness and general disagreeability.'

'Could you give us his address?' Henry asked. 'We don't have to disturb him tonight, but maybe we could arrange to see him tomorrow. And if you wanted to be present, that would be fine,' he explained.

'No need for that – he lives here.'

The vicar led the detectives through the house, via what Henry would guess was called a drawing room, to a huge Victorian-style conservatory jutting out into an overgrown garden at the back, though now the trees and shrubs were bare. It was cool, but not chilly, and an old man sat on an armchair, his feet up on a stool, a blanket draped over his legs, reading a large print hardback book. He laid this down and looked at his visitors through thick-framed spectacles.

'Dad, these gents are from the police. They'd like to have a chat with you, if you don't mind.'

'Ahh . . . my years of rape and pillaging have caught up with me then?' He laughed croakily, adding, 'I wish.'

Bateson junior shot Henry a short, warning glance and laughed nervously. 'They want to talk about Belthorn School . . . when you were there.'

'What is Belthorn School?'

Henry thought, Oh-oh, not a good start, but then the old man said, 'Just kidding.'

He gave his son a look of scorn. 'He thinks I've lost my marbles, so I just humour him. My mind is as sharp as it's always been, it's the body that's letting me down, particularly my liver. Take a pew,' he said to Henry and Tope, smiling wickedly, and Henry warmed to him. He made an expansive gesture towards a cane sofa for two opposite him. To his son he said, 'Brews all round – and make mine a double.'

The vicar smiled good-naturedly. 'Can I offer you two gents a drink? Tea, coffee, something stronger?'

'Tea for me,' Henry said. Tope said he would have the same.

'I thought you said you were cops?' the old man said.

'On duty cops,' Henry said.

'Bollocks.' To his son he said, 'You know what I want.'

'Oh yeah.' He turned away muttering, 'Burying in your own graveyard.'

'My hearing's good,' his father said, tapping the discreet hearing aid curled behind his right ear. 'And this thing's turned right up.'

Bateson junior walked away, still muttering, his head rocking from side to side as though he was having an animated conversation with his father.

'Gay, you know,' the old man said. 'Well, not married . . . makes you wonder. My wife's dead, by the way.'

'I'm sorry,' Henry said.

'Don't be. She was an ultra-bitch.'

Henry chuckled and shook his head.

'Whaddya want, guys?'

'I just thought you might be a good port of call for some gossip, maybe.' Henry started to explain why he was here, but before he'd even got into telling the story, the old man held up a gnarled hand.

'Let me stop you there. Funny, I always wondered if there'd be any future repercussions. Just a feeling . . . you're right, I was the vicar for that school and to be honest I found that Belthorn itself was a hive of nefarious activity, shall we say? A mass of secrets . . . adultery, inbreeding, abuse and violence . . . satanic worship . . . oh, yes . . . but mostly behind closed doors. It's a place with many dark secrets, or was. Just like anywhere else, I suppose. Probably not the same now, because it's more like a little town than a village these days. And I think I can guess what you're going to talk about – or at least, who.'

He stopped talking as his son shouldered his way into the conservatory bearing a tray with two mugs on it, a plate of chocolate biscuits and a glass containing a large whisky. He set it down on the coffee table and rubbed his hands.

'OK – bog off,' his dad said.

He turned, left without a sound.

'Names,' the old man said. 'Cromer, Peters, Blackshaw, Milner and some others. But they were the main ones. All kids from school. And like kids, very, very cruel to each other. And the cruellest of them all . . . Terry Cromer . . . and the main object of his cruelty, his slightly younger brother, Freddy. Just because they were brothers, it didn't mean they loved each other, quite the opposite. Now hand me that whisky.'

Christmas Eve.

On this special day, the last day of term, the school closed at 1.30 p.m. after the turkey dinner and Brussels sprouts. The children, excited and keyed up for the day after and the holiday ahead, rushed out on the bell. They poured into the playground, screaming and shouting. All thirty of them.

Strolling casually out behind them all was Terry Cromer and his little band of cronies: David Peters, Christine Blackshaw and Ella Milner. These were the kids who ruled the school when the teacher wasn't looking – and only when Terry deigned to attend. His truancy was already legend.

Freddy Cromer had run out ahead with the bulk of the other children, about twenty-five of them. But although he was with them, he was alone because of his difference. His size, his low intellect, his weirdness, his unpredictability.

Most of the kids dispersed and Freddy stayed at the school gate, waiting to go home with Terry.

He and his gang were still in the playground, huddled together, discussing something. The huddle broke up and they started walking towards Freddy.

'You comin', Tel, or what?' Freddy called to Terry.

'Do you want to come with us?' Terry responded secretively.

'Why, why, where you going, Terry?'

'Come with us, we'll show you . . . it's a secret.'

Doubt crossed Freddy's face. 'But where?'

'You like kittens, don't you?'

Freddy's face brightened. 'You know I do. I love kittens . . . why, Terry?'

'Want to see some?' The words could have been spoken by a stereotypical child molester. Terry didn't really know what a child molester was back then, but he understood the temptation behind the words, the lure of expectation . . . the trap.

'Where are they, Terry, where are they?' Freddy jumped up and down. He loved little animals so much.

He was fourteen months younger than Terry, who was eleven then. But there was something about him that hadn't quite developed, something missing that ensured he wasn't just right and stayed more childish than he should have been, even at that age.

'Follow us.'

They dashed across the quiet, narrow road in front of the school and vaulted the stone wall with Freddy following, so excited he wanted to pee. And he did so, cringing as he ran, unable to stop himself, hoping the others wouldn't notice the stain on his short trousers.

They were on land owned by a farmer called Jacques. Grazing land for sheep and cattle, although none were present that cold afternoon as flecks of snow started to drift in the air and dark clouds scudded across the sky from the east. The famer didn't really mind kids on his land. These were the days when health and safety legislation, or at least its implementation, was just a pipe dream and kids on farms, doing dangerous things, were not unusual.

Led by Terry, the gang raced across the large, wet field, mud splashing.

The field dropped steeply towards a perimeter wall and soon they were out of sight and hearing of the road, the farm buildings and nearby houses, in a secret world of their own with no witnesses.

A place that had been carefully prepared by Terry. At the age of eleven he was already a villain – like his father – who terrorized local old people, openly stealing from them and promising violent retribution should they grass on him. His criminal planning was quite advanced.

Beckoning them on, he knew he was taking them to a disused chicken coop on the edge of the farmer's land. It was a place they'd hung out on many occasions and used as a den. Although virtually abandoned by the farmer it was structurally still quite sound, a warm place to go and have a secret cigarette, or get a girl to show her fanny. Some hens still roosted there and laid eggs fertilized by the huge rooster that strutted around the farm.

Terry had found some eggs in the coop that he had hidden and cared for, kept warm in a cardboard box packed with straw. They had hatched into healthy chicks.

In another part of the coop – quite a large, sectioned off building – a feral cat had given birth to a litter of four kittens, away from the chickens.

It was to these newborns that Terry led his little gang – and his brother. His stupid, hated brother.

'Come on, come on,' he urged them all.

Terry had stolen a padlock and key from elsewhere on the farm and had used it to keep the coop secure. He opened the door to let everyone in ahead of him and they crowded in excitedly, having to almost crawl because of the low roof.

With a flourish, Terry revealed the chicks in their box. He had rigged up a lamp to hang over them to provide extra warmth. They were only days old, chirping healthily, gorgeous little creatures, tiny, frail, easily broken or crushed.

The girl Christine made motherly noises.

David Peters sneered, not taken in by them at all. He preferred action men and cars.

But Freddy was entranced, dropping to his knees and gently scooping one of them up, feeling its warm fluffy body in the cupped palm of his big hand. He was mesmerized. 'Ahh, baby hens.'

Terry tapped him on the shoulder. 'Over here. Look at these.'

Freddy replaced the chick carefully and followed his brother, who slid open a hatch to reveal his next treasures. Four mewing kittens, bundles of fur, big eyes, only weeks old.

Freddy gasped in wonderment and reached for one of the tiny cats. This time he could feel the delicate bones throughout its body, its shoulder blades and rib cage. He lifted it gently and started to stroke it.

Terry stood behind him, head lowered, a terrible look on his face and a three-foot plank of wood in his hands. He gestured for the others to stand back. He needed room, an arc, and he drew back the plank, gripped it tight with both hands and smashed it across the side of Freddy's head, sending him sprawling.

Unconscious for a short time, Freddy came to with Terry straddling him, the three other kids holding down his body and legs.

In Terry's right fist was a handful of dirt, dust, bird shit and hen feathers that he'd scooped up off the floor of the shack. With his left hand he held Freddy's face rigid and tried to force open his mouth. Freddy was still stunned and uncomprehending, aware only of Terry's blazing, hate-filled eyes and the look of determination as, successfully opening Freddy's mouth, he forced the handful of muck and feathers into it, ramming them down with the palm of his hand.

He spoke no words.

Then Freddy started to writhe and fight and he choked on the foul-smelling, germ-laden mixture, until a wave of sheer panic made him buck Terry off and break free, like a wild bear from chains, from the grip the other kids had on him.

On all fours he gasped and spat and cried and snuffled, inhaling the horrible dust and debris.

Terry bent low and spoke into his ear. 'I hate you,' he whispered. He jerked a come-on gesture to his mates and they left Freddy wheezing in the shack.

Once outside, Terry quietly locked the door then hurled the key across into the next field, trapping Freddy inside, although at that moment, Freddy did not realize this.

He lay there in a foetal position, sobbing massive, chest-juddering breaths. A chick walked around him. A kitten mewed in his ear. It took a few minutes for the sobbing to subside, then he sat up slowly, drawing his big knees up to his chin, rocking back and forth.

He picked up a kitten and stroked it. Then a chick. 'You didn't know about this, did you?' he asked the yellow ball. Then he scooped up another kitten and posed the same question to it.

The floor of the coop was constructed of roughly hewn planks, nailed together to form floorboards. Not a great job – sturdy, as was the rest of the construction, but there were gaps of varying width in the floor, and the whole shed-like building rested on a series of breezeblocks to keep it off the cold, wet ground.

Freddy didn't blame the animals at that moment. They were not part of the conspiracy. He held a kitten in one hand, a chick in the other, rubbing his face with their soft down and fur, feeling their vulnerability.

His anger rose at the thought of Terry.

Next moment, somehow, the kitten was dead. He dropped it onto the floor in disgust. And so was the chick, squeezed to death in his huge hands. He dropped it too and stared blankly at the two corpses.

Then he sniffed something and saw smoke curling up through the gaps in the floorboards. Freddy watched it, again not quite understanding what he was seeing.

Smoke. It rose. Then he felt heat underneath his bottom. And there was a glow and a flicker of flame, licking up through the gaps. The heat became intense. Freddy threw himself at the door, expecting it to be open, as the fire, set from below – the stuffed paper, dried straw and firelighters, all prepared in advance by Terry – quickly engulfed the chicken coop.

'I was at the school that day. Took a short service for the kids, as it happened,' the old man explained, as Henry and Tope sat back, stunned by the story. 'Back then I was a bit of a twitcher, though they didn't call birdwatchers twitchers back then, just anoraks. And, as I'd finished my work at the school, my dog collar came off, my anorak went on, with my boots, the bins went around my neck, and I went birdwatching on the moors. I wanted to see if I could clock some harriers that had been seen up there. No luck. As I trudged back I saw smoke rising from the old coop and heard Freddy banging and screaming in terror from inside. I managed to prise the door open with a bit of old piping, I think. He got some minor burns, his face and the back of his legs, I think . . . but he could have died very easily.'

'And was this reported to the police?' Henry asked.

'No. Hushed up.'

'Really?'

'It was put down as an accident . . . the reality being I actually saw Terry running away from the coop with his friends and I'm convinced he tried to burn his brother to death.' The old man looked at Henry. 'Freddy might be the mad one, but Terry is the evil one. His family said they would deal with it. They were a criminal family even back then and Mr Cromer told me he would burn my church down if I said anything. Even a man of God can be a coward,' he admitted. 'But at least I saved Freddy's life, although from what I gather, he's not had much of one since.'

Henry exhaled. 'Possibly explains Freddy's more extreme behaviour . . . that on top of his mental health problems. Not a good combination.' Henry thought back to the dead animals he had found strung up and laid out in the bedroom at his aunt's house in Rawtenstall on the day Freddy had had his first attempt at strangling Henry. A gruesome, unsettling find.

'Would you give a statement about it now?' Henry asked.

'I would. Chances are I'll have turned my toes up by the time it gets anywhere near a court anyway, so what have I to fear? Just an audience with the Lord, which I'm kind of looking forward to.'

Henry twitched his eyebrows at Tope, who said simply, 'Revenge.'

'Simmering for years,' Henry agreed. 'One thing for certain, we need to speak to Freddy properly now and make sure we pre-plan everything, see what he has to say about it. I'll bet he'll be an easy can of worms to pry open.'

Already Henry was mentally rubbing his hands together.

'I'm just surprised he hasn't gone for Terry yet.'

'Maybe saving the best till last,' Henry said. 'Who knows . . . let's find out.'

SEVENTEEN

S ince leaving the company of the old, retired vicar in
Oswaldtwistle, having listened to his astonishing story,
the following days had been monstrously busy for Henry,
and other than the cloud looming over him that was his
hospitalized mother, he had enjoyed himself immensely.

He had been at the helm of a complex, multi-layered police
operation which involved lots of doors being kicked down
and gang-related arrests made, alongside various media
appearances for which a range of sound bites were prepared.
These appearances included an early morning visit to Media
City in Salford, where by chance he had shared a sofa on the
BBC breakfast show with an ageing pop star he had longed
to meet and who was on a comeback tour that had hit
Manchester the night before. Henry was there to talk about
the Lancashire manhunt, which had captured nationwide
interest, and the meeting with the old rocker had been a bonus.
Henry had got the man's autograph in his pocket notebook
and had excitedly phoned Alison with the news, although she
huffed at it, unimpressed. He was also given a pair of tickets
for a London concert later in the week, but doubted he would
be able to make it.

Despite the police activity, which was very intrusive to a
lot of criminals in Lancashire, Terry Cromer remained at large,
as did Freddy.

Henry knew they would come. Just a matter of time.

He was also keeping an eye on missing persons, but none
who were reported seemed to fit the victim profile he was
interested in. One misper did turn up floating in a reservoir,
but his demise had no connection to Henry's inquiry.

They reached New Year's Eve without any real success and
Henry's team was dismissed to enjoy the festivities, have the
next day off and come back on the second of January ready
to get stuck in again.

That day's debrief had taken place at 4 p.m., after which Henry and Rik headed across to Blackpool – Henry to visit his mother, who had been watched over by Lisa for most of the day; Rik to pick Lisa up.

As Rik and Henry walked through the hospital corridors up to the cardiac unit, Henry had said, 'I'm not saying you can't have a drink at midnight, but I'd rather you erred on the side of caution.'

'Why's that?' Rik had been looking forward to getting plastered with Lisa.

'Dunno . . . instinct? We've had a quiet few days . . . I know the crims have had cops up their backsides all week and we've ruined a few New Years, but something might kick off tonight and I'd rather have one or two of us capable of reacting in a sober fashion.'

Rik shrugged an 'OK'. He wasn't about to argue. Henry's influence had managed to get his love life back on track and secure him a promotion, albeit temporary. He needed to keep on Henry's good side.

His mother looked like a shadow in the bed. After a brief resurgence of health, she had gone downhill fast and life was something she now clung onto only tenuously.

Lisa crossed over and gave him a hug, then kissed Rik.

'How is she?'

Lisa shook her head, unable to find words. Henry touched her shoulder tenderly. 'You go, I'll stay for a few hours. Not a problem.' A day earlier Henry had pinned her down and they'd had the unpleasant DNR conversation, sadly concluding that their mother's wishes should be followed. Henry thought with a hint of cynicism that Lisa had reached that decision a bit too quickly, but immediately chastised himself, for being mean spirited and judging her as the old Lisa, the selfish, self-centred Lisa who only cared about herself, the daughter who saw her mother only as a pain in the neck. Even though it was early days, a great change seemed to have come over his sister since making peace with Rik and rekindling their relationship. She was much more serene and laid back now, as if she accepted that her unstable past was over and her future was with Rik. For ever. And she was happy about it.

Henry sat next to his mother, who lay there as if she was already in her coffin, hands folded across her chest, legs out straight. She wore an oxygen mask, but her breathing was ragged and unsteady. Before he settled down, he decided to buy himself a coffee and a sandwich, returning a few minutes later with his goods and laying them out on the bedside cabinet. He ripped open the sandwiches, a noise that seemed to wake his mother, who opened her eyes as though she'd been prodded and ripped the mask off her face in a panic.

'Hey, Mum, it's all right.' Henry gently helped remove the mask and plumped up her pillows to raise her slightly. He could hear her chest rasping as she breathed.

'Not long now, eh?' she said.

He stayed with her until nine that evening and left her sleeping. As ever he made certain the nurses had his phone numbers – that of the Tawny Owl and his mobile – on their information sheets. Then he drove back to Kendleton and entered the crazy world of New Year's Eve at the Tawny Owl, where at midnight he allowed himself a small glass of champagne and bawled out 'Auld Lang Syne' without any thought for melody.

He and Alison stepped away from the crowd in the bar and went outside into the chill of the night, where most of the population of Kendleton were singing and dancing and a bonfire and fireworks were lighting up the New Year.

They stood side by side, watching the flames and the rockets, Henry's arm around her slender waist. He said a few romantic words to her, which had the desired effect, and they shared their first proper public kiss, although hardly anyone saw it.

Not long afterwards he was in bed, alone. Alison slid in about 2 a.m. after shooing out the last of the revellers.

At 03:48 the bedside phone rang.

Henry walked a few metres after he had ducked under the cordon tape, then stopped and breathed in the cold New Year's Day air. Further down the track he could see the side of a factory unit and the car park next to it, the police cars drawn up, blue lights rotating unnecessarily.

The phone call that had awakened him just over an hour earlier could have been either one thing or the other – his mother, or work. It could easily have been from BVH informing him of the worst.

But it had been the FIM – who, having been on duty for most of the previous week, knew what was happening and what Henry was interested in. Hence her opening gambit, 'Boss, I think this could be one of yours.'

It was now that Henry found himself standing in the en-suite shower room, half-wondering if the FIM was visualizing him naked.

He hunched down into his jacket – a surprise extra Christmas present from Alison, one that was of immediate use – and was about to set off towards the unit when he heard another car pull up on the main road. He turned to see that Rik Dean had also arrived and parked behind the Audi, and was now walking quickly towards him, flashing his warrant card at the PC guarding the entrance and ducking under the tape.

Rik was wrapped up in a thick outer coat.

'Henry,' he said in acknowledgement. 'Looks like you were right. What've we got?'

'I probably know as much as you,' Henry said. 'Let's see.'

They started to walk. Rik said, 'How was your New Year's Eve?'

'Nice, but short of alcohol. Yours?'

'Ditto – no sex either.'

Henry and Rik were making their way to a light industrial unit at the bottom of the village. Though disused it wasn't old; built of breezeblock and panelled metal, it was the end one of four units. The other three were in use: one as a garage, another by a storage company, the third by a manufacturer of window blinds. All, though, looked dilapidated.

The night duty detective emerged from a personnel door in the wall of the unit, adjacent to a roller shutter, and walked across the car park to meet Rik and Henry. They all knew each other. DC Oxford was a steady detective in the middle years of his service who had the possibility of making DS if he wanted. He briefed them, they fitted their latex gloves and snapped elasticated paper coverings over their shoes, then followed him inside.

It was quite a large unit – Henry would have to be told its cubic area, he couldn't even begin to guess the figure. But as he entered the unit proper through the door, then a small vestibule, he stopped, astounded and almost overwhelmed by the thick aroma that seemed to clog the steamy atmosphere.

'Bloody hell,' he said.

'Just had a quick count-up and I reckon there's about eight hundred,' said Oxford.

Henry and Rik blew a low whistle each.

There were rows and rows of them. Eight hundred cannabis plants, all very healthy-looking, with overhead lighting and heating and a sophisticated hydroponics set-up to water and feed them.

Henry was no great whizz at maths, but he knew that the street value of each plant was somewhere in the region of five hundred pounds. Multiply eight by five and add the zeros – that meant he was looking at somewhere in the region of four hundred thousand pounds' worth of illegal drugs. He blinked. Good money.

'Who found them?' he asked.

'Local couple came down here in a car for a bit of nookie,' Oxford said. 'Parked up outside to get down to business, security lights came on and they noticed that the door we just came through was open . . . through their steamy windows. They called it in, and the lad says they didn't even look inside, which I've no reason to doubt.'

Henry nodded, his eyes scanning the jungle of leaves, his head shaking at the enormity of the find.

Which was not the reason he was here.

'One of the Oswaldtwistle patrols eventually made it up here to check it out and wandered through and poked his head in the office down there.' Oxford pointed to the office at the far end of the unit, door open, light on. 'And that's where he is. This way.'

Oxford led the two detectives around the perimeter of the unit, using the route that everyone attending would now have to follow. Reaching the office door, he stood aside and let Henry and Rik sidle past him.

Henry stood at the threshold and let his eyes do the walking, as he experienced the strange feeling of dread and excitement that always engulfed him at such a scene.

In terms of an office, there was a desk and a chair and a laptop computer but little else. The walls were bare. His eyes roved. He saw the rucksack propped against the wall, a stack of clothes, the Primus stove with a small saucepan on top of it. There was half a loaf of bread, some cans of soup, a cheap-looking kettle, a carton of milk, a jar of coffee and a mug. Two newspapers were folded up next to two pillows. There was also a small two-bar electric heater of a type he had not seen for years, and a couple of raggy-looking blankets and a stack of clothes.

Someone had been living here, hiding out.

And that person now lay splayed like the letter X on an unzipped sleeping bag on the cold office floor. The head wound was dreadful. The entry of the bullet on the right side of the face was about the size of a five pence piece, the exit wound on the left had removed about a quarter of the skull, most of which was splattered against the office wall. The sight made Henry's lips twitch. Even so, the man was easily identifiable. And very obviously dead.

'Jeepers,' Rik said. He was looking over Henry's shoulder.

'Jeepers indeed,' Henry agreed.

'So this is where he's been hiding out,' Rik said.

'Looks that way.'

'Oh dear, Terry Cromer,' Henry said. 'What a terrible end, even for a man as villainous as you.'

Henry stepped back into the unit, easing Rik back a step with him.

He looked at Oxford. 'Who've you got coming?'

'Scenes of crime, and I've turned out a pathologist . . . seemed pretty obvious he was dead. And a couple more uniform patrols, just to get the scene sealed properly.'

Whilst Henry couldn't disagree with that diagnosis, he always felt it prudent to get paramedics on the scene. Cops could make mistakes in assuming that people were dead when actually they weren't . . . But he let it slide. He would bet his commutation that Terry Cromer was dead. 'Have you checked the rest of the unit?'

'Not yet.'

Henry looked across the hundreds of plants – clearly one of the Cromer family's cash cows as cannabis was still very, very popular and its possession hardly even merited a slap on the wrist. It was always the importer and distributors the police were interested in cracking down on, not the end users. Along one side of the unit was a set of steps leading up to what appeared to be another office, supported by a metal framework, which would give a supervisor a view across the unit.

'What you thinking, Henry?' Rik asked.

'Er, nothing, nothing really,' he said absently.

'Looks like the Costains found him before we did,' Rik said. He looked back into the office. 'Also looks like he's been living like a tramp.'

Henry said nothing. He always found it best to ingest serious crime scenes slowly. Soak them in, let 'em permeate; start hypothesizing but don't reach any conclusions. Too early for anything like that. But it did certainly look like this was the place where the fugitive Terry Cromer had been hiding out and living rough, no doubt fed and watered by his family and other members of his organization. Even for someone like Cromer, this was an existence that would have been short-lived, unless it was just a stop-gap before leaving the country. And it was the place where he had met his maker . . . but already Henry had his misgivings.

The Costains were on the warpath and killing Terry Cromer was no doubt high on their agenda, yet it seemed unlikely they would have discovered his whereabouts, unless someone in Terry's set-up had betrayed him. That was a likely scenario in a world where allegiances were fickle, and it would be one line of enquiry . . . but Henry wasn't convinced.

The yellowish glow of the lighting suspended above the cannabis plants made for an eerie radiance, not really suitable for searching properly – that would have to be carried out in daylight, with proper lighting rigs. But before focusing on the body in the office, he wanted to have a quick look around the place without spoiling any evidence there might be to find.

He switched on his Maglite torch and began to edge around the perimeter of the unit, right up by the wall, until he reached the steps that led up to the elevated office. He stopped here and shone his torch up at the office door, which was closed. From this position he looked across the bushes, most of which were as tall as he was, then flashed his torch up the wooden steps again, to the door above him.

Then he froze.

With measured deliberation, he ran the torch beam downwards across each step, and saw what had made him stop abruptly.

Blood. Tiny drops of it on a couple of the steps. He flashed his torch on the breezeblock wall and saw more blood, and in it a big handprint. On the stair rail there was yet more blood where a hand had gripped it. His torch flicked up to the door and there was blood on that, too, another handprint by the door handle that he hadn't seen on his first arc of the torch.

Henry swallowed and turned to look over to Rik and Oxford, chatting quietly by the office door. He could hear the murmur of their voices.

He gave them a little wave but they didn't look over at him.

He coughed – still no response.

He flashed his torch wildly at them and both detectives squinted over at him. He put a finger to his lips and beckoned them over. Rik opened his arms in a 'What?' gesture.

If he could have read Henry's lips, they would have said, 'Just fucking come here.'

Instead, Henry beckoned again, this time with a more urgent hand signal, and shook his head despairingly.

They seemed to move with reluctance, but joined him a minute later. As they made their way towards him, Henry kept his finger to his lips.

'What is it?' Rik asked.

Henry flicked his torch beam onto the wall, up the steps and onto the door of the upper office, showing him the blood smears.

'Shit,' Rik hissed.

'No – blood,' Henry corrected him. Then, 'I'm going to have a look.'

'Is that a good idea?'

'Probably not.'

He put his right foot on the first step and went up slowly, avoiding the blood and not touching the wall. At the top of the steps there was a small, railed landing. Having reached it, he touched the door silently with a knuckle to see if it would swing open. It was shut, but maybe not locked.

He crouched low, squatting on his haunches. Rik was three steps behind him. Oxford watched from the bottom of the stairs, mouth agape.

Henry rapped on the door and shouted, 'Police!' then cowered slightly, expecting bullets to strafe the door from inside the office. There was no response, no indication of movement. Henry knocked again and once more said, 'Police!', but kept low and to one side of the door.

He gave it a few seconds and then reached up for the door handle, a basic latch type, easing it down with his thumb and forefinger. He pushed the door open and ducked to one side in case anything unpleasant came out of the room . . . like chunks of lead travelling at fifteen hundred miles an hour. The door swung open to an unlit room. Nothing moved or responded.

Henry counted to thirty – not certain as to why, but it seemed a good number to aim for – then shouted, 'This is the police. Is there anyone in there?'

Still nothing. He shuffled himself around and then, with his back to the wall by the door, he rose to his full height, aware that the wall against which he pressed his back seemed to be made of MDF or some type of hardboard. It wasn't solid . . . and if there was anyone in the office, desperate and armed, the wall would not give him much protection. He reached around the door jamb with the fingers of his left hand, feeling at a height at which he would expect to find a light switch. He touched it and his forefinger ran up the curved slope of a rocker switch. He hesitated a moment and then flicked it. A strong light came on in the room.

Henry jerked away from the door and dropped low again, but nothing happened.

'Police,' he said again. There was no harm in making sure that everyone knew, he wouldn't like to have anyone arguing in court – either Crown or at an inquest (including his own) – that they had not been clearly informed the police were

there. 'I'm a police officer and I'm going to come in through
the door,' he said clearly. 'I am not armed and you will be
able to see my hands . . . OK?'

He had passed the point of expecting feedback. He rose to
his full height again and sidestepped into the doorway, his
muscles tense, expecting the whack of a bullet.

It did not come.

The office was devoid of any furniture, bare – with the
exception of the second body of the night, another male,
wedged in the far corner of the small room.

As at the first door, Rik came up behind Henry and peered
over his shoulder. 'Jeepers,' he said again.

Even though Henry could not clearly see the face, he knew
it was Freddy Cromer sitting there, legs splayed out, head
lolling forwards on his chest which was drenched with blood
from his head wound. In his right hand his fingers were loosely
holding a snub-nosed, six shot revolver. Henry could see the
entry wound in his right temple, half an inch in front of his
ear. There was no exit wound this time, the bullet having
lodged inside Freddy's head.

Henry edged forward, carefully watching where he placed
his bootee-clad feet. Rik stayed at the door.

Henry squatted down again in front of Freddy, peering
closely at him, angling his own face into a position to see him
clearly.

'Definitely Freddy,' Henry said.

Then Henry blinked and uttered urgently, 'Get an ambulance
. . . I think he's still alive.'

EIGHTEEN

'I heard a breath and then I saw his chest move,' Henry
explained to the A&E consultant. This was the same doctor
who, a week before, had come to meet Henry at the hospital
on Christmas Day – it seemed so long ago now – when Freddy
Cromer had taken the poor nurse hostage. Then, physically at

least, Freddy had been in excellent health. The same doctor
was now battling to save Freddy's life. 'Just barely,' Henry
continued. 'I didn't know if it was just a death rattle, to be
honest – you know, the last expulsion of breath, that sort of
thing. Then I heard it again, felt a pulse in his neck and realized there was life still in there.' He did not add, tempting
though it was, 'But not as we know it.'

'You did well to notice it,' the doctor said. He had spent
the last two hours treating Freddy, whose condition was
described as critical. 'I'm surprised he's still alive, actually
. . . the X-rays show that the bullet in the brain lodged' – here
the doctor touched the back of his own head, just behind his
right ear – 'somewhere in this vicinity. Obviously there's
massive swelling and bleeding and until we have control of
both, it's impossible to say what the prognosis is. At the
moment he's in a coma, which is a good thing because it'll
give his body an opportunity to settle . . . but to be fair, I
don't hold out much hope for his recovery. As corny as it
always sounds, the next twenty-four hours will be critical.

'Anyway' – he clapped Henry on the arm – 'you did well,
you saved his life for the time being at least. Get yourself a
brew. That machine' – he pointed to a hot drinks dispenser
– 'does a great filter coffee, believe it or not.'

'Thanks – and I will.'

The doctor pulled his surgical mask over his face and turned
away into the maze of the A&E department.

Henry took a deep breath, then followed doctor's orders.

It was now past eight in the morning. He carried the
steaming coffee out into the dawn and stood on the paved
area outside the A&E entrance at Royal Blackburn Hospital,
sipping the surprisingly good brew, taking in the view across
to the motorway and up the hill beyond towards Belthorn.
He thought, Who could have believed I could have had so
much fun in such a small place?

Daylight had only just crept in, but it was still grey. At least
the threatened snowstorm had not materialized, yet as Henry
searched the sky, the possibility still existed. There seemed
little chance that the sun would shine on the beginning of this
brand new year.

He phoned Rik, who was still up at the factory unit in charge of the murder scene. The circus had arrived en masse and got to work. It was only a short conversation – as he talked, he was focusing on an Astra van being driven up the curved driveway to the hospital. He ended the call and sipped his drink whilst watching the occupant park, pay and hurry in his direction.

He took a long swig of the coffee, then dropped the plastic cup into a waste bin and prepared himself to meet and greet Janine Cromer, daughter of Terry, niece of Freddy. He was already thinking this was going to be fun.

She halted abruptly in front of him, challenge in her manner.

'Janine, I'm so sorry.'

She blinked away her disbelief and said cynically, 'I'll bet you are.'

'Oddly enough, I don't like people dying.'

She surveyed his face with hard-edged eyes. He could almost see the turmoil inside.

Henry had to agree that this wasn't the way he would have chosen to deal with the relative of a murder victim and an (attempted) suicide. But he had wanted to stay with Freddy when the ambulance turned up fifteen minutes after being rousted and he did not really want anyone else to deal with them. When Freddy had been rushed into casualty, he had called Janine, using the mobile number he had logged in his phone, but there had been no reply. He'd left a message and then had a uniform PC to go up to the house in Belthorn – but there had been no reply there, either. And as the surveillance team had been taken off the house a day before (because of the cost), there was no way of knowing if there was actually anyone in or not. According to the patrol, the place seemed completely empty.

So Henry had left another message for Janine. And another. And eventually she called him, sounding tired and irritated.

He had asked her to come to the hospital to meet him. His idea had been to tell her face to face what he had found in the factory unit, but she had insisted that he tell her over the phone.

So he did. To silence. Not the best way to deliver the news of a death, and Henry was very uncomfortable with it – but that was what she wanted. So she got it.

Finally she'd said, 'My dad's dead, but it looks like Freddy might live. Is that what you're saying? Freddy might live?'

'Yes – so I need to speak to you, please. And also to your grandmother, their mum.'

'I'll come,' she said. And hung up.

And here she was standing in front of him. Suddenly her hard shell cracked and she said, 'Can I see my uncle, please?'

'Yes, I think so . . . I'll come if you don't mind.'

'I do, actually, but I need to know what's going on, what's really happened, and sadly you might be the only person who can tell me.'

It would have been easy for Henry to shrug and say 'Whatever.' Instead he bit his tongue and remained professional. 'We need to talk,' he said.

'Yes, we do.'

She stalked past Henry through the automatic doors, but once inside the reception area she stopped unexpectedly and spun on him. 'I don't even know where he is. You take me.'

'Follow me,' he said softly, walked past her touching her arm, leading the way to the A&E wards. He was sympathetic to her mood – something as enormous as this was hard for anyone to deal with and get right in their head. She had only just learned some terrible news about her family and Henry understood that she would probably hate him, love him, despise him, pretty much all at the same time. That's the way it went, whether people were members of crime families or not.

As they entered the A&E wards, he bumped into the consultant again. A busy man.

'This is Janine Cromer, the patient's niece. Can she see him, please?'

The doctor looked at her. 'We met last week. I'm very sorry about your uncle, but yes you can see him.' To Henry he said, 'You know where he is.' To both he said, 'We're going to have to take him to Preston Royal Infirmary. They have the surgical facilities and expertise for this kind of thing . . .'

'What kind of thing exactly?' Janine demanded crossly. 'I've only got part of the picture here . . . The police haven't been very helpful, to be honest,' she said with feeling and gave Henry that hostile look again. 'But that's not surprising as they hate and harass my family.'

'OK, look, I'll tell you what,' the doctor suggested, sensing the aggression, 'let this officer take you to see your uncle first. I'm afraid you won't be able to touch him, or anything like that, but you can speak to him if you so wish. He's been seriously wounded, he's in a coma and critically poorly. When you're ready, come up to the office and I'll tell you everything I can. And I'm sure that Mr Christie' – he looked pointedly at Henry – 'will tell you all he can.'

Henry nodded helpfully.

Henry then led her to the single treatment room, in which Freddy lay spreadeagled on the bed. His clothes had been unceremoniously cut from him and a single folded sheet was laid across his lower stomach and upper legs. A machine was helping him to breathe steadily, making a sucking noise, and he was attached to two drips running into the veins in the back of each of his hands. He was connected to a monitor that showed the weak blip of his heartbeat and his dangerously low blood pressure. The head wound was covered by a dressing and bandage and although the area around it had been shaved, cleaned and disinfected, there were still streaks of dried blood down his cheek and neck.

He was a huge, hairy man, Henry saw. A massive barrel of a chest, enormous biceps and thick legs. Although Henry knew that Freddy had mental problems, he wondered why he'd allowed Terry to dominate him so. Terry was a big, tough guy, but he didn't have Freddy's physical presence. Henry knew the answer was psychology not brute strength. A powerful, evil personality was all that was required to cow others into submission, and Terry had certainly had that. Until now.

Janine's hand went to her mouth, stifling a squeal of shock. 'My God,' she said into her palm. 'My God.'

Henry, standing behind her, managed to catch her before she pivoted forwards and hit the hard tiled floor.

'Seriously, I'm OK,' Janine said, waving off the attention and taking a sip of water from the glass Henry had provided for her.

Henry had caught her and dragged her gently to a chair in

the corridor before lifting her onto it, again gently. The nurse who had been attending to Freddy swooped across to assist and it was established that Janine had simply gone woozy and lightheaded, not actually passed out, although Henry had seen the whites of her eyes as her eyeballs rolled right back into their sockets.

She sat with her head well forward, breathed and fanned herself. The nurse had checked her blood pressure, which was low but OK.

'It's just this whole week, what's been going on, then this morning . . . Dad, Uncle Freddy . . . just too much to bear,' Janine explained. 'But I feel all right now.' She smiled feebly at Henry. Her face was the colour of ash, but a healthier-looking tinge was creeping slowly upwards.

The consultant came out of Freddy's room and bent down in front of Janine, checking her pulse and eyes, nodding as everything seemed to be in order.

'Do you want to come up to the office?' he asked. 'I'll tell you what I know.'

'Please.'

He helped her to her feet and the three of them went to the office further down the corridor. Henry stood to one side whilst the doctor explained Freddy's wound to Janine, using the X-rays, laying out the possibilities for recovery (slim, but miracles did happen) and what would be happening to Freddy in the immediate future. The air ambulance had been requested, he said, would be on site within an hour and Freddy was going to be flown to the trauma clinic at Preston Royal Infirmary.

There was a little shock in Janine's face that Henry didn't quite understand. She said, 'So quickly?'

'Within an hour and a half he should be being operated on,' the doctor claimed. 'I will accompany him, of course, and assist in the procedure.'

Janine shook her head at the news. 'I just thought that if someone shoots themselves in the head, they'd die.' She sounded a tad disappointed.

'Every gunshot wound is different, every body different,' the doctor explained. 'It all depends on angles and the condition of the weapon used and the ammunition. From the X-ray, as you can see, the bullet entered his head at a very acute angle and was not fired directly into the brain. Had that been the case, the injury would certainly have been fatal and we wouldn't be having this conversation. But we are. Mr Cromer is still alive, we'll do our very best to save him. Maybe he will live and talk again.'

'Thank you, thank you, doctor,' Janine said. Henry thought that rather than being elated or hopeful, she looked mortified by the news that he might survive.

'For the moment we need to concentrate on keeping him stable and preparing for the arrival of the helicopter, which is based in Preston. I need to do that now.' He rose from his chair, gave Henry a glance and left.

Janine blew her nose on a tissue she found in her shoulder bag. She wiped her red-raw eyes. Henry perched on the corner of the doctor's desk.

'How you doing?'

'Not good.' She looked up at him. 'Are you going to tell me what you know?'

'As much as I can.'

'What the hell does that mean?'

'It means as much as I can.'

After giving him another antagonistic gaze, Janine relented. 'OK – fire away.'

Due to his conditioning as an SIO – and the fact that informing the relatives of murder victims was always fraught with difficulty – Henry kept it as brief as possible. Not least because there was always the chance that the 'live' relative might also have killed the 'dead' one.

He wasn't to know, yet, if Janine had killed her father and put a bullet into her uncle's head. It was always possible. Not that he thought this was the case here, but he always had to keep it in mind. There was a lot of work still to be done at the scene to piece together exactly what had happened.

First glance gave the impression that Freddy had killed Terry, who had been hiding out in the factory unit, and then turned the gun on himself in a fit of remorse. Henry didn't phrase it in those terms for Janine, though. All he did was state facts.

He was interested in her conclusions, though. And he had

a lot of questions to ask her, but they would have to come later. The first priority was to get Freddy treated and until the result of the surgery at Preston was known, Henry doubted if he could morally pin her down. He did wonder where Freddy's mother was. Janine said she had gone to the Canary Islands to get away from all the 'shite' that was going on and that she, Janine, would speak to her later.

Janine snuffled and wiped her eyes. 'So it looks as though Freddy killed my dad,' she said, catching a choke in her throat, 'and then shot himself. Is that what you're saying?'

'I'm not really saying anything just yet, Janine. The scene needs very careful analysis before we reach any conclusions and that may take a while. And, hopefully, Freddy will recover enough to be able to tell us exactly what did happen.'

Henry saw her reaction to this idea and did not quite know what to make of it. It was like a cloud had scudded across her face, then it was gone.

'I know this is a tough time for you, Janine, but at some stage I'm going to need a formal identification of your father.' She inhaled sharply at this in terror. 'Unless we can do it some other way,' Henry relented quickly. 'You know, dental records, fingerprints, DNA . . . but you may have to, yeah?'

'I know.'

'And we will have to sit down and have a chat . . . but for the time being, I realize you have to be with your family and be there for Freddy,' Henry said, all heart.

'I don't suppose they'll let me fly in the helicopter with him?'

'I doubt it.'

Once more she exhaled long and hard. 'This is unbelievable. My dad and my uncle.'

'They weren't the best of buddies.'

'No – but murder and suicide? That's so extreme.' She stood in front of Henry. 'I need to get up to the house, sit down and try to contact Gran. Then I'm going over to Preston and be there when they operate on Freddy.'

'I could give you a lift.'

She shook her head. 'I'll manage. I'll just have a quick look in at him.'

'OK.'

'What's going to happen with Dad . . . his body, you know?'

'When we've done what needs doing at the scene, he'll be brought to the public mortuary here, but that could be a few hours yet.'

'I understand.'

Henry asked, 'Did you know about the cannabis factory, by the way?'

'No . . . no, I didn't.' Suddenly she moved to Henry and hugged him unexpectedly. He patted her shoulder and she seemed to relax into him. He inhaled her aroma, which made his nose wrinkle. Then she drew away and wiped her eyes. 'I'll go and see him, then go.'

Henry walked her to the room and stood back as she entered and went to Freddy's side. All Henry could think was, 'I hope you recover, you bastard.'

After touching his arm, Janine left the room and made her way towards the hospital exit.

Henry folded his arms and considered Freddy for a few moments, visualizing Janine standing next to him. He frowned. Then he spun away as a nurse entered the room, and headed out. He passed the consultant's office and saw the doctor was speaking to the nurse who had been with Freddy a little earlier. He was briefing her, Henry guessed, as to what would be happening to Freddy.

As he reached the hospital foyer, Henry's mobile rang and he stepped outside to answer it.

'Henry . . . it's Lisa.' Her voice was strained.

In the distance Henry heard the clatter of a helicopter and saw the air ambulance approaching from the west. But he wasn't really thinking about it as he walked towards the car park where he'd left his Audi, and only part of his mind clocked that the small van Janine had arrived in was still parked where she'd left it – and that she wasn't in it as he would have expected. He was concentrating on Lisa's words.

'Henry . . . you need to come . . . it's Mum. They reckon she's only got a little time left . . . she's really deteriorated overnight . . . Henry, what should I do if . . . if . . . you know?'

Henry upped his pace to his car. 'Do exactly what we've

decided and what she wanted, if it comes to it. The hospital know.'

'Let her die?' she sobbed.

'Yes,' Henry said firmly, an answer he truly did not want to give. He wanted his mother to live for ever and his instinct was that the doctors should do everything in their power to save her, but it wasn't the right thing. He almost vomited on the word.

'Oh God, Henry.'

'I know, I know, sweetheart.'

'Is Rik with you?'

'He's at a crime scene.'

'Can he come, please? I think I need him.'

'I'll see what I can do . . . are the girls there?'

'No.'

'Phone them, get them there, and I'll be there as soon as I can.'

'OK.'

Henry hung up and approached his car, noticing there was a missed call on his phone which must have landed at the same time as he talked to Lisa. He got into the Audi and started the engine to heat it up before returning the call,.

He sat back in the comfortable driver's seat and waited for the connection, again noticing that Janine's van was still parked – she must have gone to the loo or something, maybe to wash and freshen up. He cricked his neck and peered up through the windscreen to see the air ambulance up above, manoeuvring over the big H of the helicopter landing pad about a hundred metres from the entrance to A&E. Standing on the edge of the circular pad were the consultant and the nurse, ready to greet the crew.

'Jerry – you called?'

'Yeah,' the DC said gruffly. 'Another public holiday.'

'I haven't called you out – yet.'

'No – but I know what's happened and you were going to ruin another day off, weren't you, so I got in first . . .'

'And ruined your own day, all by yourself?'

'Something like that. But you were going to call me, weren't you?'

'Hard to say,' Henry teased. 'This could just be a murder/ suicide and a lot of things will be sorted by the deaths, unless Freddy lives, that is . . . So why call me? You should've gone out for the day, made yourself unavailable.'

Henry's mind wasn't really engaged in the conversation. He was thinking about his mother, how long it would take him to get to Blackpool. Would she still be alive when he got there? How would he deal with it all? His eyes wandered lazily from the always spectacular arrival of a helicopter, landing with just a little bounce, back to the hospital, where he thought he saw Janine Cromer entering the A&E department through the sliding doors.

Tope was saying, 'I don't know if this is of any interest, but I'm telling you anyway . . . just some things I got back late yesterday, was going to tell you tomorrow when we all rolled back in.'

He started to explain.

Less than thirty seconds later Henry leapt out of his car and sprinted fast and hard to the hospital entrance, a very bad feeling in the pit of his stomach as his arms and legs pumped. His vision was blurred from the exertion and his hearing distorted by the *whump-whump* of the copter rotor blades.

The automatic sliding doors opened with agonizing slowness, but then he ran through the reception foyer and into the A&E department, his eyes jerking left at the reaction of the startled receptionist and down towards the treatment room in which Freddy Cromer was located.

He swerved into the room.

The nurse who had been treating Freddy was on her knees, clutching the back of her head, and Henry was too late.

The drips had been ripped out of Freddy's hands.

The sticky pads that connected the wires from the machines monitoring his vital signs were torn off and dangled uselessly by the bed.

The soft pillow that had been used to smother and suffocate the comatose Freddy lay diagonally across his chest.

Henry bent by the nurse, and she glanced up at him and gasped at the pain in her head. 'Somebody hit me,' she said and swooned. Henry caught her, twisted her round so she was sitting on her backside and pulled her back to the wall, where he propped her up.

'Did you see who?'

'No.'

He went to Freddy and checked for a pulse in his wrist. Nothing. Then he pushed his thumb and forefinger into the soft flesh underneath the jaw and felt for the jugular vein, but could find no pulse there either.

This time Freddy was dead.

'Shit.'

Henry spun out of the cubicle and stood in the corridor. Which way?

He chose left and ran, coming to a T-junction in the corridor, his head jerking both ways. Seeing an arrow that pointed towards an exit to the left, he ran in that direction, knowing that Freddy's killer had maybe a minute, maybe ninety seconds on him. Not long, but plenty long enough to make an escape.

He set off and passed an emergency exit which was still secure.

The corridor ahead of him had a ninety-degree turn in it. He rounded the corner, skittering on the polished floor, pushing himself off the wall and using his momentum to power on.

At the next turn Janine was fifty metres ahead of him, hurrying but not running down a deserted corridor. She must have sensed or heard him. She stopped, turned and faced him for the briefest of moments, then hared off down a corridor to the left. Henry upped his pace and as he came around the corner, he found he had her trapped – the corridor she had shot into was a dead end with a fire door which had halted her. She was rattling the bar desperately, unable to get it to open.

Henry stopped, caught his breath. 'Janine,' he called.

She stopped instantly, stood upright, revolved slowly. 'Henry,' she whispered, defeat in her voice.

'That's far enough, love,' he said and walked towards her, his chest rising and falling. He made a calming gesture with his hands, palms down, patting thin air. 'You're going nowhere now.'

He took four more steps, then her right hand slid into her shoulder bag and emerged gripping a small revolver, snub-nosed, six rounds.

Henry stopped. 'Put it down.'

She shook her head.

'Let's talk.'

'What's to say?' There was that hostile, unforgiving look in her eyes again.

'All sorts of things.' Henry's hands still made the calming gesture, but they were now rigid. His eyes flickered between the gun and her face as he spoke. 'Come on, talk to me, Janine.'

'I have nothing to say, Henry.'

'Really? Nothing?'

'Not to you.'

'Not even about Terry Cromer not being your real father?'

The gun came up slightly. It was in her right hand, supported by her left, which was cupped underneath it, steadying it. It was pointed at the centre of Henry's chest.

'How do you know?'

'DNA . . . you were arrested a few years back in Manchester, weren't you? You're not the sweet innocent you make yourself out to be, are you? Doing a bit of dealing, I believe. Anyway, your DNA was taken. I took Freddy's DNA last week, if you recall, and we already had Terry's on record. One of my staff fast-tracked a comparison.'

'Why?'

'Because I told him to investigate your background. I'm a cop – that's what we do. I mean – the more I thought about it – a member of the Cromer family being a solicitor! Christ – you've never been near a university, have you? Just what have you been doing?'

The gun wavered. Just a little. Henry saw her forefinger tighten on the trigger. He was still ten metres away from her, and he knew if he had any sense he should be reversing not advancing. *Let her go. Let her run.* That was the intelligent thing to do.

'You *are* Freddy's daughter, aren't you? Not Terry's. I saw the resemblance a couple of times, just thought it was a general family thing, but it's striking in some lights. Like I said,' he shrugged, 'I never thought about it. But you don't look anything like Terry when I *do* think about it.'

'Well spotted.'

'And I saw the way you were with Freddy.'

'And how was that, Henry? Do tell.'

'Loving,' he said truthfully, and saw the word hit the mark – at least for a second. Then she refocused her ire.

There was a door on either side of her down this dead-end corridor. She edged sideways to the door on her left and tried the handle. The door opened, so she pushed it wide and glanced quickly inside before stepping back and jiggling the gun.

'In here, Henry.'

'Why?'

'Because when I shoot you in here, it'll take longer to find you and that can only be good for me. Not that anyone knows what I did, or saw me. I hit that nurse from behind.'

'You might be surprised.'

'Get in,' she ordered him, waving the gun, keeping him covered, keeping her distance.

'If I don't?' he challenged her.

'Then you'll die in a dead-end corridor as opposed to a storeroom.'

'You're clearly not the best of shots, though, are you? I assume you put the gun to Freddy's head?'

'I did – but he pulled the trigger. It just sort of slipped, which is why the bullet didn't go straight through his ear, which it should have done. IN! I won't say it again, Henry.'

Henry, still with his hands out flat, but not so much in a calming gesture now, more a 'please don't shoot' one – slid past her and into the room, which was simply a store with stacks of chairs. He walked in, turning to face her as she came in behind him, closed the door and leaned against it, the gun up, aimed at his body.

He swallowed, amazed at how effective adrenalin was at drying up throats. He folded his arms and tried to look casual and unafraid, when in reality he felt as though someone had rammed a broomstick up his arse, he was so tense and terrified. He wondered if it had come to this: a thirty-odd year career as a cop ending in either a corridor or a storeroom.

Thing was, he knew for certain it would end here if Janine was truly as ruthless as she had to be in order to leave no witnesses behind.

'Let me tell you something, Henry,' she said rapidly. 'This isn't confession time. I'm not going to tell you about my freakin' childhood, the abuse, the terror my mother had to endure because of one stupid mistake she made – getting shagged by Freddy.'

'Sounds like a confession to me,' Henry observed.

'Don't be a smart arse – doesn't suit you.'

'But you must have a tale to tell,' Henry said. He needed her to talk, he needed her to blab, to get emotional, to drop her guard. 'All that stuff that drove you to self-harm . . . yes, I saw the scars,' he said, responding to the surprise in her face. 'And I know the pain that drives someone to mutilate their own body . . .'

'You know fuck all, Henry,' she growled in rage. Her breath came in short gasps. 'You know nothing about shitty family secrets and having a mother who suffered at the hands of a . . .' She uttered the worst word in the English language. Her face contorted into a hideous mask of anger and pain. Tears cascaded down her face. 'You know nothing,' she said weakly. 'Nothing about loving a man who couldn't be called Dad or taking revenge with him for the wrongs he suffered as a kid – and as a grown-up. Yeah, yeah,' she sneered, 'we killed them all one by one. Each year on the day they almost burned my father alive . . . and the last one, the pinnacle, was always going to be Terry. My dad – Terry,' she almost spat. Her face glistened with flowing tears. 'Not my fucking dad, actually . . . trouble was a gang war kinda screwed it up . . . so we improvised. Just sad we didn't get the chance to make him eat feathers. That would've been a real trump.'

'But why kill Freddy? Or try to kill him?'

'Because he was a nutter . . . isn't that what you called him? The medical term? Didn't you snigger at him? Nutter! You arrogant, fucking, uncaring bastard, Henry Christie. Phh!' Her voice had risen almost out of control, but now she calmed herself, though Henry saw the gun was shaking with her fury. 'Freddy couldn't have lived with what he'd done . . . to the others, maybe, but not to Terry, because really he loved him. He was his brother, but he had to kill him . . . a story as old as the hills.'

'And you manipulated him into doing just that, didn't you? I should have realized as soon as I smelled weed on you,' he said, recalling the aroma he had sniffed when she had hugged him earlier. 'It was obvious you'd been in the factory.'

'He wanted to do it. So we took Terry some food and a gun and killed the fucker where he was hiding out from you . . . saved you a job, didn't it? Saved the taxpayer a lot of money . . . least it would've if Freddy had died too, like he was supposed to have done.'

'Whoa.' Henry held up his right hand. He gave a short laugh. 'I think you're the nutter here, Janine. Freddy was the most sane man in the world compared to you. You're a sick, twisted individual.'

'And guess what? This sick, twisted individual is about to take over the family business. How's about that!'

'Oh, now it starts to make sense.'

'That cannabis factory? There's ten more of them. Four million quid in the making. And they're mine.' She gave him a rueful smile. 'I bided my time, then I struck. And by the way – all the shit you cleared out for me this week, cheers. Good policing. Some good arrests. Real dross.'

'So there is a family business after all and you just want the money.'

'I want everything, actually.' She winked conspiratorially at him and his heart skipped a beat, because he knew then that he had lost. He had somehow hoped that he could talk this young woman down, drive a wedge into her emotions and make her crack, fall apart and sink down the wall, sobbing her heart out, seeing the error of her ways, overwhelmed by the enormity of her awful life. That was not going to happen, Henry knew. She was mad, and she was determined that no one would be a witness to her crime – and she would kill Henry right here, right now.

'Just so you know . . . I'm going to pay a little visit to the security office before I leave . . . just to check the CCTV cameras. Wouldn't like to get caught, would I?' She gave a playful, childish shrug and a wrinkle of her lovely nose at the exact moment Henry's mobile phone rang.

Her eyes flickered down, momentarily distracted – and Henry launched himself at her.

In his mind he knew exactly where he intended to take her. In the midriff. It would be a bone-crushing, organ-compressing tackle, underneath the gun, slamming her back against the door and using his shoulder to heave upwards, at the same time pinning her right arm against the wall. He had it all worked out in that micro-second. Visualized the point of impact, driving the breath out of her lungs, crushing and disarming her.

He dived like the rugby player he had been many years before.

Difference was that when he was nineteen or twenty, he hadn't weighed almost fifteen stone and had been fit, agile and super-fast. Thirty plus years ahead, too much spread, too much weight, had slowed him right down. For his age he knew he was pretty fit, could still run three miles a day, visited the gym regularly . . . but it was all relative. In fact he was older and slower than his brain led him to believe.

Janine reacted instantly.

Whilst Henry was in mid-air, she pulled the trigger. In the confines of the small room the sound of the discharge was ear-shatteringly loud, accompanied by a spectacular muzzle flash and a bad recoil that jerked her hand up.

The bullet still connected, hitting Henry with such force that he felt like he'd slammed into a brick wall. The impact stopped him, spiralled him off course, threw him back and he landed face down in an untidy heap, almost at the point from where he'd jumped.

There was no pain. Just a huge, spreading numbness radiating out from somewhere around his neck and right shoulder. He tried to move but his limbs didn't respond to any of his brain's demands. With a great effort of will he pushed upwards, but then his hands slipped in something thick and oily and warm and went from under him, and his face hit the floor in the wetness.

With a surge of panic he realized he was lying in his own blood and that he had been shot.

His eyes were open. He saw Janine's feet. His mouth popped like a stranded fish and he tried to speak.

She was standing over him.

More immense effort. He moved his head slightly and looked up through the corner of his eye to see her pointing the gun down at his face. The black circle of the muzzle was maybe four inches away from him. Her finger curled around the trigger. The cylinder started to revolve. Henry could just about focus on the tips of the bullets seated in their chambers, fitted snugly like mini-missiles.

It rotated.

The hammer went backwards. The trigger was pulled. Henry didn't even have the energy to wince, to prepare himself for the impact into his brain. There was a metallic clunk as the firing pin smacked down onto a dud. It didn't fire. In anger, she yanked the trigger back twice more – both duds.

'Shitty fucking ammo,' she said.

Henry's eyes closed slowly. His face relaxed into the spreading pool of his own blood. He heard footsteps, a door closing . . . then blackness.

NINETEEN

Because his mother had not been particularly religious, the funeral service was conducted by a humanist preacher who had spent a couple of hours in the company of Henry, Lisa and Henry's two daughters a couple of days before. It had been good to talk about his mother, and the preacher had been skilled at getting the four of them to open up. Henry actually enjoyed the process, which was something of a catharsis, recalling not only the significant events in his mother's life (such as his twenty-four-hour birth, which she often described as excruciating) but also more trivial, funnier ones. From their chat, the preacher had put together the speech he was to make at the crematorium.

His mother's body had been brought to his house in Blackpool before the funeral cortege rolled from there out to a crematorium near Kirkham. It was only a small convoy; first the hearse, then a long funeral limousine carrying Henry, Lisa, Leanne and Jenny, and behind that another limousine with Rik and Alison and her step-daughter Ginny, plus Henry's old friend from the FBI, Karl Donaldson, and his wife Karen. A few other cars followed, carrying a couple of distant relatives Henry didn't even know existed and a few of his mother's friends. There were not many: the old dear had proudly outlived most of her contemporaries and most of those still drawing breath didn't have the physical capability to get there.

Henry liked this. The fewer the better as far as he was concerned.

It went as well as any proceedings at a crematorium could, and afterwards they adjourned to a local hostelry near Kirkham where a meal had been booked.

It was ten days since Henry had been shot and he had been warned by his doctor not to do anything strenuous. Anyone, who for whatever reason, had almost bled dry and then been given a transfusion of six pints of blood, he was told, should take things easy for a long, long time. Henry argued that attending his only mother's funeral was unlikely to be too taxing; overdosing himself with powerful painkillers, he had hobbled there, paid his respects, said goodbye and stifled his tears.

Throughout the service he had held Alison's hand and when he glanced at her she was crying a river.

The meal was muted, but pleasant enough, and afterwards he sat back and sipped the green tea he had opted for, pulling his face at each sip and wishing it was a pint of Stella with a JD chaser.

He rolled his shoulder to keep it moving. Ten minutes of inactivity made it stiffen up and become very sore.

'How are you doing, darling?' Alison asked, sitting next to him. This was the first time he had ventured either beyond his house or the Tawny Owl. Although pleased by her concern, it was getting a little OTT for his understated taste. He did not like being fussed over.

'I'm good.' *For the hundredth time.*

She squeezed his hand. 'I'm so sorry about your mum.'

'I'm just gutted I wasn't there when she died. But at least

Lisa and the girls were – and the DNR thing didn't have to be addressed. She had some familiar faces around her when she went. Of course I would've been there if I hadn't been contemplating the end of my police career in a puddle full of my own blood.'

'Thank God that hospital porter spotted your blood pooling out under that storeroom door.'

'I'll always be grateful to a hospital porter,' Henry said. 'And the fact that the gun was loaded with home-made shells.'

Sometimes, at night, he could hear the metallic smack of the firing pin hitting the useless bullets in Janine's gun. And sometimes, the bullets fired.

Alison's face creased at the thought. She turned and looked earnestly at him. 'Henry, I don't want to go through that again.'

'It was just a bit of bad luck, really.'

'What – being shot by a madwoman! You take it all so . . . so . . . God, I don't know. Like it's a joke.' She was infuriated by his attitude. She smacked her fists down onto her thighs. She found she couldn't say anything else and her eyelids fluttered over new tears. She had lost her first husband in a very ugly incident in the Middle East where she and he were both serving in the armed forces. Henry was aware the memory still affected her even eight years down the line. 'Look,' she eventually said firmly, turning her whole body to him to make her point. 'You asked me to marry you and I said yes. I'm not going to rush you or anything, but I really would like to get married as soon as possible . . . it means so much to me, honey. And I'd really like you to retire from the police. You keep saying you will, but you don't do it. But I absolutely hate you turning out to murders and horrible stuff like that.' She paused. 'I know you think you were born to hunt killers, but can we get on with our life without that at the Tawny Owl? I know you want to, and I want it – us – to be a success, but I want you to be by my side all the time . . .'

Henry looked up to see Rik Dean crossing the bar, mobile phone clamped to his ear, looking urgently at Henry and making excitable gestures.

'What do you say, love . . .?'

Before Henry could answer, Rik said bluntly, 'Henry – look,

sorry to cut in, I can see this is a lovey-dovey moment, but there's a bit of breaking news here . . .'

Alison stared incredulously at Rik. Henry saw her reaction and for a moment was torn . . . what the hell was so important? He did the balancing act in his head and it came down in Alison's favour.

'Just give us a minute, pal?' He arched his eyebrows pointedly at his friend, trying to get the message across.

'But—!'

'One minute,' Henry insisted.

Rik's eyes narrowed. He ended his phone call and walked over to the bar where Karl and Karen Donaldson were standing, glancing back at Henry, curious and a little alarmed.

'Alison.' He touched her knee. 'I will retire in the near future, I promise, and I can't wait to get legitimately serving beer to all those sozzled villagers in Kendleton . . . though I do have the feeling that me running a pub might be akin to Herod running a nursery. But I do have a few things to sort and a desk to clear . . . but for the first time in my life, I'm going to have a very long period off sick and milk the system, during which time I will do the decent thing by you and go down on one knee somewhere a bit tropical. But only when I know I can get back up without having to use a cane or a crane.'

'Sod the painkillers.' Henry slapped Rik on the back, having managed to creakily get to the bar. 'I need a pint . . . and what's so all-fired important on that telephone of yours?'

'They've tracked her down.'

'Where?' Henry gasped. His insides did an empty spin.

'Marseilles, would you believe?'

'France?'

'I think that's where Marseilles is . . . but get this . . . she's holed up in some grot-flat near the seafront and has opened fire at the bloody gendarmes . . . there's a bloody siege going on.'

Henry shook his head. 'Who'd've thought it . . .'

'Told you she was a black widow.'